KILLERS DON'T TALK

I0671409

A

PaPa Sak

Novel

KILLERS DON'T TALK

PaPa Sak

2

Introduction

This book is probably one of my most violent stories. It is a book that takes you through the mind of a killer. There are many criminals in this world we live in but the killer is the most distinctive. In more cases than you might believe, many killers have a particular moral belief. Some killers are not necessarily evil people but are commissioned to kill because of certain circumstances. There is a difference in killing and murdering someone. Killing someone may be justified if it involves protecting yourself and your family. I may even say when it comes time to avenge your family the judicial system is not working in your best interest. Many people, especially law enforcement will suggest that you should never take the law in your own hands. Man's justice is always debatable because it is always perceived through the eyes of each man's biases, prejudices and other things that hinder the proper perspective. Killers have a distinct mindset that makes them clean up the diseased people of the world without compromise. I'm not referring to serial killers that harm people for the sake of killing or for some demented joy out of making people suffer. I'm referring to killers that have a particular objective that must be carried out because of an injustice that lingers.

Weeks before I released this novel a woman was just acquitted for the charge of murdering her 2 year old daughter. I'm not going to get into details of the case. What was amazing was the outpour of anger and disappointment when she got off free. There are so many cowards in the world that justice is a stranger in many cases. A man like Charles Manson can convince teenagers and young adults to kill people including a pregnant woman but still be allowed to live and do interviews for decades. A young man sells a small amount of crack cocaine and he gets life in prison because it's his third strike. The scales of injustice are not in balance and eventually nature has to respond to the cries of the people that continue to get injustice. It is the universal order of things. Nature purifies itself just like our body purifies itself. When it does purify in the way of death, it is usually silent and swift without mercy. Thus the title is Killers Don't Talk.

I would like to thank Shay Fresh for her wonderful photography. She is a queen that very few measure up to and a rare talent in her craft. I also would like to thank Rafael Rodriguez for his great graphic design. I would like to thank Proverb C. Wisdom, Laverna Beed, Shannon Fisher, Brian Duckett and everyone in my literary community. Mostly I would like to thank the fans of my work, you are the blessing to me and I appreciate that you enjoy my work and I will never take it for granted.

PaPa Sak
The Kingpin of the Inkpen!!!

TABLE OF CONTENTS

You have the right to remain silent!

What about the code people have forgotten their way
Cutthroats are in play and honor among thieves has blown away
Tears fall for the man that stands firm on his belief
He doesn't grit his teeth for the life he chose
He knows his choices and accepts the consequences
Hustlers keep hustling, Gangsters keep riding
Killers don't talk while informants keep hiding
Who knows what's in a man's heart until he faces some pressure
But when it becomes clearer can he look himself in the mirror
It ain't always about right and wrong as it is weak and strong
Can only enjoy the good times and when pain comes their word is gone
No pride, no passion, no rules or regulations
I respect a gangster that sincerely believes more than a preacher
that fornicates with his congregation
It's about principle, it's about believing in something
Or falling for anything because dishonor is what so many bring
From the vagrant to the president your word is bond
But some are blinded by their own pain to really respect the game
Shame on you because you're empty at the core
Choosing to live your life in a lie
I rather die the good death for what I stood for

1
THE RELEASE

The life of man upon earth is a warfare!
Job 7:1

Present day:

The cold was refreshing as Tango strolled down the long pathway to be released from Folsom State prison. His eyes were sharp and focused as he kept his head up and face straight ahead. His 5'11" stocky frame had the mannerism of a man that had suffered insurmountable pain. His dark brown complexion blended in well with his mustache, beard and handlebars that were speckled with gray. He taught himself how to be patient and resolved. He taught himself for ten years how to meditate on the exact moment. He couldn't reflect on the past to such a point that he forgot about the present. But the past was no doubt embedded in his psyche and heart. No tears would fall as he reached the final gate, greeted by two correctional officers.

"You are now free to go, Davenport."

Ignoring the comment Tango stepped outside of the gate. There was no reason to look back at that place again. He knew somehow that this day would one day come. It took long enough, he pondered. He casually strolled to the closest bus stop sorting out his thoughts. He had close to nothing when it came to money but he wasn't worried. A lot of things had changed within ten years, but once again he wasn't worried. His lips curled up as he noticed the bus arriving on time. The bus driver instantly noticed the sullen faced man and took note that he must have been a recently paroled inmate. He nodded and let the man on the bus.

Once the fair was paid he sat down and went further into himself; further into his thoughts.

Within thirty minutes into his ride he had fallen asleep. He had a long way to go and he needed to rest his mind. When he awoke he found himself cruising on the 101 Highway into a city called Paso Robles. California was really a desert state for the most part. Down the coastline was a different story. He could look on both sides to observe the beauty spots of this large state. Since he was going south towards Los Angeles, on his right side was the ocean and on his left was wine country. He remembered taking his beautiful wife, Loretta, up to the country from L.A. Those were the times they would escape from the kids and enjoy one another. He chuckled, reminiscing on how Loretta considered herself a wine connoisseur. She was a beautiful Creole woman with long pretty jet black hair and gray eyes. Her death happened while he was incarcerated. He hadn't been in that long and solitary confinement was the only thing that stopped him from killing someone. He had actually requested to be isolated after the passing of his wife. Now the ocean view was in front of him and for a time he had peace. He learned many years ago how to avoid the shedding of tears. He stood up momentarily to stretch and noticed the bus driver staring at him through the mirror. He wouldn't even entertain the fear that showed in the eyes of the timid man. There was bigger fish to fry like figuring out how he would make a living. His businesses had been closed down for years so his source of income was obsolete. He had pulled some strings before he went in that should cover him but that wasn't guaranteed. All he could do was hope for the best.

The view kept him up for the rest of the way to Los Angeles. He would end up in downtown L.A. near skid row, close to the Greyhound station. The city air was definitely different but it didn't matter; he was a lion that had been released from his cage. His focus intensified and his resolve was cemented. He walked the littered city streets considering what cigarette smoke infested motel he would reside in for the night. The polluted debris irritated his senses, but he still stayed sharp. The raggedy earthquake ready buildings in downtown were decayed with paint peeling before his very eyes. The concrete was scattered with homeless men and women wrapped in blankets, using cardboard for shelter. He had roamed these mean streets many years ago as a boss. His family was well respected among Crips and Bloods. He grew up on the border lines of both sides of the color line so there was no problem with him working with either. He once had it all and now he had nothing.

He only had a niece that was his last remaining family member. She was just nineteen years old when he went away. Her mother, his sister had passed away while he was incarcerated. He heard through the grapevine that his niece, Melanie, was married and living in the suburbs. Years later she found a way to contact him when her mother passed. He appreciated her letters and her words and he promised himself that he would contact her once he got himself settled. She sent him a picture and she was the spitting image of her mother when she was that age. Good ole Missy was his sister who was renowned for fighting men and women. She was only a couple of years older than him, but she had a way of acting like she was his mother. They were close, but breast cancer had gotten the best of her.

He had a lot to think about as he walked up to a downtown motel he thought to be relatively clean. They had weekly rates and that gave him somewhat of an advantage to readjust to his situation. Before he went into the pen he had prepared for the worse or so he thought. He definitely planned to be financially secure for the rest of his life if he was given the opportunity to get out. If there wasn't clear proof that evidence was tampered with, he would have never won his appeal. He pondered on how politics got him ten years in prison then overturned on a technicality. He definitely had to count his blessings. But now he could start anew with a different outlook.

"Yes, can I help you?" An Arab man answered the window after Tango pushed the buzzard.

"What are your rates?" Tango looked down as he dug in his pockets.

"Forty dollars for one night and two hundred and thirty dollars for the week. We only accept cash and there is no prostitution or drugs allowed." He replied.

"Let me get a room for one week."

"I need your I.D. and a do you have a car so that you can write down the license plate number?"

The Arab man's voice irritated Tango because it sounded as though he was nagging. He had a high pitched voice, dark tan and receding hair line. Tango stared at the man momentarily, trying to correlate the voice with the face. He hadn't paid attention earlier.

"I have a form of I.D. but not from the DMV and I don't own a car."

The Arab man showed a look of disdain, but Tango knew that the man wanted the money more than anything.

"Okay but I don't want any problems out of you or I will call the police." He sharply stated.

The man must have expected a reaction but Tango didn't dignify the statement with even a facial expression. He kept his sullen face and laid the money on the counter. He slid the money under the bullet proof glass and patiently waited for the key.

After receiving the key he walked up to the second floor and went into his temporary residence. He didn't have much when it came to material things but he had what so many people didn't have; peace. But is peace a lie? War was a natural part of life even on a social level. He fell backwards onto his bed and stared up at the ceiling. His thoughts wandered on his plans. He had known plenty of people who claimed to be gangsters. He had known many people who claimed to be men. He also met plenty of people who claimed to be women. It was usually the misconception that age and not principle defined you as a gangster, be it a man or a woman. Tango considered at a young age that there had to be guidelines to all of those titles. A standard of measure was vital to these titles in order for them to truly hold value. These were the things that he would usually ponder on when he was locked up.

He lifted his head slightly to look around the room. The small room was shabby at best. It was kept moderately clean but the residue of sitting without use floated in the air. He cut on the heater to keep warm. After several jerks from the air conditioning motor it finally started blowing out air. Naturally it started off cold then slowly heated up. The walls around the room were an off white color that was past due for a new coat of paint. The raggedy television hung from the wall in the corner with buttons missing from it. It was painfully obvious to him that he would only be able to operate the TV with a remote. He glanced at the smaller blue dresser that had chipped paint on the corners with a telephone and phone book next to it. The drawer matched the nappy blue carpet. He opened the top drawer, noticing the traditional bible sitting inside. He walked over to the other side of the bed near the television and went to inspect the bathroom where he saw four white towels and two small bars of soap.

"It's better than a prison cell," he said aloud.

He fell asleep shortly after that. He woke up early that next morning ready to make some moves. The first thing he did was hit up his old comrade Leonard. They went to high school together and were really good friends. If there was such a thing, he considered Leonard to be that. They watched out for each other from time to time. Leonard wasn't big on writing any letters, but he made sure to put some money on his books. When Tango got big in the game he made sure that Leonard was taken care of. He didn't know what to expect from the man after ten years but he had to see how he was doing. Leonard had a habit of keeping his ear to the street. Tango had to respect him for that.

He walked up to the yellow house with the dirty shudders and windows. It brought some old memories back to Tango. He had a moment of nostalgia before he walked up the walkway. When he reached the front door he hesitated before knocking then rung the doorbell once and knocked twice just in case Leonard couldn't hear one or the other. Eventually he heard the heavy footsteps walking towards the door. He didn't call so he was anticipating the response. Without even looking through the peephole the door swung open and Leonard stood right in front of him. Neither man said a word for several moments.

"I can't believe my eyes. Am I looking at Kevin Davenport, a.k.a. Tango?" Leonard announced.

"What's happening; my man?" They embraced.

"Just chilling at the house with this broad. Come on in nigga, I can't believe they let yo ass out. I thought you were sitting on twenty-five years?"

"My lawyers finally won my case on appeal." Tango replied.

"Well that's good you had enough for a lawyer…Come on in. I thought when the police cleaned you out; you didn't have money for shit."

"I paid my lawyer a bunch of money in advance. That was why I was able to keep him working on my case."

"I can't forget how crazy paid you were. Take a seat. Are you hungry?" Leonard pointed to the plush brown suede couches.

They simultaneously sat down diagonally across from one another. Leonard sat on the couch while Tango chose the love seat.

"I could use a bite to eat." Tango replied.

"Debbie, come in here for a minute. I want you to meet a good comrade of mine."

A young woman in her late twenties to early thirties walked into the living room with a robe on. She was a very pretty woman with a beautiful mahogany complexion and dimples when she smiled.

"Nice to meet you." She held out her hand.

Tango lifted up to return the gesture then she glanced over at Leonard. Leonard was still looking in amazement at Tango. Then he caught himself and looked up at Debbie.

"Go get us some breakfast take-out so that me and my boy can talk on a full stomach. You can drive the Cadillac." He said while handing her a hundred dollar bill.

She glanced over at Tango with a slight look of surprise. The two men didn't really say anything as she went to the back to put on some clothes. Within ten minutes she was out the door snatching his keys in the process. Once they heard the door slam that was when Leonard started in.

"First and foremost I want to give you my condolences for the loss of your family. That was some real fucked up shit. You know if you need anything from me in any kind of way I got yo back." Leonard began.

"I appreciate that. Right now it is about me getting on my feet. I think about that shit from time to time. I was locked up though, so it wasn't like I could have stopped anything. I just have to chalk it up, regardless of how painful it is."

"How are you going to handle that other thing though?" Leonard asked.

"I'm not. I have to live for the moment." Tango replied.

"I guess those ten years gave you plenty of time to put everything in perspective huh?"

14

"Yeah you can say that. I see you have done pretty good for yourself. You have decked the house out since I last seen it. I'm really happy for you." Tango observed the surroundings.

"That was more of taking my time and eventually getting to my goal. Now it is a different time and the streets is uglier than before. Here…Let me give you a little bit of paper to get on your feet."

Leonard walked into the bedroom and within minutes came back out with ten crisp one hundred dollar bills.

"I know it ain't a lot, but it is enough to at least give you some leverage."

"I didn't come over here to ask for any bread, even though I appreciate what you're offering. I just came by to catch up with an old friend." Tango replied.

"I know my man, but take it so I can feel a little better. I know you ain't any leach type nigga and I know you are about getting your own. But take the money so that I will know you got something to move on." Leonard explained.

Tango nodded and accepted the money. He folded the bills and glanced down at his pocket while sliding the money inside.

"So what's gotten so ugly with the streets?" Tango asked nonchalantly.

"These wild niggas today got everybody walking on eggshells. Both the Bloods and the Crips have gone off on the deep end. Some muthafuckas is robbing they own homeboys and everything. And these little niggas don't respect their OGs. All these young niggas today respect is money. If you can't put some money in their pockets they are quick to peel yo cap. It's wild out here now Tango. Nowadays even Blood hoods go to war with other Blood hoods." Leonard explained.

"What about the dope game; how is that nowadays?" Tango frowned.

"More cutthroat than ever. It was bad when you were running things but it has gotten worse. Now gangbanging type niggas is shot callers when it comes to moving major weight. Don't you remember when a gangbanging type nigga ran a few corners or spots but he's the one copping the weight."

"Yeah things have changed. Well it's a good thing that I'm out of that mess. If I can live my life in peace I will be content with that." Tango replied.

Leonard decided to change the subject. He didn't want to dwell on the times since his old comrade didn't hunger for the game anymore.

"So all of your family is gone right now?"

"Yeah! I have a niece somewhere but I don't know where she is at right now. It would be good to catch up with her." Tango sighed.

"Missy's daughter, right?"

"Yeah, she moved somewhere, and I had the address when she was married. We lost contact when she got divorced."

"Yeah I remember Melanie. She has to be pushing thirty by now, huh? I wonder if she has any of the traits of her mother. Your sister wasn't any joke when it came down to serving a nigga his nuts. I don't understand how you grew up under that much pressure." Leonard chuckled.

"One day at a time. But when Missy loved you, she loved you hard. I never had a fight with her. But I never had a reason because she was more like a mother than a big sister. I miss her friendship." Tango smiled slightly.

Twenty minutes into the conversation, Debbie, walked into the door with bags of food. Tango and Leonard glanced up and followed her into the dining room.

"Damn baby, I was beginning to ask if you went out and killed the food yourself." Leonard commented.

"Nigga I wasn't gone that long. I did stop at the grocery store to grab some orange juice to drink this shit down." Debbie smiled.

After they sorted out the Styrofoam plates and ate, Leonard walked Tango outside. They walked down the walkway to the front of the yard.

"Well its good you came by...Where is your car? How did you get over here?" Leonard asked.

"I caught a couple of buses from downtown L.A. I got a little room down there for the time." Tango replied.

"Aw I can't have my people catching the bus. Let me grab my keys so that I can give you a ride back down to your spot."

"I appreciate that, but I need some time to clear my mind. It is cool to look at the scenery while I'm on the bus. It is a trip to see how L.A. has changed in the last ten years. Some things are the same though."

"Well if you need me to pick you up from somewhere or you need a ride here is my business card. Hit me up and I will find a way to get at you." Leonard smiled.

They embraced one last time then Leonard watched him walk down the street. After Tango turned the corner Leonard went back inside.

Tango wanted to catch several buses to another destination before he went back to downtown L.A. It took him about an hour and a half before he reached his destination. He observed the address on the 3x5 card he had received while in prison. He walked down the street of the relatively quiet neighborhood until he reached a white apartment complex. He smiled when the numbers on the card matched the numbers on the building. He glanced at the apartments then realized that the place he was looking for was on the second floor. As he climbed the stairs he glanced around to see the open fields and dry lands. Based upon the sequence of numbers the apartment he wanted was at the end.

He knocked on the door several times then patiently waited for a response. It was the middle of the day he considered. Suddenly the door swung open and he was staring at a beautiful chocolate bombshell in jeans and a T-shirt with her hair wrapped.

"Uncle Kevin!?!" The girl blurted out.

"How are you doing Melanie? I'm sorry I showed up unannounced but I didn't know when I might catch up with you. I never had a number on you." Tango smiled.

"Never mind that, come on in. You are the only family member on my mother's side I have left and you are worrying about calling." She waived her hand for him to come in.

He walked inside and noticed the immaculately furnished apartment. He stood in the living room admiring the décor.

"Take a seat anywhere you like, Uncle Kevin. It is really good to see you. I honestly didn't think that I would be able to see you unless I went to visit you in jail." She smiled.

"It is good to see you as well. You remind me of my sister so much that it seems like I'm looking at her when we were younger." He replied.

"That's what everyone says that knew Mama before she passed. I wasn't as strong as she was though. I always got the impression that she could knock out a horse or something. So when did you get out?"

"Yesterday. So this is the city of Rancho Cucamonga? I never had any interest with anything out this way so I never knew about the surrounding cities. It looks like you are doing good for yourself. Your mother would be proud." Tango smiled.

"Other than robbing Peter to pay Paul from time to time I can say that I'm blessed."

"Well things can always get better. Aren't you married now? You have a son; where is he at right now?" Tango asked.

"He's at school right now. I will be picking him up in about an hour or so if you wait around you can meet him. He is five years old so my mama got to see him right after he was born. As far as my husband we are separated and the divorce should be final early next year. That trifling nigga can't keep his dick in his pants but that's a whole different story."

"I know how that can be. But it looks like despite your problems you are doing pretty good. I just came by to see you and let you know that I'm out. I would love to meet your son."

"Of course but if you don't have a place to stay you can take little Terrell's room and he can sleep in the room with me. At least until you get back on your feet." Melanie eagerly offered.

"I have a place to stay for now but I will be sure to come visit you on a regular basis. If it is possible I might try to move out this way to get away from the L.A. scene. I'm a face that might not be fully accepted if I return...You know what I mean?"

"I do understand what you mean Uncle Kevin that was why I offered for you to stay up here with me. You are really the only family I got besides my son and there is cold low down people out there in L.A. That is the main reason I moved out here." She passionately explained.

Tango noticed the tears well up in her eyes. She was a beautiful girl that didn't deserve to be exposed to some of the things she experienced. He noticed her strength and silently acknowledged that she had the same strength of her mother.

"Uncle Kevin, it was really horrible. I'm sorry I hid in the closet and didn't come to their defense but I was scared." She cried.

Tango walked over to her and put both his hands on her shoulders. It was obviously difficult for her to look him in the eyes. By now the tears had fallen down her face.

"If you would have tried to defend them it would have resulted in you being gone just like they are gone. A higher power decided that it was best that you lived. But never mind that, let's talk about the future and put that past behind us. I'm free now and we can start over. I've did all the crying that I'm going to do right now."

She stood up to hug him. He was the only real man that she knew. He was the only father figure she knew until he went to prison. Her biological father wasn't ever around. He didn't want her to be sad but secretly he was seething inside. Solitary confinement was the only place that seen all the tears he would ever let fall from his face.

"So is your little boy big now? Is his father at least in his life nowadays even though you two are separated?" He carefully changed the subject.

"He sometimes comes around but not as much as he should. He's trying to take me to court for joint custody but that is so that he doesn't have to pay as much on child support. I was going to fry some chicken, with mashed potatoes and some string beans for dinner...Are you hungry?"

"I could use something to eat."

She took her arms from around his neck and her face from being smothered in his chest and walked over to the kitchen. She wiped the tears from her face as she grabbed things from out of the cabinet. Tango sat back on the couch trying to breathe out calmly. Some old feelings had resurfaced and for a long time he didn't want to dwell on it. He heard that it was a horrible situation but he could only imagine what Melanie went through considering she was there. He also knew that it must have been tormenting for her not to be able to protect them. It tormented him and he was locked up miles away from the scene. He let his head drop trying to fight his anxiety.

"Are you okay Uncle Kevin?" Melanie asked.

"Yeah I'm fine; I just wasn't feeling good for a brief moment."

"Go in my room and lay down for awhile. I'll get everything ready for dinner and when I pick up my son we can sit down and eat." She pointed towards her bedroom.

He walked into the master bedroom and noticed the brown carpet with the queen sized bed and oak bed frame. He sat on the edge of the bed before he laid his head down. When he finally laid down he quickly fell asleep.

A couple of hours later he was awakened by the noise of someone running in the house. He had to regain his composure; for a brief moment he had forgotten where he was. He looked around frantically and calmly came to a realization that it was the place of friends not enemies. He sat back up on the edge of the bed rubbing his eyes. He walked into the living room to see a toddler running across the living room.

"Boy I told you to stop running like that before you wake up Uncle Kevin." Melanie whispered.

The little boy noticed Tango before she did so he pointed at the tall stranger. Melanie peaked out of the kitchen to see her uncle standing right by the bedroom door.

"Uncle Kevin, I'm sorry he woke you up."

"That's okay; I needed to get up anyway. The food smells really good and who is this active little man?" Tango gently smiled.

"Tell him your name." Melanie glanced at the child.

"My name is Royce and I'm four years old." The child smiled.

"Well everyone come to the table and I will fix your plate." Melanie announced.

Everyone sat at the table while Melanie prepared the food. She helped Royce in his high chair then fixed his plate. When she finished piling all the food on Tango's plate he questioned if he would be able to finish the plate. The conversation at the table was relatively quiet until the end of the meal.

"I have a key that my mother told me to give to you if you were to ever get out."

"I wondered if she decided to give it to you or not." Tango replied.

"Yeah she gave it to me a couple of months before she passed. She believed that I wasn't supposed to have survived that whole ordeal so it was probably a sign that you would one day come home. That is amazing that they overturned your conviction on an appeal. Well let me go in the room to get the key."

Melanie disappeared in the room. Tango glanced over at Royce who was watching a cartoon by now. He was so engrossed in the television that he didn't even glance up when his mother walked in the other room. Tango appreciated the innocence of the child. He just stared at his great nephew with admiration when Melanie walked back inside. He wondered how good it was to be innocent and guiltless.

"Here you go Uncle Kevin. I made sure I kept it in a little box where I would always have access to it."

He took the key and prepared himself to leave. She offered one last time for him to stay with her but he politely declined. They hugged each other with the promise that they would see each other regularly.

He headed back to Los Angeles but decided to make a stop at a cemetery near the city of Pomona. The Home Depot was nearby so he went inside to purchase himself a shovel and other odd tools. Not too far from Forest Pine Mortuary he dug up a spot that was about three or four feet deep. He moved the stiffened duffel bag around until it loosened. Once he was able to pull the bag loose he unzipped it and found that what he was looking for was still there.

He grabbed his duffle bag and discarded the tools then hopped back on the bus back to Los Angeles. When he made it back to the hotel room he opened up the bag and didn't bother counting the money. He knew that there was enough to last him until old age. Now he could rest knowing that he had the resources to do what he had to do. In America money meant freedom and now he felt like he had truly been released from confinement. Now he had to visit some people after he used the key that his niece just handed him.

2

THE BLOCK IS HOT

No one is so brave that he is not disturbed by something unexpected!
Julius Caesar

Past- ten years ago:

Tango was relaxing while munching on steak and lobster in his living room. He wasn't even worried about the money run he had to do later on. His people understood that their money needed to be right. Besides he took care of everyone and people that were a part of his team ate well. His wife was in the bedroom watching television while his daughter was nibbling off of his plate sitting right next to him. He glanced at her being playfully annoyed.

"You know I would have fixed you some too?" Tango smiled.

"I know daddy but I just want some of yours. When is Auntie Missy bringing Melanie over so she can do my hair? We're supposed to go to World on Wheels tonight." Samantha commented.

"I know, I know. You know Missy is not going to keep you two away from each other. I'll take ya'll after I get done with my business, ya hear?"

Samantha nodded then leaned back on the couch after taking some food from off his plate. Tango stood up and stretched looking down at his lovely daughter.

"You can kill the rest of it. Let me talk to yo mama before I go and I will see ya'll back here around seven. If yo Uncle Cisco calls tell him I will be stopping by to holler at him in about an hour."

Samantha got up to hug and kiss her father then resumed her scavenging of his plate. Tango walked into the room to see his wife laid out asleep with the television blasting. He leaned over the bed and gently kissed her on the lips. Her eyes slightly opened to see her husband standing over her. She softly smiled and glancing up at the man she adored.

"You are about to do your runs huh? Be careful and be ready to make me feel good tonight. Melanie and Samantha can't wait for you to take them to World on Wheels. But you and I will have some alone time." Loretta slyly grinned.

"Don't threaten me with a good time." Tango smiled.

He gave her one more kiss before he walked out of the bedroom door. He couldn't help but look back one last time at the love of his life. When he made it back to the living room he noticed the plate of food was abandoned and the front door was slightly open.

"I guess Missy and Melanie finally made it." He smiled then walked out the door.

Samantha was already near the fence waiting for Melanie to get out of the car. Tango stepped on the porch looking around on both sides to make sure there wasn't anyone or anything he should worry about.

"What's up big sis?" He yelled to Missy.

"Nothing Kevin, how have you been? These two, right here, are worrying me to death about going to World on Wheels tonight. Melanie was worrying me so much I thought she was the mother and I was the daughter." Missy pointed at the two teenage girls.

Tango laughed while three of his favorite four women came walking up the walkway. They all walked past him staring then simultaneously they all began giggling.

"What's so funny?" Tango asked playfully.

"You are always looking so serious. By the way, if you see our knucklehead cousin Cisco, tell him he hasn't been coming by to see us lately." Missy replied.

"I've been keeping him busy, plus Dionne is pregnant now. If he is not taking care of business, he's tending to his pregnant girl." Tango replied.

"Okay, Okay, but he could at least make an honest woman out of that child. Tell him his cousin said he needs to go ahead and marry that girl. Seems to me, like this generation is going to start producing only baby mamas and baby daddies and not husbands and wives." She playfully complained.

"I know big sis, you are old school like me. Things are changing nowadays though. These young people want freedom without responsibility. The new generation of hustlers are even different. Well I got to go…but I will be sure to relay that message to Cisco." Tango chuckled while walking out the gate.

Drew Dog walked out of the house as fresh as he wanted to be. His creased Levis laid over his blue Puma tennis shoes. His white T-shirt easily lay over his body, revealing his bulging muscles. He walked with a slight limp from when he was shot several years before. His fresh blue golf hat tilted slightly to the side, laying over his small afro. He had finally figured some things out and wanted to act on it. His road dog, Shook expected him to show up any minute. They had some kinks to work out before they put everything into action. Drew Dog kept his thirty-eight revolver tucked under his waist just in case some trouble came his way. As he approached his road dog's house, Shook, stepped on the porch to greet him. Shook was a stocky man with a light brown complexion. He had to constantly prove himself because he was considered a pretty boy. Whenever one of the homies had to prove himself by fighting one of the homies he would always be the one they chose. Before long, his big homies would shake their heads whenever he was chosen because he had quickly become nice with his fists. His reputation was well known by the time he had reached the tender age of fifteen. That was how he got his nickname. People used to brag about his physical abilities like this. "He shook another big nigga off of him the other day."

Shook walked up to the fence to embrace his comrade and road dog. They walked outside of the gate before anyone said anything. Shook had grown hard in the face at the age of nineteen. After a three and a half year stint in Youth Authority he was a battle tested soldier. His comrade Drew Dog was more of a thinker when it came to making moves for some serious money. They balanced each other out.

"Look here cuz, we gone have to get our hands on some serious paper. That nigga Tango ain't trying to put a nigga on for shit. That nigga Cisco is his cousin so maybe we can get at him." Drew Dog began.

"I thought you already got at the nigga about putting us on and all he wanted us to do was curb serve," Shook replied.

"I don't mean talk to him. I mean we run in on his spot and take care of that nigga. We lay that nigga down then we can open up some shit for ourselves." Drew Dog explained.

"But Cisco is from our set. That nigga is one of the founders of our hood. Besides we gone be the first people they would blame for that shit if that nigga comes up missing." Shook said.

"We wouldn't do that shit ourselves. We would get someone else to run up on that nigga. He is the muscle that Tango has and he is the only nigga that is really holding down his stash. We get that nigga out the way then we gon' be good. I'm telling you cuz, fuck that nigga Cisco. He's making major paper with his cousin while the homies is walking around broke. If that nigga had real love for the hood he would put us hungry niggas on first; but instead he's keeping that shit between him and his punk ass cousin." Drew Dog bitterly explained.

"Okay, so say we get some niggas to do that shit? Who would be the niggas that will run up in his house and smoke OG Cisco and Tango if it ain't us?" Shook inquired.

"I was thinking about these slob niggas that's been trying to holla at Tidbit. She was telling me that she had some niggas over there where she moved trying to get at her all the time."

"We gon' have some slob niggas kill one of our OGs? Cuz, have you lost yo muthafuckin mind?" Shook said in disbelief.

"Hell nah, nigga. Think about it. We make sure we have an alibi then we can have them niggas smoke Cisco while the other homies will want to war with them niggas behind that shit. We will be killing two birds with one stone cuz. Tidbit told me that those niggas like jacking fools. We let her tip them niggas to the spot then we don't have to worry about Cisco moving weight in the hood. Then we can move on some connections I got because niggas got to fuck with us because he's dead. It ain't any way this shit could go wrong. Even if those slob niggas live after everything hits the fan, none of the homeboys will believe we sent them to do that shit." Drew Dog elaborated passionately about his plan.

Shook pondered on his words for a brief moment. He didn't like smoking one of his own homeboys, but Cisco hadn't helped any of the homies go any higher than the curb. Tango wasn't really an issue because he didn't live in the hood. Matter of fact, he didn't know where Tango lived. If the high roller had some bite, he would more than likely go after the Bloods that smoked his cousin.

"I'm with it cuz, but you better make sure that your cousin Tidbit is careful." Shook said.

"Yeah, I thought about that. It's going to take a little time before she can get those niggas to listen to her. She might have to go as far as fuck one of the niggas. She said that one of them she thought was cute. I ain't really cool with my little cousin fucking with a slob nigga but this is business."

"You got some more of that weed you were smoking last night?" Shook asked.

"You better believe it."

Drew Dog pulled out a joint already rolled out of his side pocket. He had to straighten it out because it had bent a little from being in his pocket. He lit it up with his blue lighter and puffed on it several times before he passed it to Shook. Shook slightly smiled, barely cracking open his obvious weed lips. He puffed on the joint several times allowing the marijuana smoke to flow through his lungs. He held it in for several seconds before exhaling.

"You know that nigga Fat Rat is barbecuing today. That fat ass nigga gon' be cooking ribs, chicken and everything. All the homies supposed to go over there for his birthday. Even that nigga Cisco supposed to shoot through."

"Yeah I heard about that shit. You want to step through there in a little bit? I wanted to run by Kelly's house so I can get some pussy. Let me hit that ass while her moms is at work then we can link up after that and bail to the party together."

"Alright then cuz, get at me later."

They finished the last remnants of the joint then went their separate ways. Drew Dog only had to walk a couple of blocks and around a corner to get to Kelly's house. She was a sexy light skinned bombshell with an unusually large backside. She only stood about five feet one and she always wore her hair in a ponytail. She had grown used to niggas worshipping her but Drew Dog knew how to keep her in line. That was what made her like him so much. He walked on her block and noticed that her mother's car wasn't there. He looked around cautiously trying to avoid nosy neighbors. He knocked on the door then turned around again to see if anyone was looking. The door swung open immediately.

"Damn Andrew, I thought you were coming over here about an hour ago." She playfully complained.

"I had to take care of some shit cuz. You're wearing the shit out of those jeans though. You gon' let me in or you gon' let one of yo nosy ass neighbors see me on yo porch?"

She opened the door then peaked outside to see if anyone was looking after he walked inside. He glanced around the house before sitting down on the couch.

"Aw snap, those are the new blue Pumas. When did you get those muthafuckas, they are fresh as fuck?" She said enthusiastically.

"I picked these up at the Slauson swap meet about a week ago. Those 62 Brim niggas almost got me and the homie Shook but we rolled up out of there before that shit went down." Drew Dog gloated.

"My homegirl Chante is really trying to fuck with that nigga Shook. She's been getting on my nerves about his ass. You need to go ahead and hook that shit up." She smiled then sat next to him on the couch.

"We'll set up a double date or something. But I didn't come over here to talk about them." Drew Dog put his hand in her shirt.

"What you come over here for?" She asked rhetorically.

He began kissing on her neck while unbuttoning her shirt. He struggled to loosen her bra.

"Nigga you gone give me a hicky." She moaned.

"You shouldn't be fucking anyone else but me, anyway." He replied.

"I'm talking about my mama tripping out about that shit."

He ignored her complaints and continued kissing her neck and her chest. Once he finally pulled her bra loose he began to suck hard on her pink nipples.

"Oooh that's it right there Andrew." She moaned.

He allowed his tongue to explore her upper body while grabbing the back of her ponytail. She loved the way he took total control over her. He finally stood her up and made her ease out of her skin tight jeans. She let her panties drop with her jeans to the ground.

He stood her up in front of him and grabbed a hold of that enormously fat ass. He then stood up to lay her on the couch. He spreads her legs to opposite sides of the couch before letting his boxers and Levis drop to his ankles. She looked at him with complete lust, submitting to his aggressive domination. He quickly plunged his dick inside of her with hard and forceful thrusts. Her legs shook as she felt a small orgasm. He continued to beat it up, pounding furiously into her. She wanted him to do it that way; she wanted him to fuck her hard. After making her cum for a second time he lifted her up and bent her over the couch. That large redbone fat ass tilted upward over the couch in his direction. He moaned as he penetrated once again with force and determination. He grabbed a hold of both ass cheeks then put his right foot on the edge of the couch. She tried to run but he had too good of a grip of those ass cheeks. She had to take the rough penetration that he was giving to her. She began to enjoy the pleasure pain and in fact started pushing her ass into his pelvis with more fervor. He started stroking harder and faster while she kept up with his momentum. Sweat began to drip from his chest to her ass making it glisten in the dimly lit living room. She could feel it. She knew it was on its way. In a matter of seconds he gave out a low moan then released inside of her. His body shook while she kept pushing her ass into his pelvis. She continued to push upward until she felt his dick go limp then slip from out of her. He still had a tight vice grip on her ass while breathing profusely.

He stood stiff trying to intake the experience to the fullest extent. She broke from his grip and began wiping the sweat from off his chest. She gently puckered her lips and kissed on the tip of his dick. He was extremely sensitive to the soft kisses. He backed away trying to resist her feminine wiles. She slowly leaned on the couch to give him time to regain himself. He walked over to the couch and collapsed next to her. It would take several minutes for him to feel up to doing anything else. She had drained him from all his energy.

"Where's yo phone at?" He asked.

Kelly got up to hand him the phone. He glanced at her as she stood over him while he dialed the number. His facial expression was clear that he wanted to have some privacy. She backed away then smacked her lips.

"You better not make a long distance call. My mama will go the fuck off." Kelly commented.

"Girl, I'm calling my little cousin Tidbit. You know she done moved over there in slob territory. I'm just checking on her."

Kelly waived him off while he waited for his cousin to pick up the phone. Tidbit snatched up the phone after the third ring. She was breathing hard when she answered the phone.

"Hello?"

"What's up, little Tidbit?"

"Who is this?"

"You don't recognize your own family when they call you? I mean, you just moved over there and you already forgot about yo own cousin. Do they got you claiming they set by now or what?" He berated her.

"What's up Andrew? I thought you were some bill collector mama was trying to dodge. What the fuck you doing calling me so early in the morning?"

"It ain't that early. Matter of fact, the early bird gets the worm." Drew Dog replied.

"Nigga what do you want this early in the morning? I don't know shit about a worm, all I know is if you want to talk we can do that shit this weekend. Other than that I'm about to bounce."

"Where are you going? Auntie Janet ain't letting you run around here like you're grown or some shit." He interrogated her.

"I'm gon' hang up Andrew if you don't want anything."

"Alright, alright...I got something you might want to pass on to them niggas you say be doing all the jacking. They should come up on a few of those things if they do that shit right."

"Are you talking about that nigga Big Red? You want me to tell him about doing a lick. That nigga been trying to get with me since I've moved over here. Why don't you do that shit yourself if they coming up like that?" She asked.

"Quit asking so many muthafuckin questions. I just need you to pass the word down to them as if you know of a spot that they can come up on the next time he tries to talk to you. Say the shit in passing, and then bring it up another time when I've given you more details to the shit. We don't want those niggas thinking that you set them up. You still got to live over there."

"Okay but you gon' need to make more sense when I come by yo house this weekend."

"For sure." Drew Dog smiled.

When he hung up the phone Kelly looked at him suspiciously without commenting. She figured it would be unwise to ask any questions because it would clearly indicate to him that she was listening. She decided to walk in the kitchen instead.

"Are you hungry? I can cook something up if you want me to."

"What ya'll got?"

"A lot of shit...Are you hungry or not?" She sassily replied.

"Yo ass can't cook." Drew Dog laughed.

"Well fuck it then. Since I can't cook, yo black ass can starve."

"I'm just fucking with you. Yeah, fix me something to eat. So I can build up my energy to hit that ass one last time before yo moms gets home."

Drew knew that he would be living the good life at least until four in the afternoon. Might as well make the best out of it before he went to the barbecue one of his homies was throwing. Just so he wouldn't take any chances he planned on leaving before noon.

By the time he met up with Shook, Fat Rat already had most of the meat cooked. They walked in the backyard observing everything that was going on. Fat Rat was behind the grill. He nodded to them when they walked in. Cisco and three other OGs were playing dominoes and drinking beer.

"Damn Fat Rat, cuz, you gon' have to hurry up with that grub. You got grown men over here starving." Bullet yelled.

"Alright nigga, give me a few minutes and this shit will be ready." Fat Rat replied after putting chicken in a pan.

Drew Dog watched Fat Rat prepare everything while he and Shook stood near the gate entrance. Drew Dog and Cisco made brief eye contact without either man saying anything. Cisco's eyes followed Bullet's hands while he shuffled up the dominoes. He felt something subtle coming from Drew Dog and Shook so he observed them through his peripheral.

"The food is ready." Fat Rat announced.

Everyone jumped up and headed for the table. A few of the homegirls that were inside fixing accessories came outside. They had potato salad, chips and a few other items to go with the barbecue. When everyone finally grabbed a plate and went over to their side of the backyard Fat Rat went up to Cisco and put his arm around him.

"I got major love for this nigga right here. If it wasn't for Cisco I wouldn't have been able to put this thing together. This is a real muthafuckin homie, cuz."

Cisco felt a little embarrassed but he nodded his head once. When Shook and Drew Dog went over to the corner they were holding their paper plates and talking as low as possible.

"I'm telling you nigga, everything we talked about earlier is about to come true. Once we got everything in place we gon' be straight. I even got an alibi. We can be at this muthafucka when everything hits the fan." Drew Dog whispered.

Shook just nodded not realizing Cisco was looking at them both from time to time.

Two weeks went by; Drew Dog and Shook were once again hanging out at Fat Rat's house. Down the street and around the corner Cisco was preparing to close up shop. He had plans to hang out of the homie Fat Rat's house and get drunk. He had the spot closed down early plus he had spoken to his cousin Tango earlier in the day. He had explained that it would be another party at Fat Rat's house and he wanted to shut it down early. He was selling a quarter of a kilo or better of that raw Columbian cocaine. But everyone had already copped their dope today so he didn't have to worry about any late customers. He sent his homeboy Lazy to the party because he figured he wouldn't need any muscle. If some shit went down he should be able to handle his own. He had his thirty-eight tucked away in his Cadillac.

Unbeknownst to Cisco there was a couple of criminals waiting for him to step outside onto the porch. They watched his homeboy leave as they patiently waited for him. Before he could set both feet on the porch he was rushed at gunpoint. They pushed him inside the house and to the hardwood floor. He grunted as his head slammed onto the hardwood.

"Aw cuz, what the fuck is ya'll niggas doing?" Cisco yelled.

"Come up out of everything you got up in this house Blood. Yo ass is getting jacked, crab ass nigga." Big Red replied. A mask covered his face.

"Who are you niggas? I'm telling you cuz you don't want to fuck with me. My cousin is a connected nigga and you don't want the problems that come with you fucking with me." Cisco pleaded.

Lavelle walked over to him then leaned down to slam the nine-millimeter pistol into his mouth. Blood started pouring from his mouth.

"Where's the muthafuckin dope, Blood?" Big Red barked.

"I don't know what you're talking about." Cisco said. His words were muffled from the gun held in his mouth.

Lavelle slammed the pistol into his head another time. He allowed Cisco to regain his senses then he cocked his gun.

"I'm telling you Blood, if you don't get to talking nigga we gon' work yo ass slow. All yo muthafuckin homeboys is at a party right now so this shit can be slow and painful or quick and easy." Lavelle whispered up close.

"It's under the floor board in the closet in that first room to the right." Cisco surrendered.

Big Red pointed his head in the direction of the room and Lavelle went inside with his pistol ready. After a few minutes he came out with a box that had a dead bolt lock on it. He dropped the box right next to Cisco and glared at him.

"The key is in my pocket."

Big Red went through his pocket for the keys then found the key that would open the lock. When they opened the lock it was dope and cash in the box. Lavelle and Big Red looked at each other and nodded.

"Look man, you can take that shit and bounce. Ya'll go your way and I go mine. This shit ain't got to be brought up again."

"You talk too muthafuckin much Blood." Big Red replied.

"I'm just saying it doesn't have to go any further than this. Take what you came for and we all can go our seperate ways." Cisco subtly pleaded.

"Nah Blood, yo crab ass got to get yo cap peeled nigga. We ain't supposed to leave a witness after a score like this." Lavelle commented.

"Come on now. I don't know how you look because you got those masks over ya'll faces. I won't even speak on this shit and will take the loss with no problem." Cisco replied.

"What about yo relative? If we let you live and he finds out who we are ain't he gon' handle us. But if there are no witnesses how can he find out?" Big Red said; he was obviously amused. He wanted to see how much Cisco would beg for his life.

"Look man, I'll let bygones be bygones because my girl is pregnant right now and I want to see my baby." Cisco continued.

Big Red and Lavelle both looked at each other. There were smirks on their faces because they already knew they were going to kill him. They were told to make sure he was dead or there would be hell to pay. Cisco observed the exchange and finally realized that he was doomed.

"I know those niggas Drew and Shook had something to do with this shit." Cisco sighed.

"That's what the homie is talking about Blood. You talk too muthafuckin much. We don't know any niggas named Drew and Shook and if they were right here, right now we would peel they cap just like we about to peel yours."

Lavelle made sure he secured everything in the bag. Both of the Bloods looked back at the helpless Crip and began to let off fire. In a matter of moments his body went limp after being riddled with bullets. Before they walked out the door they peaked outside. The house on one side was vacant and the house on the other side had all its lights out. They both walked in the direction of the vacant to their parked car that was a little ways down the street. They had to pick up the pace knowing that they were in enemy territory and could get killed. They didn't say a word to each other until they made it inside the stolen car they had secured. Big Red started up the engine with his screwdriver as they rolled away from the scene as quietly as possible. They didn't relax until they were dipping on the back streets of their own neighborhood.

"I'm telling you Blood, we came up like a muthafucka. That little bitch Tidbit is gon' always have a place in my heart." Big Red laughed.

"Yeah that little bitch knew what she was talking about. You think she knew those niggas that crab nigga was talking about just now?"

"Probably so, but she knew they probably wouldn't have the heart to do that kind of shit. That little bitch knows that we don't give a fuck. And she's not gon' drop dime because her name might come up in the mix. So it's a win-win situation for us Blood." Big Red replied.

They dumped the car off in an alley then went to Big Red's garage to count up the profit they made on one night's work.

3
SETTLING IN

It is not the same when a fighter moves because he wants to move; and another when he moves because he has to!
Joe Frazier

<u>Present day:</u>
Tango lay in the bed of his new apartment nearby his beloved niece. He wanted to be out of what was going on in Los Angeles. He didn't want to disrupt anything with his sudden appearance. He had laid low for about two months by now. He recently found his cousin Cisco's baby mama. It took a little time for him to find out that she had moved to the city of El Monte. He promised to go by and visit Dionne soon so that he could talk to her and see his ten year old second cousin. That was his only link to his dead cousin by blood. He heard through the grapevine that she had given him the name, Denmark. It was a different kind of name for a young black boy he considered. He wondered even more if Cisco would have approved of the name since his legal name was Kenyon.

His mind wandered to the day he found out his cousin Cisco was killed. It wasn't until the next afternoon he realized Cisco had been robbed and killed. He didn't begin to worry until by mid afternoon Cisco hadn't returned any of his pages. When he went to the spot to see what was going on, that was when he saw the police and paramedics out front. There were a bunch of people crowded around the area as the paramedics rolled Cisco's corpse out on a gurney. Tango had made his way through the crowd to the front of the house. He noticed a few familiar faces before he made it to the front. The police had everything secured so at some point he wasn't allowed to go any further. The sun was extremely bright that day, Tango remembered. When he seen that the body in the gurney was covered from head to toe, he realized what had happened. Two homicide detectives in business suits walked outside on the porch looking for potential witnesses. They scanned the crowd to only find people turning their heads when eye contact was made. Tango didn't budge from his position and stared at the two detectives. They walked outside of the yard and approached Tango.

"Who is that laying up in that gurney?" Tango asked, knowing the answer.

"Kenyon Roe." The stocky Black detective replied.

The Hispanic detective watched Tango's reaction and it was obvious that Mr. Roe was a loved one. He pulled out his pen and pad while observing the bystanders through his peripheral. Tango had his face in his hands trying to not let anyone see him cry. He couldn't give them the satisfaction. More than likely they had something to do with it or knew who had something to do with it.

"I'm Detective Maldonado and this is Detective Banks. Are you related to the victim sir?" Maldonado asked.

"Yeah, he is my cousin."

"What is your name sir?" Maldonado continued.

"I'm Kevin Davenport."

"First off, we are sorry for your loss. It appears that it was a robbery/murder and we want to get to the bottom of it. Do you have any information that might lead us in the direction of finding who did this to your cousin?" Maldonado asked.

"Not really, I don't even know of any enemies he might have had. You will have to excuse me. I have to let my family know about what happened to a member of our family." Tango turned around and walked away.

"Okay Mr. Davenport. Maybe we can talk some other time."

Tango didn't respond he just walked towards his car until he noticed two young Crips that looked familiar to him. There were other members of Cisco's set but something had drawn him to these two. He walked towards them and they appeared uneasy. He got within a few feet of them and nodded his head.

"That's fucked up what happened to Cisco cuz." The darker one commented.

"Yeah, that was my favorite cousin. What are ya'll names again?" Tango asked.

"I'm Drew and this is my homeboy Shook. We were at Fat Rat's party the night that shit went down. But I bet you it was some slob niggas on the other side. Those niggas always be trying to rob niggas. All the homies were at the party, even Lazy was at that muthafucka and he always got Cisco's back." Drew replied.

"Well Drew if you find out who those niggas are, be sure to let me know." Tango replied.

"For sure cuz, for sure." Drew nodded.

Tango remembered that day like it was yesterday. He woke up out of his slumber and prepared to take a shower. He had to go out to El Monte and he didn't know what to expect. He didn't know if Dionne would give him a warm welcome or become disgruntled. He braced himself for the worse and prepared and hoped for the best. He remembers her taking Cisco's death pretty hard, which was why it didn't make sense why she didn't name her son after him.

It took him about an hour to get dressed and drive down to El Monte. He had bought a used black Honda Civic to get around in. He wanted to be as discreet as possible. He drove down the block twice once he arrived. For some reason the address numbers on the house were hard to locate. When he found the address he had written down, he parked in front of the house. It was a gated yard with a nice lawn in front of a black and blue house. As he put the car in park, he saw a figure walk by the window. He sighed, knowing that someone was home. He didn't have any excuse that he could give himself now to why he didn't contact Dionne.

He slowly went up the walkway. When he reached the porch he rang the doorbell twice then put his hand behind his back. He heard the footsteps walking toward the door then he noticed the person trying to look through the peephole.

"Who is it?" The woman barked.

"Tango, Tango Davenport?"

There was a pause for a moment. The person behind the door was hesitating. Tango patiently waited for her to recover from the shock. Everyone assumed that he wasn't going to see daylight. It just might be a little hard to believe that he had been released from prison. It was also the fact that there might be some hidden resentment towards him. Cisco was working for him when he had gotten killed. He let his thoughts wonder for a moment, considering all the possibilities. Finally the woman peaked out of the side window to get a better look. She was satisfied with her assessment. The thick wooden door swung open to reveal a more mature but still attractive Dionne. Her eyes got big because it was still hard to believe Tango was in front of her despite the fact she was looking at him. Maybe it was a dream or some form of hallucination.

"How have you been, Dionne?"

She still didn't respond. She took some time to take it all in. Without saying a word she opened the door wider then stepped out of the way for him to come in. He glanced around the room to notice the cluttered living room. There was too much furniture in this small space. It made the room feel stuffier than it actually was.

"I'm sorry Tango but I still can't believe that you are standing in front of me right now. My eyes are telling me one thing, my ears are telling me the same thing, but it is still hard to swallow."

"You look beautiful." Tango replied.

"Thank you, but I could have sworn they gave you life in prison. You didn't break out or anything?" She sounded nervous.

"I won my appeal. It is hard to believe, but my lawyers were able to prove that evidence was tampered with and I didn't have a fair and impartial trial. When they read that verdict at first, ten years ago, I didn't think I would be walking free either." He chuckled.

"Well have a seat. I'm going into work a little later today and I was just unwinding. I got to ask though, how did you find me?"

"I went to visit your cousin Colleen. She still has that house in north Long Beach. I knew that she owned the house so I figured she still might be there. Her mother was home; so she was telling me that Colleen went out of town on business and wasn't returning for a few weeks. I got your address from your Aunt June."

Dionne laughed for a brief moment. She knew her auntie well enough to know that he wasn't lying.

"She talked your head off, huh?"

They both started laughing. Tango sat down as she maneuvered through her living room into the kitchen.

"I'm making some tea, do you want some." She yelled from the kitchen.

"That will be fine. How has everything been going with you?"

She walked back into the living room within a minute with two coffee mugs. She handed him one of the mugs before she responded.

"I've been fine as of lately. You know I had to move away from that whole little scene in L.A." She shook her head.

"I've been hearing that a lot lately. I seen my niece Melanie and she told me the same thing."

"I felt so sorry for that poor little girl. I guess she's a grown woman by now. How is she holding up nowadays, I know she went through a lot back in those days? I was devastated when I heard about everything." She commented while taking a seat.

He took a few sips of the tea before responding. He didn't want to dwell on what Melanie went through because he knew how angry he would become. Instead he wanted to know what Dionne knew.

"What did you hear about everything that went down with Cisco and how is my little cousin Denmark doing? Is he big now or what? Does he look like Cisco?"

"Denmark is doing good. He is in the fifth grade. His full name is Denmark Kenyon Roe. When I was pregnant with him I started hearing a whole bunch of shit after Cisco was killed. I didn't want too many people to know his real name. I remember Cisco telling me that little bitch Tidbit kept openly flirting with him days before he died. He said she was coming on real strong the weekend before he was killed. It was amusing to him; but not to me, because he looked at her as jailbait. I just didn't know if someone would try to hurt my son or me after Cisco was killed."

"Who is Tidbit?"

"Some little fast tale bitch that was related to Drew Dog but now lived in Blood territory. I heard she got a baby by one of those slob niggas now. That was what Colleen told me about four or five years ago."

"I've never heard of her before today. Did she do something to threaten Denmark or you to make you think that she might try to harm you?"

"I wouldn't say all that. It was just crazy to me that everyone from the hood was at the party when Cisco was killed. It just seemed too convenient to me. Cisco was throwing parties for the hood and everything. He had just thrown a birthday party and barbecue for Fat Rat's fat ass. It was somebody in the hood that heard or seen something but everyone acted dumb. I didn't know what to expect from any of those muthafuckas. Tango I was scared." She honestly explained.

"Yeah but it is all over now. I wouldn't even worry about it now. I know you loved him just as much as I did." Tango replied

"Yeah, and every day I look at Denmark he looks more and more like his daddy. Sometimes it can be haunting." She shook her head.

"Well don't just sit there, show me some pictures of my little cousin." Tango jovially replied.

"Yeah sure, I just got back his fifth grade pictures anyway. Let me go in the room and grab them." She walked into another room.

Tango laid back on the couch thinking about everything she said and he was secretly seething inside. He had to remain calm because some things he didn't have any control over. His thoughts wandered off for a moment before she returned with pictures of Denmark.

After showing him the pictures he realized how realistic her description of him was. He looked as though Cisco had spit him. He might have been a little chubbier in the face, but they were almost identical. This observation brought tears to his eyes he tried to hold back. They reminisced for about thirty more minutes then he got up to leave. He promised her he would visit frequently. Right now he was all about settling in he told her. He didn't want anything to do with Los Angeles and what was out there. It was several times he had to fight back his tears which was strangely unusual to him. Besides the bitter moments down memory lane he felt happy to have seen Dionne. He climbed into his Honda Civic and drove home.

When he made it back home he realized how tired he was. He had to run a few errands before he went to sleep. It was still very early in the day but at the very least he needed a long nap. The anticipation and the anxiety of reconnecting with Dionne was somewhat draining. The first thing he did was fix something to eat. He laid out some clothes for later on then left to pay a few bills. When everything was said and done he was so tired he could barely keep his eyes open. He was hoping to go by Melanie's house to check on her and her son, but there wasn't any hope for that tonight. He quickly got undressed then climbed into bed. Once his body hit the bed he suddenly fell into a deep coma like sleep. He didn't realized how exhausted he was until he got in bed. He was officially dead to the world for the night.

"Look here Blood, I was gone fuck the nigga up anyway. Ole young ass nigga can't even piss straight and acting like he some kind of shot caller. He's down to put in work, but fuck that little nigga. It's all about the paper nowadays. You know what the fuck I'm saying Vell?"

"I Bee what you saying Blood. He's a little rider for the set but some of these young niggas nowadays don't know how to respect their elders." Lavelle replied.

"That's what I'm talking about, nigga. True, he's a little Damu rider but that shit don't mean shit to me. I was putting in work when that little nigga was in a stroller. All I'm saying is I got a gun too."

"So what are you about to do? You gon' cut the little nigga off from his money? If he's complaining about not getting paid right now, what you think he's gone do when you cut him all the way off?" Lavelle considered.

"Fuck that little nigga, Blood. That's on everything I love." Big Red vehemently replied.

It was on his mind though. A flash of fear ran through him, considering what one of his little homies was capable of. His little homeboy, Boston, was a trigger happy nigga that didn't mind shooting anyone. He had proved to be a formidable foe against the Crips whenever a feud took place. Big Red had paid Boston less than what was the normal rate and Boston somehow found out. Naturally the OGs would back Big Red, but he was beginning to get a reputation for being shady. His own homeboys that grew up with him started looking at him as a nigga that could be a snake at times. Big Red pulled out a 380 double action when his homeboy Porky wanted to fight him over some money. Big Red had size but he didn't want a fair one with Porky. He told Porky he was too rich to fight. All the homies was outside so it left a bad taste in everyone's mouth. Porky just realized it was best to stop fucking with him. Now he had this dilemma with Boston. Boston didn't have any problem pulling a gun just as much as him.

"I'm going to have to get at the little nigga somehow. If I give the nigga the money then its gon' make it seem like he's punking me. So I got to feed the nigga some bullshit hope and then serve his ass when he gets comfortable." Big Red replied.

"Yeah that might work. If you come straight at that nigga it's definitely gon' to be war in the street" Lavelle replied.

They were standing in front of Lavelle's house smoking some Entica Skunk weed. This is what it was called before it was called Chronic and Kush. They were considered two of the high rollers in the hood. They had money, cars and bitches. Tidbit had a baby by Big Red by now but he couldn't make her his lady because she was a crab bitch at heart. Deep down though he didn't love any woman more. If it wasn't for a lick that she tipped them on to ten years ago he might not be in this position. Lavelle had a lot of respect for her as well. That little petite frame but round backside made her a favorite among many men but she just had love for the other side. Big Red stretched and yawned, feeling the day wind down on him. It was a clear night outside and it almost appeared as though there wasn't a cloud in the sky. He thought about taking it home to this little bitch he was fucking with named Brenda.

"I might as well take my ass home to Brenda and suck on those big ass titties. What are you about to do Blood?" Big Red asked.

"Shit, I might go inside and listen to Cindy talk major shit before she gives up the drawers. You know I had to beat her ass the other day for talking shit?"

"Yeah, yo ass better be glad she's dark skinned. You socked that bitch in her jaw. You could have broken that shit or something." Big Red chuckled.

"If the bitch can talk tough like a man then she should be able to take a hit like a man."

They both laughed. Big Red yawned again, obviously ready to take it home. He glanced in the direction of Brenda's house and looked at Lavelle.

"I'm about to bounce Blood. You B' up, B' down and B' bool." He shook hands with his comrade.

He walked away from the yard watching all sides an enemy could approach. He wasn't particularly worried because they weren't warring with anyone. He also understood that that didn't mean anything. Any given day of the week someone can decide to start a war on either side. This thought made him wonder about his troubles with Boston. He knew that the young soldier was always eager to put in work. He had rank on the youngster but that didn't mean much in this generation. Some of these young niggas went against the code of respecting your elders. He walked half a block when he heard noise coming out of the bushes. He almost reached for his gun safely hidden under his belt until he realized it was just a cat.

"I need to stop being so fucking paranoid." He said out loud.

He had deliberately parked his 69 Chevy down the street from where he was at. His car was starting to be known as a Damu vehicle. He's never put in work in the ride but certain Crips remembered what he drove. He pulled his keys out of his pocket then looked both ways before he climbed in the car. His rearview mirror and other mirrors in the car suited his paranoid nature. He made sure no one was following as he pulled into Brenda's driveway. Brenda's porch was unusually dark but he figured it was probably a light bulb out. He made sure he had his skunk weed and some Zig Zags papers to roll up the weed. Brenda was definitely going to want to smoke before and after they finish fucking. He organized everything while sitting in his car. He knew to leave his money in the car because Brenda loved to go through his pockets while he was asleep. She had no problem lying to his face when he would confront her about stolen items. He chuckled, realizing he had someone that can be just as conniving as him. He rubbed his eyes one last time before climbing out the car.

"I might not even feel like fucking this bitch…nah I'm at least going to get her to suck my dick." He laughed.

He walked up to the porch staggering slightly. He had his eyes focused on what was in his pockets. He didn't notice the large figure standing behind a tall plant that Brenda neglected. He was in his safe zone when he came to Brenda's house. That was where he was able to relax and unwind. He slowly worked his way up the stairs. He was already high so smoking more weed would only put him to sleep. He pulled out everything he had just to make sure he was straight one last time. He dropped his bag of weed accidentally.

"Damn Blood!"

He picked the weed up from off the ground and finally made it up to the top step of the porch. He didn't have any keys to her house but he had forgotten for a moment. He glanced up for a second to his right.

"What the fuck…"

Everything went black. He couldn't understand what happened to him until he awoke. His eyes slowly opened and he realized that he was lying next to Brenda but they were both tied up and gagged. Big Red couldn't believe his predicament. He looked around frantically trying to make sense of the whole thing. Then suddenly a large figure walked into the living room. He couldn't make sense of who the guy was because he was wearing a black ski mask. The mask covered most of his face except his eyes. The man didn't say anything to him at first but moved around quickly. The masked man was apparently setting something up. When he was finished he walked over to Big Red and squatted down to talk to him. He removed the gag from Big Red's mouth.

"They call you Big Red, right?"

"Nah homie you got the wrong nigga." Big Red lied.

The masked man's gun quickly slammed into Big Red's forehead. Then he paused for a moment then repeated the act.

"Alright Blood, it's me. But I don't have any money on me, but I can tell you where to get it. We can definitely work something out." Big Red pleaded.

"I don't want yo money."

"I don't have anything to do with what you beefing with me about. I'm telling you Blood if that nigga Boston sent you after me, I can pay you more than he paid you." Big Red replied.

"I don't know anyone named Boston. But I'm going to need you to clear some shit up with me. If you answer the questions right then you get to live. If you try to bullshit me then I will kill yo ass slow. Yo broad will get taken care of just as well.

So think carefully about the questions I asked you. Oh by the way, I'm not any of your Blood or Cuz."

"Alright my man, ask your questions." Big Red nervously replied.

"Ten years ago you robbed this dope spot over in Crip territory. Who was it that tipped you off to the lick?"

Big Red was worried sick after hearing the question. He never thought that he would have to answer to the robbery. His mind raced back and forth because it was obvious that his captor knew that it was him. He wondered if Tidbit gave him up. Then he began to wonder if Tidbit was even alive. Nah…she must have turned on him and let the people know who did the lick.

"My time is valuable muthafucka. Who tipped you to the dope spot?"

"It was this little hoodrat crab bitch named Beverly but everyone calls her Tidbit." Big Red admitted.

"How did you do the nigga you killed? Did you make him suffer or did you kill him off real quick?"

"We killed him off real quick. But I'm telling homeboy it was my home Chef that killed that nigga not me. Chef is dead now but I told him we should spare the nigga but he wasn't trying to hear it." Big Red pleaded.

"You are fucking lying. In the coroner's report you shot him a few times before you even killed him."

The masked man pulled out a pistol with a silencer attached to it. Big Red's eyes got big as the gun was pointed at his knee caps. With one quick pull of the trigger a bullet pierced his knee cap. Big Red began to scream but the masked man covered his mouth. Brenda lay next to him crying her heart out. They were utterly at the mercy of this masked maniac. It was apparent that he had no intentions of showing mercy.

"Okay my nigga it was my homeboy Lavelle that done that shit. We didn't want any witnesses." Big Red cried.

"What makes you think that I want any witnesses?"

Brenda looked at Big Red with total disgust. She couldn't believe that he would turn on Lavelle like that knowing that the man would probably kill them anyway. She had very little respect for him after that and it showed on her face.

"Even your woman doesn't respect you anymore. And I am not your nigga."

Big Red glanced at Brenda then lowered his head in shame. The masked man made sure that his gun was loaded and prepared. He walked over to them both and began shooting Big Red from his groin all the way up to his torso and chest. He finished the last shot to his head. He looked at the woman and realized he had to kill her too. Her eyes showed some hint of fear but she had silently accepted her fate. They stared at each other for a while then he squatted down to look her directly in her eyes.

He put the pistol to her head and fired one shot to her dome. He did her quick and easy even though she didn't really have anything to do with it. She was in the wrong place at the wrong time. He carefully took the pistol and unscrewed the silencer. He had on gloves, but was easily able to pull out his clip and tossed them right next to Big Red and Brenda. Then he went back into the kitchen and began to pull loose all of the gas pipes and then he lit a match. He pulled a can of lighter fluid from out of his bag then walked a trace back to the bodies. He twisted up some newspaper then lit everything on fire. He allowed the fire to grow before he walked out the door. Still masked and careful he walked out of the house and quickly walked down the street. He walked half a block down the street from Brenda's house to an empty house that had been vacant for over a year. With his bag in hand he jumped into his raggedy bucket parked in front of the vacant house.

He didn't take off his mask until he was miles away from the murder scene. He finally pulled into an alleyway where his own car was parked. He made sure there was no evidence that linked him to the car. He climbed out of the bucket then put his mask and silencer in the bag. He was finished for the night so he could get some rest. He headed back out to the Inland Empire area quickly jumping on the 10 freeway. Breathing out he began to relax as he blended in to the light traffic.

"I'm settling in my new role just fine… Just fine." He said out loud.

4

THE KINGPIN

Don't depend on the enemy not coming; depend rather on being ready for him!

Sun-tzu

Past- ten years ago:

The gloomy sky drizzled rain as mourners gathered at the grave site of Kenyon Roe also known as Cisco. There was a chill in the air that everyone had to acknowledge. When people dispersed after the services, Fat Rat lowered his head as he somberly walked over to pay his respect to Cisco's cousin, who he only knew as Tango.

"Ay my man Tango, I just came by to pay my respects. I had major love for that nigga Cisco and it fucks me up that he's gone." Fat Rat began.

"Yeah you are the one they call Fat Rat, right? He always told me you were one of the coolest people from his neighborhood. We buried a good nigga today." Tango replied.

"Yeah but the shit don't add up. How did someone know he was going to be there by himself? Did someone know that everyone was going to be at my party or what? It's just a bunch of shit that doesn't make sense. Who else but niggas in the hood would know about the spot?" Fat Rat explained.

"Was it anyone from your hood that didn't show up to the party?" Tango inquired.

"Everyone was there except for the homies that was locked up or dead. It could have been a civilian but more than likely they would have just called the police." Fat Rat replied.

"I don't know my man. I appreciate you taking the time to give your condolences. The entire family wants to thank you for your attendance and your loyalty." Tango nodded.

They made eye contact for a brief moment then Fat Rat walked away. A few minutes later Leonard walked up to Tango. Tango glanced up and gave a half hearted smile. Tango had sat down by now so Leonard decided to sit next to him. Neither man said anything for a few moments. Finally Leonard felt compelled to say a few things.

"It might be good if we find out who was behind this shit. Next thing you know they will be coming after you." Leonard began.

"They don't know where I rest my head. Revenge is on my mind but I'm not about to start shooting in the dark. There are plenty of suspects but then there are no suspects. I got to keep my eyes open for awhile before I can make a serious move on anyone." Tango replied.

"Well let me know any way I can help because we shouldn't be coming to your cousin's funeral this early in his life. What did that fat nigga have to say just now?" Leonard glanced at Tango.

"He's just got a whole bunch of unanswered questions just like the rest of us. I think he is real broken up behind that shit like everyone else."

Missy walked over to Tango grief stricken with Dionne and Melanie close in tow behind her. She tapped Tango on his leg so that he would look up at her.

"Are you ready to go?"

"Yeah, I guess so."

Tango stood up and quickly embraced Leonard who stood up right after him. It wasn't a good time to talk but they looked at each other knowing they would talk soon. Tango walked toward the limousine with his family behind him. It was time for Tango to hibernate and keep away from the outside world. If he was going to get over this he had to regroup and think things out.

Drew Dog and Shook were both sitting on the couch at Shook's house smoking weed. It was the way that Drew Dog was able to unwind and plot out his next plan. Now that Cisco was out of the picture he had to start making his next move. Shook passed him the joint and he puffed away before explaining what was in the works. He dragged on the skunk weed long and hard and found himself coughing. It took him several minutes to recover as Shook laughed at him.

"Look here cuz, now that nigga Cisco is out the picture we can start putting shit in motion. But I got a feeling that nigga Tango will start serving Fat Rat's fat ass before we get started. So we gon' have to get rid of Fat Rat and probably that nigga Tango. If we knew where he lived we might be able to touch him." Drew Dog passed the joint.

"Yeah, did you see how cuz went up to that nigga Tango crying and shit? More than likely if he still gon' be putting dope in the hood he gon' do it through Fat Rat. You think Fat Rat told that nigga something about us?"

"He doesn't know shit about us to tell that nigga. I doubt that he even knows that we tried to get put on with Cisco and the nigga wanted us to be curb-servers. But I got a way to get at that nigga Tango without getting our hands dirty."

"What's that?"

"We gon' put the police on that nigga Tango. When he comes to serve Fat Rat we gon' have the police waiting on that nigga; especially if we make him out to be this big time kingpin nigga." Drew Dog smiled.

"Snitching and shit. I don't know about that shit cuz." Shook frowned.

"You want to get rid of this nigga right? The only way we gon' rid of him without smoking that nigga is getting the police to do him. It ain't like he's one of the homies anyway. We might be able to find out where he lives after we get rid of him. He more than likely left some money for his family. Once again I don't see a way we can lose." Drew Dog passionately explained.

"That nigga Tango ain't from the hood though." Shook considered.

"That's what I'm saying. We scope game on that nigga Fat Rat then tip 'One Time' to expect a drop off from Tango." Drew Dog replied.

"We're probably gon' have to smoke that nigga Fat Rat too. I mean he's going to start asking questions when we start moving weight. If we gon' be scandalous we might as well be that shit all the way." Shook glanced at his road dog.

"I know cuz, we gon' have to get rid of that nigga too…Well, I guess we won't be having anymore barbecues in the hood." They both laughed.

Tango had been waiting for thirty minutes for Leonard to show up and he still hadn't come. The last thing he needed was for him to hear about another person close to him dying. He had waited long enough. Now it was time to roll over to Fat Rat's house and give him the dope that he told him he would give to him on consignment. It wasn't that much, but it was enough to see if he could trust him. If things went well he would be able to buy wholesale from Tango like Cisco once did. He yawned as he began to put the car in drive. He pulled over when he got a phone call on his mobile phone. Tango wasn't big on using his mobile phone because it was expensive and it was only supposed to be for emergencies.

"Hello?"

"Kevin baby, this is Loretta. I just got a collect call from Leonard and he wanted me to tell you that he won't be able to make it because he is in jail. We didn't talk too long, but he was saying they were trying to charge him with carrying a concealed weapon and assault with a deadly weapon." Loretta frantically explained.

"Okay, that's why he's late. We were supposed to do something together, but I was worried when he never showed up."

"Yeah, I know that you don't like getting calls unless it's important, but I thought this was important." Loretta explained.

"Thank you baby, I'm glad you called. I'll be home in about an hour so I will see you in a little bit."

He hung up the phone and sat in the car thinking about his comrade. The plans would be altered a little but that didn't matter. He still would make the drop off. As he drove down the street the song 'What's Going On' from Marvin Gaye was playing on the radio. He sang along with the words allowing his thoughts to wander in different directions. The music of various songs began to cloud his thought and take him away from the task at hand. He stayed that way until he turned the block to where Fat Rat lived. As he hit the block he noticed an unmarked car was parked across the street from Fat Rat's house. It wasn't directly in front of the house but several houses down. Two men were sitting down waiting patiently inside the car. Tango caught a glimpse of them and noticed their alertness when he drove up. He kept his eyes on them through his peripheral and decided to pass by Fat Rat's house. It just so happened when he passed by Fat Rat walked outside his house and noticed his car. Tango tried his best to waive Fat Rat into going back into the house. Fat Rat had a puzzled look on his face as he passed by.

"That's a hint and a half past my monkey ass." Tango said aloud.

He allowed himself to get a little distance down the next two blocks before he turned left. He drove around for awhile trying to figure out what he was going to do. He was sitting on a quarter kilo of raw cocaine so he didn't want to go home. He decided to pull up to a donut shop and post up to call Fat Rat. Fat Rat would have to meet him somewhere because for some reason his house was hot. He looked around before he pulled into the parking lot.

"That fat nigga don't take me as the type to set a nigga up."

He sat in his car contemplating his next move when suddenly the same unmarked car pulled into the parking lot. He was briefly startled, but tried to remain calm. They didn't know who he was unless Fat Rat had them staked out like that. He wondered if the man was that conniving. Both detectives climbed out of their car and went on both sides of his car. The detective on his passenger side knocked on the window first. They had smirks on their faces like they knew something he didn't know. He glanced at the detective on the passenger side then glanced at the one on the driver's side.

"You mind getting out the car Tango?"

Fuck!!! He knew at that point that he was caught up in some shit. He lowered his head trying to decide what he should do. They have to have probable cause to search my vehicle, he considered. He slowly rolled down his window trying to pretend to be confused.

"What's going on officers, how do you know my name?"

"We know a lot of things about you Tango; so just step out the car so we can get this over with as soon as possible." The detective on the driver's side replied.

"First and foremost, do you have a warrant or probable cause to even bother me in the first place?"

"Look nigger, either you can do this the hard way or we can handle this the easy way. It doesn't matter to me regardless, you piece of shit." The same officer barked.

"Well you have to show me a warrant in order for me to submit to any kind of search. Then you will also have to point out any probable cause." Tango remained calm.

Suddenly the detective grabbed Tango from out of the window and began to choke him. As Tango resisted the detective began trying to pull him out of the car. In a matter of moments the second detective was also on the driver's side helping his partner. Tango began to gasp for breath as the strangle hold became tighter and tighter. Within several minutes they were able to pull him out the car and he struggled against the two officers. He fought, but the other detective grabbed a hold of one of his arms and began to handcuff him. With the end of the other handcuff the officer pulled Tango's arm back, twisting it in the process. Tango yelled in pain as the handcuffs found his other arm. He groaned as they slammed his face down on the ground. The second detective that handcuffed him immediately began searching the car.

They searched it thoroughly, trying to find something they already knew was there. High and low they tore the car apart trying to find some form of contraband. One of the detectives finally took the keys from out of the ignition and went inside the trunk. After digging through a few things they finally came up with what they were looking.

"Ah hah!" One detective announced.

Tango was lifted from off the ground and read his Miranda rights. He had gravel all over his face as onlookers stared at him. He wondered why Fat Rat would set him up. It would benefit him to make good money unless he had another supplier. He tried to make sense of the entire thing while being shoved into the police car. He wanted to lash out in a fit of rage but couldn't. Within a few weeks everything had fallen apart. The two arrogant detectives laughed and joked all the way to the police station. Tango just lowered his head and prepared for the worse. He would eventually get his phone call and tell his wife to pass the word that Fat Rat was a snitch.

Loretta relaxed at the house waiting for her husband to get home. She knew that he was going through a few things as of lately. His cousin Cisco just got robbed and killed; and now his closest buddy Leonard was looking at some jail time. She promised herself that she would cater to her man's every desire when he got home. It was starting to get late and she wondered what was taking him so long.

"He better not be dealing with that bitch Colleen." She said out loud.

"What did you say mama?" Her daughter Samantha asked from the other room.

"Never mind."

She lay on the bed, patiently waiting until she fell asleep. She was dreaming about her man coming home to make love to her when the phone broke her dream. She struggled to open her eyes in the dark. The television was blaring so she had to focus in on finding the phone. After the fourth ring she was able to grab the phone. She looked at the time by the bed and realized that it was two in the morning. Before putting the phone on her ear she glanced over at the other side of the bed to see if her husband was home.

"Hello Tango? Baby where are you at?"

"This ain't Tango this is Leonard."

"They let you make phone calls in jail at two in the morning?" She asked.

"No I'm out. I was able to make bail so I should be going to trial in a month from now."

"So are you with Tango? Did he tell you to call me or something? I was knocked out." Loretta yawned.

"Nah, I was calling hoping that Tango was at home and he could come and pick me up." Leonard replied.

"He hasn't made it home yet for some reason. Do you want me to tell him something when he gets home?"

"Well it is more about what's going on right now. I'm stuck way out here and the buses stop running and there isn't a taxi anywhere in sight…never mind, I will have to figure some shit out on my own." Leonard sighed.

"I got the Chevy in the driveway. If you want me to come and get you that's not a problem? If Tango was here I know he wouldn't have a problem doing it." Loretta offered.

"That wouldn't be taking you too much out of your way though, would it?"

"It's cool. Let me tell my daughter that I'm stepping out for a minute and I'm on my way. You are stuck in downtown L.A. right?"

"Yeah."

"I know where the county is at so I'll be down there in a little bit. Let me throw something on."

Within fifteen minutes she was dressed and knocking on Samantha's door. Samantha reluctantly answered after several knocks.

"Look baby, I'm going to pick up Leonard from somewhere so just wait for your daddy to get home, okay?"

"Okay mama." Samantha sleepily replied.

She jumped into the Chevy and sped off to pick up Leonard. Her main concern was where her husband might be. She didn't want to worry just yet. She glanced up to see the sky cloudy as if rain was on its way. She wondered if that was an omen. She didn't want to think that way so she shifted her thoughts. I wonder why the people that bailed Leonard out didn't come and pick him up? Within fifteen minutes she was pulling up on the man. Leonard smiled from ear to ear after seeing her pull up. He quickly jumped into the passenger side and sighed.

"Thank you Loretta. You ever find out where Tango was at?" He asked.

"Nope that nigga ain't come home yet. I was beginning to worry about his ass but there's no telling where he's at. I doubt something happened to him."

"Well I needed to talk to him about a few things and now he's MIA. Let that nigga know that he should link up with me as soon as possible."

"If you want to you can come back to the house and wait for his trifling ass to come home." Loretta offered.

"I haven't been to the new spot since ya'll moved. Yeah I can wait for that nigga and crash on the couch or some shit."

"I thought Tango let you come by when we weren't there. I didn't know he never brought you to the new pad."

They pulled up to the house in a matter of minutes and Leonard smiled at the landscaping. He got out the car and followed closely behind Loretta. He walked up the walkway admiring everything about the house. When he walked inside the house he was instantly taken aback by the beautiful décor. Why would Tango ever want to leave this place, he considered.

They were both tired so he didn't waste any time once he got inside. She walked into the bedroom while he admired his surroundings.

"Could you pass me a blanket Loretta?"

Leonard had no problem crashing on the comfortable couch. They both went to sleep in a matter of minutes until the phone rang. By that time daybreak had crept through the window and Loretta was able to see clearly. She had slept long and hard, answering the phone with a groggy voice.

"Hello?"

"Who is this?" The familiar voice asked.

"Who is this? This is Loretta!" Her voice began to clear.

"Oh baby you had that morning voice going on and I couldn't make out who you were. Baby, this is Kevin?"

"Yeah nigga I figured that much after your first few words. The question is where you were all night?"

"I'm in jail. These muthafuckas picked me up with some dope in the trunk of my car. They got me for resisting arrest and all kinds of shit. I need you to gather some money from some spots so that you can get me a lawyer." He replied.

She climbed from out of the bed, rubbing the sleep from her eyes, in shock from the revelation.

"I need you to hit some spots in the house as well as a few key areas. They are denying me bail because those punk ass cops got a bunch of charges on me. But once you talk to the lawyer I will be okay." Tango explained.

"But Kevin how are we going to get through all this shit while you are in jail. Baby I don't know how to handle all this…"

"Calm down Loretta, everything is going to be alright. I just need you to be cool for right now. If you do what I'm telling you to do then we should be just fine. Even if I catch some time we still will have enough to get us by until I get out. You might have to get a job but that's about it." He continued.

"Where am I supposed to get the money and when?" She frantically asked.

"I'm going to guide you through the motions, but call Missy and she will be able to help with some of this shit." He calmly replied.

"I don't know Kevin I'm scared. This is something you always handled."

"Would you shut the fuck up and be cool. Damn Loretta, you act like you are the one in jail. Now I told you I got this if you do what the fuck I'm saying to do. Now is not the time to be a punk bitch. I need you to saddle up and be a soldier or we are all in trouble." Tango viciously replied.

"Okay, okay, I'm calm and listening. You want me to get some money for your lawyer. Is some of the money stashed away in the house?"

"Yeah, some of it, but most is in different places I know couldn't get raided. That's why you need to holler at Missy and she will help you get to the other spots." Tango explained.

Loretta was frantic. "Okay, well first tell me where the places are at home and then we can go from there. By the way, Leonard was able to get out so I picked him up from jail. He tried to get in touch with you but you were in jail. He spent the night on the couch hoping you would come home."

Tango didn't reply right away. The phone was quiet for a minute before he spoke again.

"Hello? Kevin, are you there?"

"Yeah, let me speak to that nigga then I will call back later with the places you need to hit up."

"He might still be asleep." Loretta suggested.

"So what? Wake that nigga up." Tango barked.

Loretta sat the phone down. She understood that he was in jail, but still didn't appreciate the tone. She slipped on her robe then walked into the living room to find Leonard snoring. She slightly shook him hoping he would open his eyes. He didn't move initially until she shook him a second time. He coughed then slowly opened his eyes to stare at her. He hurriedly jumped up out of his sleep.

"I didn't mean to wake you Leonard but Kevin is on the phone and he wants to talk to you." Loretta smiled.

"Damn I didn't even hear the phone ring. Where is that nigga at?" He yawned.

"He's in jail and told me he wanted to talk to you on the phone." Loretta reiterated.

"Alright, do you have a phone in the kitchen?"

"Yeah."

Leonard walked to the kitchen and picked up the phone. He put it to his ear then breathed out.

"What's up Tango? How in the fuck you get caught up?" Leonard began.

"I think that nigga Fat Rat is snitching. I seen the police staked out down the street from his house. When I rolled past his house he came outside and waived his hand wondering why I didn't stop. I kept rolling because I seen those muthafuckas. Then I roll up to that Donut Stand, off Vermont and the same two detectives rolled up on me. They beat my ass and everything. They got me out to be some kind of kingpin or something." Tango explained.

"You think that fat muthafucka got something to do with my charge? Some police rolled up on me the same way but it was before I even got to my car. They searched me right on the spot and found my thirty-two." Leonard replied.

"Yeah something is going on. How did you get out?"

"I made bail. I had some money in my pocket and I put that shit up. They ran a check on the pistol and didn't find any bodies so they charged me with carrying a concealed weapon. My bail was only ten thousand for a first offense so I paid the thousand dollars in cash and was out by two in the morning. It would have been earlier than that if those muthafuckas didn't take so long processing a nigga."

"You gon' fight that shit or you gon' plea down. You might get probation if you get a lawyer." Tango replied.

"Yeah that's what I'm gon' try to do. But now we have to talk about getting yo ass out of jail. If there is anything that I can do just let me know."

"Just be a friend in some troubling times. Loretta will take you home probably a little later so I will call you collect so that we can talk in more detail. My time is about up on this phone so I'm about to back off. Tell Loretta and Samantha that I love them and tell Loretta to do what I told her to do." Tango quickly explained.

The phone went dead before Leonard could respond. He glanced at the phone for a moment then hung it up.

"What did he say?" Loretta's voice trembled.

"He told me to tell you that he loves you and Samantha and for you to do as he says."

"Okay! Are you ready for me to take you home?"

"Yeah might as well. He told me he would call me later on at the crib."

Loretta hurried in the room to get dressed. She woke up Samantha so that she could have someone to roll with back from taking Leonard home. Samantha grudgingly got out of bed and followed her mother to the Chevy.

Fat Rat came outside to roll to the grocery store to put a few things on the barbecue grill. He had one of those propane grills so he was able to cook barbecue style food whenever he liked. It had been a few days since Tango rolled by his house without stopping. He wondered what that was all about, but never heard from the man after that day. He climbed in his Monte Carlo sporting his blue golf hat, white T-shirt and blue khakis. He had just bought the latest blue Nike tennis shoes. He was an obese gangster but he always knew how to sport his clothes in a way that still made him look fresh. He pulled his keys out his pocket then looked down the street. He reminisced about his boy Cisco and lowered his head.

"That was one of the realest muthafuckas I knew, cuz." He lamented.

He fired up the engine and sped down his block hitting corners like a gangster would. He turned a couple of blocks to find himself quickly pulling up to the parking lot of the local grocery store. He planned on being in and out. He jumped out of his car and quickly walked inside. Making his way to the meat section he began to savor the taste in his mouth. A couple of steaks on the grill and he would be straight. After grabbing a few accessories he went to the longest line in the store. He didn't necessarily want to wait that long but the cashier in that line was really good looking. He would flirt with her from time to time and she seemed interested.

"She just doesn't know, us fat niggas can work it." He laughed.

She gave him the look as he drew closer in the line to the front. He smiled at her and she smiled back. It was only three customers ahead of him. When he finally reached the front he gave her another smile.

"What's up baby, you gon' quit playing with me and slide me that number. You ain't fucked with a real nigga." He smiled.

"Let me get a pen and paper and I will write my number down."

"Cool." He calmly replied.

He didn't want to seem too eager so he kept it cool without saying anything else. Inside he was excited as hell but he couldn't let her see that. She handed him the piece of paper and gave him another one of her pretty smiles.

"Alright then Ashley, I'll call yo fine ass later."

He walked out of the store as cool as he wanted to be. After all this time he finally got her number. He took the paper from out of his pocket and glanced down at it. Even her handwriting was pretty. The bag of groceries wasn't that heavy but he still walked slowly to the car. He glanced up for a moment and seen fire flash right in front of his eyes. He heard the first gunshot but couldn't hear anything else after that. Several bullets riddled his body before he fell on his back hitting the pavement hard. There was no time to scream or catch his breath. In a matter of moments footsteps ran off in the night and the gangster known as Fat Rat lay dead in a grocery store parking lot. The dead corpse had a bag of groceries in one hand and a piece of paper in the other.

5

WORD OF MOUTH

Life is war against the malice of men!
Baltasar Gracian

Present day:

Tidbit had wrapped her son up in his coat then threw on her coat and scarf to walk out into the cold air. She had to go view the body of her baby daddy Big Red whose legal name was Jerome Devoe. He had been murdered in his girlfriend's house and then the house was burned down. There wasn't much left of the man except charred remains but she still had to visit the body and see for herself. In recent times Big Red had become a high roller so it could be many reasons why someone wanted to kill him. He was tight with his money even when it came to his son. Jerome Jr. barely knew his father but she thought it was best that he knows what happened to him. She figured Lavelle was probably losing his mind. Big Red and he were road dogs for years. There was no one she could think of who was closer. Naturally he would want revenge but who would he look for? There were so many people that had been salty with Big Red at one point or another. That wouldn't be Lavelle's only problem. When the killer or killers burnt the house down they didn't leave any evidence. There was nothing the homicide detectives could go on.

"I wonder who that nigga pissed off this time." Tidbit mumbled.

"What did you say mama?" Jerome Jr. glanced at her.

"Never mind, let's just go." She replied while hopping in the Buick.

She turned over the ignition and as she began to put the car into drive a Brown Cadillac pulled in front of her. The Cadillac was familiar, but she couldn't understand for the life of her why he double parked with his car slanted in front of hers. She climbed out of the car trying to make sense of the situation.

"Damn Vell, why you pull up all crazy and shit." Tidbit yelled.

"Bitch I need to know if you had anything to do with my homie getting killed. So you can miss me with all that shit you talking." Lavelle retorted.

"What!?! Nigga have you lost yo goddamn mind. Why in the fuck would I want to kill or do anything to the father of my son?" Tidbit angrily replied.

"You and that nigga were having problems. He was telling me you wanted more money for child support and shit like that." Lavelle replied. His pistol was noticeable as he approached her. She glanced at it but paid it no mind.

"So I want him dead over some child support? You know how much muthafuckin sense that makes. Big Red crossed a lot of niggas so you need to check off a long ass list before you get to me." Tidbit frowned with her hands on her hips.

"Fuck! I just can't believe that my nigga is gone. Whoever done this to him has to get got. He can't even have an open casket." Lavelle cried out.

"Yeah I heard through word of mouth that his body was charred when they pulled him out of Belinda's house. It was somebody that really had a problem with him. I was on my way to the coroner's right now." Tidbit began to calm down.

"You think this shit has anything to do with what went down ten years ago? But why they kill Brenda too?" Lavelle racked his brain.

"That shit I tipped ya'll on to? Hell nah that don't have anything to do with that. Where the hell would you get that idea?

This is some recent shit that Big Red is caught up in. Whoever did this shit knew he was fucking with Brenda. It might even be one of your homeboys." Tidbit explained.

Lavelle began to pace pondering on her words. A person came to mind after hearing her say that. He slammed the palms of his hands into his forehead. His embittered heart couldn't wrap the fact around his head that Big Red was dead. He glanced at Tidbit then turned around to walk back to his car. Lavelle hopped in his Cadillac, put the car in reverse then sped off backward. Tidbit watched him make a three-way turn, drive off so she just shook her head.

"Little Jerome, just stay in the car and mama will be right back." Tidbit ran inside the house.

She quickly dialed the number. It took about three rings before her cousin picked up the phone. He didn't answer right away which indicated to her that he was preoccupied.

"Hello?"

"Hey, what's up Andrew; this is your cousin Tidbit."

"What's up Tidbit?"

"I was calling to tell you that Big Red from over here got killed the other night. You know one of those niggas that was in on that thing we did back in the day."

"Are you serious? So somebody was able to touch that slob ass nigga huh? Well I guess I got to find another nigga to serve from the other side." Drew Dog nonchalantly replied.

"You don't know anything about who it could have been?" Tidbit pushed.

"What? If I had something to do with him getting smoked I definitely wouldn't talk about it over the phone. I didn't even know the nigga was dead until just now. Damn Tidbit, I'm related to you and you gon' come at me like that?" Drew Dog sounded disgusted.

"It ain't like that Andrew. Somebody asked me some shit and I just had to make sure."

"I was benefiting from the nigga living; just because he's from the other side don't mean I want to smoke the nigga. It's all about business with me nowadays." He sounded disinterested.

"I was just making sure." She sounded relieved.

"When did you start questioning family? I know you got a baby by that nigga but when you start feeling like I would do something like that and wouldn't let you know?" He asked.

"I guess I'm just reacting to the shock of it all. You know his road dog came to me about it and some things from the past came up."

"Well, next time you get these '*feelings*' you should know not to talk about that shit over the phone. You don't know who the fuck is listening." Drew Dog firmly replied.

She said her goodbyes and assured him that it wouldn't happen again. She had her doubts, but for the most part she believed her cousin. What made her believe him the most was the fact that he wouldn't have anything to gain from Big Red's death. As a matter of fact he would lose out on money. Big Red copped his dope from Drew Dog so he was going to have to deal with someone else from the other side to make up on that money. She knew her cousin and one thing she understood was that he was too business minded to want Big Red killed. She also knew that he was too arrogant to really give a damn at this point in his life.

Tidbit rushed back to the car to find her son sound asleep. She started up the ignition and quickly drove to the coroner's office. When she got there she was made to wait for awhile before they let her view the body. They suggested that Jerome Jr. remain in the hallway while she viewed the body. She reluctantly agreed, considering it might be too traumatizing. When she made it to the body with his toe tag on it, she gestured to the coroner to unzip the bag. When she saw his charred remains she quickly covered her mouth. Tears fell down her face as she began to sob.

"Who did you piss off like this Jerome?" She whispered.

Her lips were trembling as she tried to regain her composure in front of the coroner. She could tell it was personal. It was doubtful to her that the image of Big Red's corpse would leave her psyche anytime soon if ever.

Back in the neighborhood Lavelle was furious for the entire day. He hadn't really hung with the homies for some time. He was known as an OG but it had been years since he really put in work. The little homies had a few riders from the neighborhood that were getting a name for themselves. They had damn near blasted a neighboring Crip set that they were warring with into submission. Times were changing for a lot of people. The young Damus (Bloods) were a little more determined to bang against anyone. It didn't matter if you were a Blood like they were. The code was being abandoned more and more. Lavelle contemplated these things while sitting in his car. His eyes were blood shot red from tears and the bottle of Hennessy he was taking to the head. He wasn't in his right mind to make any sound decisions.

"Why would that little nigga kill Brenda too?" He wondered aloud.

He finally climbed out of his car. He staggered slightly with the bottle still in his hand. He had his pistol tucked under his belt and hidden behind his 3X Pro Club white T-shirt. OG Vell finally found his footing and strolled to the front yard of the vacant house where the young riders of a younger generation were hanging. It was a few that just kicked it and wasn't necessarily riders like most groups of gangsters. It was also a few OGs that were still willing to put in work with the little homies. Vell looked at them as niggas that never grew the fuck up. He walked up on the pack and the few homies from his generation instantly acknowledged him. A big dice game was going on with mostly the youngsters in the game. The one particular gangster he was looking for was actually the one with the dice in his hands.

"I bet I hit my running mate Blood." Boston made a side bet.

"You bee what this nigga said Blood? Yo point is ten and you gon' hit the running mate of four, yeah right. I take that bet blood and that on the hood nigga for a dub." The other homie threw down a twenty.

Boston threw down his twenty dollars to cover the bet and began shaking the dice. He blew hard on the red dice before letting them roll.

"Blood, you niggas got to have heart if you want to come fucking with me. That's why ya'll can't get what ya'll want because ya'll niggas is too scared to take what ya'll want."

"Quit talking shit and roll the dice Blood." Boston's road dog laughed.

Boston looked back at his homie and grinned then let the dice roll. He rolled a five. He rolled several more times until sure enough a three and a one showed up on the dice when they hit the ground.

"That's what the fuck I'm talking about Blood. Soowooop!!!"

"You still ain't hit yo point though Blood." Another homie yelled.

His next roll was an eight then he hit the ten he had been waiting for. Everyone in the circle made some kind of noise be it good or bad. Boston laughed loudly feeling like he was on cloud nine.

"Like that crab nigga Ice Cube was saying in that one song. Bucking fools now the circle's getting smaller." He laughed.

"That nigga Ice Cube never gang banged. I heard his brother is from 111 N-Hood but not that nigga. He just lived over there." His road dog replied.

"Whatever Blood, you know what the fuck I'm saying." Boston replied.

He let the dice roll again then he hit a three. Everyone started laughing when he crapped out.

"Bee Blood, you were talking all that shit." Boston's road dog chuckled.

At that point Boston backed away from the circle while passing the dice to someone else. He turned around to count his money still feeling satisfied with the game. When he looked up he had a pistol pointed at him. He froze in his tracks for a minute wondering what was going on. He tried to glance at the person holding the gun and realized it was OG Vell.

"Blood, why in the fuck are you tripping?" Boston asked.

"I know you had something to do with Big Red getting smoked. Nigga don't you know you killed the nigga I grew up with since we was toddlers?" OG Vell barked.

"Blood I didn't even know that Big Red was dead. That's on Damu I didn't have anything to do with that nigga getting killed. Me and Blood had problems with some money but I wasn't gon' smoke the nigga behind that shit." Boston sincerely replied.

"You the only nigga I can think of that would even think about killing that nigga." OG Vell kept the gun steady.

"Look Blood, I'm trying to tell you that it wasn't me. You need to get that gun out of my face. I ain't got a problem saying when I smoked a nigga but on this one I ain't got anything to do with it."

"Niggas will say anything when they got a pistol in their face."

Boston glanced over at one of the other OGs that were standing next to Lavelle. Lavelle followed Boston's eyes then took a deep breath. It didn't make sense for Boston to kill Brenda and Big Red then burn the house down. He was a rider but not that kind of killer, Lavelle considered. He slowly lowered his pistol and put his head down. His thoughts was racing because he didn't know who to blame at this point. He looked up for a moment and considered apologizing to the young gangster.

"I shouldn't…"

Boom! The sound of Boston's infamous all black forty five went off. Lavelle's body took a second before it fell on the ground. Half of his head was missing while brains and blood was splattered on the grass and concrete.

"Don't you ever put a gun to my head and don't use it Blood." Boston barked.

Not even a second later everyone dispersed and went their separate ways. Lavelle's body was laid out on the ground stiff and alone.

A few days later Drew Dog and Shook was hanging out on Drew Dog's porch. They were blazing some Chronic waiting for the football game to come on. They were laughing about a few things in the neighborhood and just enjoying the fresh air. Drew Dog's common law wife, Kelly, was inside cleaning up for them to watch the game. He had left the door cracked a little bit so that some air could circulate throughout the house. He got up from the lawn chair and closed the door all the way. He sat in a lawn chair that was closer to Shook than before.

"You know both those slob niggas we tipped off about that shit back in the day are dead? We gon' have to pick up some new clients from the other side to make up that end." Drew Dog began.

"Nah cuz, I didn't know that shit. How the fuck that happen?" Shook replied in shock.

"I don't know but Tidbit called me on the phone and told me that that nigga Big Red got killed over some broad's house. Whoever killed that nigga killed the broad also. It sounds as if it was over some personal shit not business. But fuck all that; we need to find some Damu niggas that we can start supplying." Drew Dog insisted.

"But who?" Shook shrugged his shoulders.

"I don't know but Tidbit is on her way over in a little while and we plan on talking about this shit when halftime starts."

"What happened to the other nigga that used to run with Big Red? Was he with that nigga when he got smoked?" Shook asked.

"Nah, Tidbit is supposed to tell me about that when she gets over here. I had to check my little cousin on talking about shit over the phone. So now when she needs to tell me something she knows to talk to me face to face." Drew Dog smirked.

"Oh so she was running off at the mouth over the phone?" Shook laughed as well.

"Yeah on some stupid shit. But I nipped that…"

The front door swung open and Kelly came walking up to the screen door. Drew Dog glanced at her frame reminiscing when she had a much cuter shape. After two kids she had gained a little weight, but Drew Dog still loved hitting it doggy style. He had a couple of broads on the side anyway.

"Close the fucking door." Drew Dog barked.

"Damn Andrew, it's hot as fuck in here. I'm trying to get some air up in this muthafucka." Kelly complained.

"Bitch, if you don't close that fucking door." He warned. His lips were curled up when he said it so she knew he was serious.

Kelly glared at him through the screen then closed the door. The sun was beginning to creep on the porch but both Shook and he ignored it.

"As I was saying. I nipped that shit in the bud, but she is going to help us point out a sound hustler for our shit."

Shook pondered on his words for a minute. It was always a shaky thing when you involved women in your business when your business was crime. Tidbit was pretty solid but she fell hard for that Damu and it almost clouded her judgment.

"Do you think she can handle putting another nigga on to what we're doing?" Shook asked.

"I know she had gotten sprung over that nigga at some point, but I doubt she'll fall for that shit again. But I'm gon' school her on what to look for and see where their head is at. If a nigga is about his paper then that gangbanging shit he can look past. I'm mean, this is Crip until I die but it ain't gon' stop me from getting money." Drew Dog replied.

"Yeah that's some real shit. So we serving that Crip set our set don't get along with, we serving our own homies from the hood and we serving the Damus. We are coming up like a muthafucka." Shook smiled while they shook hands.

They finished the last remnants of the weed they were smoking then walked inside to watch the game. Drew Dog opened the door to see Kelly pacing back and forth. She was fanning herself with her hands while the kids were sitting by the window near the side of the house.

"Why you got to be so selfish Andrew?" She rhetorically asked.

He walked over to her as calm as possible and whispered in her ear that it was business so it was some shit she didn't need to hear. She put her hands in the air as if to surrender. Drew Dog and Shook sat on the couch and turned the television station to the game. About twenty minutes into it the doorbell rung. Kelly answered it to see Tidbit standing behind the door.

"What's up girl? What you doing over here?"

"Came over here to talk to my knuckle head cousin. I've been good, what have you been up to besides putting up with his shit?" Tidbit smiled while hugging her.

"That's it girl, putting up with his shit. Our air condition broke and we not getting a new one until after the game is over. So you gon' have to excuse the heat."

"Girl, I ain't tripping. Where that nigga at?"

"He's in the living room watching the game with Shook's crazy ass." Kelly pointed in their direction.

Tidbit walked into the living room and sat next to her cousin. He gently tapped her on the leg to let her know she was acknowledged. She sat her purse down and started watching the game.

"The fucking Raiders do stupid shit at times cuz. It's either a bad-ass coach or Al Davis or both but they can't get shit right." Shook blurted out.

"It's probably both cuz." Drew Dog laughed.

They watched the game until halftime then all three stepped outside into the yard. Tidbit didn't want to have anything to do with speaking on the porch. Drew Dog had spooked her out and now she was extremely careful.

"One of Lavelle's own little homies smoked him. He accused some young nigga named Boston of shooting Big Red and his girl then burning the house down. Word of mouth is that he put a gun in Boston's face but didn't kill him. So once the pistol was out of Boston's face he peeled his cap. It was a gang of their homies outside that witnessed that shit. That nigga Boston gon' be locked up in a week or so. That many niggas see some shit like that the police gon' find out who it is." Tidbit explained.

"Was that shit that happened with Big Red personal too or was it over some business?" Shook asked.

"That's the big mystery but I don't think it was Boston that did that shit. He's a young knucklehead nigga that flies off the handle. The nigga that did this shit was a smart muthafucka. He knew what time Big Red was showing up to Brenda's house and everything because that nigga don't live there. He was probably just going over there to fuck that bitch." Tidbit replied.

"I don't give a fuck about that shit right now. Who was the nigga you think from the other side would be down to connect with us?" Drew Dog sighed.

"I'm thinking about this nigga named Brazy Bee."

"You mean Crazy Cee." Shook chuckled.

"Whatever nigga. That's what they call him over there because he was a rider back in the day. Now he's got two kids by this broad from their hood so he's all about his paper. He's a stand up nigga from word of mouth. He did six years up in Susanville for a dope charge." She replied.

"Alright then we might fuck with the nigga. You might have to give him some ass so that he can be convinced a little easier. You know how you do the shit. Fuck the nigga then pillow talk with him letting him know, through word of mouth that you know where you can cop some of that Yayo." Drew Dog explained.

"You act like I don't know the drill. But you gon' have to kick a little more than before because I could be doing better." Tidbit smiled.

"Alright little cousin, you earned it. But not until you make that shit happen with that slob nigga."

She nodded while counting the dollars in her head. They figured halftime was over so Drew Dog and Shook headed towards the front door. Tidbit followed close behind but with her plans in mind.

"Look here Andrew; I'm going to bone out so I can run a few errands. Mama got Jerome Jr. tonight so he can be with all his cousins over there. So I'm grabbing my purse and bouncing."

"Alright then little cousin." Drew Dog hugged her.

Tidbit went inside grabbed her purse, and talked to Kelly for a few minutes then left. She was trying to do a little shopping from some money that she remembered stashing for Big Red.

"He's not going to need it now." She considered.

She wouldn't dare think about spending his money if he was alive. He wasn't the type of nigga that would forgive some shit like that. It was only five thousand dollars that he made her promise not to spend. Now she had a chance to catch up on some bills and buy a few things for her and her son. Besides she had to set up a good environment for Brazy Bee to come through once she got him to her pad.

First thing she did was pay all her bills until they were current. Then she picked up a bunch of accessories from the department store. Then she bought herself a couple of outfits from the swap meet. She bought her son a few outfits as well. When she was done with everything she was sitting on a little less than twenty-five hundred. She felt good when she looked in the back seat of her car. She didn't have to window shop or put anything on layaway. She was a hustler by nature. Her mother always told her as long as she got a pussy between her legs she should never be broke. She remembered that but at times it seemed to her as though pussy stock had plummeted. It was hard to get a nigga to kick in some real dough nowadays. She was thinking about using the rest of the money to cop a little something on the side. She could at least maybe cop some weed if not a little bit of Yayo. She knew if she handed twenty-five hundred to her cousin he would just laugh in her face. The wheels began to turn and she figured out what she might do. She would put in on the shit that Brazy Bee might get then she could hustle some shit on the side without too many people knowing. All she had to do was get her cousin to give her the shit on consignment so it would show good faith with Brazy Bee then she would take her cut on the comeback. The more she made the more she could put into the pot and Brazy Bee or her cousin wouldn't even have to know what was going on.

She smiled at her brilliance as she was parking her car in front of the house she was renting. She and her sister took over the rent when their mother wanted to move somewhere else. Her sister had moved out a couple of years ago and she had been covering the rent on her own. Sometimes it was hard but now she had a plan to make it all better. She climbed out of her car, looking in the backseat. She knew right then and there that she would have to make two trips. She grabbed the first couple of bags and sat them on the porch. She glanced up at her porch light, realizing that it was out.

"I could have sworn I left that muthafucka on." She said aloud.

She figured it wasn't really a big deal because the light bulb probably went dead. Once she brought up the second bundle of bags she unlocked the door to her house and left it wide open. She grabbed the first bundle and quickly ran into her bedroom in the back of the house. She thought she heard some noise in the house but dismissed it after peaking out the bedroom door. She took a few things out of the bag then ran back to the porch to grab everything else. She was tired by now. She began to get undressed, dropping her clothes on the floor. She cut on the television after putting away all the groceries.

She climbed into bed and munched on a bag of barbecue potato chips. The television was showing a music video that caught her attention.

"I need me a real man to come into my life." She reflected.

As the words came out of her mouth she noticed a man standing in her bedroom doorway. For a few seconds she thought she was having an illusion. She just spoke of having a man now one just pops up. But this man had his face covered up except for his eyes. He was holding a machete and his eyes were piercing. She lied on her bed frozen stiff wondering what was going on.

"Who the fuck is you?" She blurted out.

"Never mind that Tidbit. All you need to do is answer a few questions for me. Everything will come clear in a moment."

She quickly squirmed out of her bed trying to run but he caught her by her ponytail. He put the sharp blade to her neck before she could scream.

"How do you want it? Quick and easy or slow and torturous are your choices."

"Who the fuck..."

He grabbed her by the neck and squeezed tightly until she started coughing. He dragged her by the neck into the living room and sat her down in a chair. He quickly tied her up then gagged her.

"I'm going to ask you a few questions and if I don't like the answers it will be very painful. Don't believe for a moment that I'm beyond torturing a woman; especially a low down bitch like you."

He pulled the gag from around her mouth and looked her directly in the eye. Tears began to fall down her face but he had no sympathy. He sighed momentarily before he began his questioning.

"First off who killed Fat Rat?"

"I don't know who killed that nigga. I didn't have anything to do with that shit." She trembled.

He put the gag back on her face, making sure it was tight. Then he held out her hand and chopped off her pinky finger. Her muffled screams were all that were heard through the gag.. Her face was filled with tears as she tried to deal with the pain. He patiently waited for her to calm down then he proceeded.

"Who killed Fat Rat?"

"My cousin and his homeboy Shook." She sobbed.

"Why did your cousin have you send those Blood niggas in the house to rob Cisco?"

Her face showed terror at the mention of Cisco. She couldn't hold back her tears at this point because she knew there wasn't any return from that.

"You are going to kill me anyway." She cried.

"How do you want it quick and clean or slow and painful?"

"He said that Cisco was trying to regulate them to curb serving so he had to go. They knew they would be the first suspects if he came up missing so they came up with an alibi by being at Fat Rat's party. So you killed Big Red and Brenda, huh?"

"I'm asking the questions. But put it like this, I don't have to worry about that nigga Lavelle."

"You gon' burn my house down too?" She cried.

"Nah, because then it would look like a pattern."

"Well let's get this over with. What else you want to know?" She surrendered.

"You answered all my questions."

With one quick swing he cut her throat. She was barely able to make a noise as he watched her head drop and her face fill with shock. He went into the kitchen and washed his blade off in the sink then walked out the back door.

6
GANGSTER, GANGSTER

Space I can recover. Time, never!
Napoleon Bonaparte

Past – ten years ago

Loretta began preparing a big meal for her family. Her husband Tango was still incarcerated but she had hope because they violated his civil rights. She decided to pay a retainer fee upfront to his attorney. If the lawyer proved that they didn't have probable cause and he was violated he might stand a chance at being set free. She gleefully prepared the meal for her daughter Samantha and her niece Melanie. She loved that her daughter and niece were the best of friends. Family was always important. That's who you can rely on the most. She started making her famous spaghetti that everyone in the family and out had praised for years. She would bake garlic bread then make her signature banana pudding. It was fattening but the kids loved it the most. She began boiling the noodles then getting her special sauce ready.

"It is how you make the sauce which really makes the difference. I add some ingredients that I will only pass down to you two. Everyone else will have to guess how we make this dish." She laughed while Samantha and Melanie watched.

She was hoping that Missy stayed so she could have another adult to talk with. Missy wasn't feeling too good and opted to go home and rest for awhile. Loretta figured she would watch movies with the girls. After they ate dinner they would then all eat banana pudding while watching a movie. She stirred up the pot giving instructions while preparing everything.

"Melanie, go inside the cupboard and grab some tomato sauce. Make sure baby you grab the big cans because ya'll best believe I'm making enough to last for a couple of days." Loretta smiled.

"Okay Auntie Loretta, but let me use the bathroom real fast."

"Samantha, check on the noodles and check on the pudding."

Both teenage girls scrambled off to do as they were told while Loretta stirred the sauce. Not a moment after they scrambled off the doorbell rang. Samantha considered answering the door but her mother warned her too many times about that. She looked at her mother.

"Did you hear the doorbell mama?"

"If you heard, what makes you think I didn't hear it?" Loretta replied.

She walked into the living room and passed Melanie on her way to the door. Melanie rushed past her to get to the cupboard.

"Melanie, make sure you close that cupboard door all the way so you can use that step ladder to reach up top for the tomato sauce. That cupboard is small so that ladder won't fold all the way out. You hear me child?"

"Okay Aunt Loretta." Melanie nodded.

Loretta made it to the door a moment later. It was dark outside so when she peaked outside she couldn't see who was at the door. She tried yelling through the door but didn't get any response. Finally she made sure the chain was on the door then cracked it open.

"Who is it?"

"Hi my name is Jonetta and I'm a friend of your husband Tango." A cute young girl answered.

It was dark but Loretta could tell that she was older than Melanie and Samantha. She imagined the girl to be seventeen or eighteen years old. She smiled at her, but didn't remove the chain.

"How can I help you and how do you know my husband?" Loretta kindly asked.

"I stay right down the street but he seen me sitting on the curb one day. He asked me what was wrong and when I told him I was hungry he gave me money to feed my family. I wanted to thank him for his help." Jonetta replied.

Loretta was happy to hear that and quickly opened the door to let the young girl in. She quickly took the chain off the door then cracked the door open. Before she could open it all the way the door slammed right into her. In a matter of seconds two hooded gangsters came barging inside with pistols drawn. Loretta attempted to scream but was silenced by a brutal pistol whipping. She whimpered as they dragged her on the ground. The other gangster ran into the kitchen to find Samantha balled up and frightened to death. They brought both of them in the living room and began tying them up.

"Tidbit, go sit in the car and be the lookout until we're done." Drew Dog said.

Tidbit nodded and headed out to the car. Tidbit worried momentarily because he said her nickname but she figured they weren't going to survive to remember her name. Drew Dog and Shook started tying the mother and daughter up. Once they were tied up one began asking Loretta where the money was hidden.

"I don't know anything about any money." She trembled.

He hit her in the forehead with the butt of his gun and she began bleeding. She almost passed out.

"Chill out Drew Dog cuz, if she is unconscious how is she going to tell us where the money is at?" Shook spoke sensibly.

"Bitch you need to tell us where the money is at or yo ass is about to go through some serious pain." Drew Dog barked.

"Maybe this little bitch knows where the money is?" Shook stared at her lustfully.

"I don't know anything about money." Samantha pleaded.

Shook began to untie the young teenager then stripped off her clothes. Samantha began to cry uncontrollably.

"Please the money is in the den under a few things. You can have all of it, just leave my baby alone." Loretta pleaded.

"Bitch you better not try anything or yo ass will really regret the shit." Drew Dog warned.

Even though her hands were still tied he took her down to the den. Shook had Samantha on the living room couch butt naked. He pulled down his pants and forced her legs open. Within seconds he was panting and ranting as he penetrated the teenage virgin. The pain was so excruciating that she couldn't even cry, scream or speak. Her vocals had gone away as he mercilessly pounded inside of her. Tears poured down her face while he had his way with her. He then turned her small frame around and continued raping her brutally from the back. Her body went limp as he ejaculated inside of her. He moaned then waited momentarily before climbing off her limp body. A few moments later a gunshot went off then Drew Dog appeared. He slowly walked in the living room looking through the large bag of money. When he glanced up Shook was buttoning his pants while the teenage girl lied limp on the couch. It appeared as though she was dead but in fact she was in shock.

"You gon' have to kill that little bitch cuz." Drew Dog explained.

"Yeah but I had to fuck her young ass before we bounced." Shook replied.

"Leave it up to you to get some pussy while doing a lick. We got the money so let's bounce." Drew Dog smirked.

Shook looked down at the girl and seen her start to tremble. With one fatal shot he pierced the back of her skull. She was silenced forever.

"We should light the muthafucka on fire cuz. Just in case we left some evidence that we don't know about." Drew Dog suggested.

Shook grabbed a sheet from out of the bedroom then walked into the kitchen. He passed by the cupboard but didn't notice it. He lit the sheet on fire from the stove and began spreading it throughout the house. After the fire was lit in different places throughout the house they ran out the front door and closed it behind them.

Melanie heard the car screech off but she still waited a couple of minutes before walking out of the cupboard. Her tears started falling down her face before she walked out. She knew that her cousin and aunt were both dead. What bothered her the most was the fact that she couldn't do anything to help them. The fire began to spread throughout the house quickly. Nevertheless she tried to find where both bodies were. If one survived then maybe she could get them to the hospital. She first hit the living room to find her cousin Samantha laying face down with a bullet hole in the back of her head. She screamed but quickly covered her mouth. She ran into the den to find the same result for Aunt Loretta. She stood there in shock until the fire bringing down an ornament on the wall brought her back to reality. She rushed toward the door and ran outside into the cold air.

She quickly ran at top speed to the closest phone booth she could find. She wasn't thinking straight. She could have gone to a neighbor's house but she thought about the liquor store around the corner. She knew for sure that there was a phone booth there. When she reached the phone she dialed 911 Emergency.

Drew Dog, Shook and Tidbit were speeding on the freeway rushing back to Los Angeles. They were laughing about the lick they had just pulled off. The duffel bag was a nice sized bag and it was filled to the top.

"I'm telling you cuz; it has to be about two hundred to three hundred grand in this muthafuckin bag." Shook dug through the bag.

"Oooh shit! I figured he had some money but I didn't think that much. I sure in the hell want my share Andrew." Tidbit replied.

"You gon' get a cut. Don't even worry about that and you are also gon' help us count this shit to see how much it is." Drew Dog smiled

"That ain't a problem. You didn't see if they had any dope or something like that hidden?" Tidbit eagerly asked.

Drew Dog and Shook both looked at each other, obviously disappointed. Tidbit caught the exchange and shook her head. She knew her cousin could have a one track mind. She had to admit that he knew how to plot and plan when it came time though.

"We really just wanted the money so that nigga Tango can't have the money he needs for a lawyer. Only problem is that he has a sister that might can help him but I never seen her." Drew Dog explained.

"But that was probably the only stash he's got that was why he kept it in his house." Shook interjected.

"Even if it ain't we at least hurt him enough where he gon' have to get him a public defender at best. I mean, with all this money if he does have another stash it probably won't be this much." Drew Dog replied while exiting the freeway.

They pulled up to Drew Dog's house and went straight for the garage. They parked the car right next door to a neighbor's house. Everyone quickly jumped out of the car then ran towards the back.

"Ay cuz, we gon' have to get rid of that car." Drew Dog reminded everyone.

Drew Dog unlocked the garage door and let everyone in then sat the bag of money on the fold out table."

"It might take us all night to count this dough so we might need someone to get rid of the car while we counting this shit up." Shook suggested.

"Who gon' dump the car?" Tidbit asked.

"Why don't you go little cousin and we'll start counting while we wait until you get back. You are a female so police won't be quick to pull you over like they will Shook and me." Drew Dog suggested.

Tidbit reluctantly got up from one of the chairs and grabbed the car keys. As she was walking out the garage door Drew Dog spoke up.

"We were wearing gloves but still make sure you wipe down the seats and the steering wheel. If you find anything that can be traced back to us get rid of it."

Tidbit nodded and rushed out the door. She drove around looking for a place to dump the car. After some thought, she finally decided where to dump the car.

"I'll dump this muthafucka where Fat Rat got smoked." She thought out loud.

She made sure she wiped down the car as she was told and left it as clean as possible. It was stolen anyhow but just in case someone saw it while at Tango's house they had to make sure nothing was linked back to them. She climbed out the car with gloves still on and walked back to Drew Dog's house. She figured they were going to cut her out of most of the money but she had to be glad she was able to get some. She knew how conniving her cousin could be.

Melanie didn't move from the phone booth until she heard the sirens coming towards her uncle and aunt's house. She had called her mother but the phone just kept ringing. She worried that maybe something happened to her mom. She panicked for a moment then walked back to the phone booth after walking several yards away. It would be best that she called again. She reluctantly dialed the phone number one last time expecting to get the same result. After the second ring her mother picked up the phone.

"Hello?" Missy's drowsy voice echoed through the phone.

"Mama! Mama! You got to come over here as quickly as possible." Melanie screamed through the phone.

"Calm down Melanie, take your time and tell me what's the problem. Where is Loretta and Samantha?" Missy replied.

"They are dead mama. I'm trying to tell you that you need to get over here as soon as possible." Melanie continued to scream.

Missy climbed out of the bed while rubbing her eyes. She couldn't clearly comprehend what Melanie was saying but it sounded like she said Loretta and Samantha were dead. That was impossible. She must have heard her wrong.

"Melanie, I cannot understand what the hell you are saying. You will have to calm down if you expect me to understand you." Missy demanded.

Melanie took a few deep breaths. She knew it might be hard for her mother to swallow so she tried to be calm. Her heart and mind were on the brink of hysteria though.

"Look mama, I was hiding in the cupboard when two men and a girl came into the house at Aunt Loretta's house. They kicked in the door and robbed the place. They shot Aunt Loretta in her head and they raped and killed Samantha. It was the worst thing I have ever seen in my life." Melanie calmly explained.

"Where are you right now?" Missy finally got the picture.

"I'm at a nearby phone booth waiting for the firemen to put out the fire at their house. Whoever these people were they set the house on fire to get rid of evidence." Melanie explained.

"I'm on my way. Just stay at the phone and I will find you. If you see a car that looks suspicious you hide somewhere." Missy explained.

"Okay."

Missy jumped up and quickly threw on some clothes. Still in her house shoes and a Moo-Moo she put her twenty-five automatic in her purse. She ran outside to the car and sped off. When she pulled up close to the phone booth, where Melanie might be, she slowed down. Rolling down her window she began to scan the area near the phone booth.

"Mama, I'm over here." A voice loudly whispered.

Missy glanced in the direction of the voice to fine Melanie curled up and hiding. When Melanie stood up to walk towards the car, Missy, could see the terror on her face. She climbed in the passenger seat and Missy immediately hugged her. Melanie's tears began to fall all over again. Missy rubbed her only daughter's back and began to silently pray. She couldn't do anything about Loretta and Samantha, but she was thankful that Melanie still lived. After the long and grateful hug, Missy put the car in drive and went around to Tango's house. The smoke could be seen from where they were at. Missy reached the street to find cops and firemen all over the place. The coroner was there and both bodies had already been found and put inside the truck. Missy decided to walk over towards the police and ask a few questions. She didn't want Melanie going through an interrogation right after the incident because she was still in shock. But she had some questions that needed to be answered. She instructed Melanie to stay in the car.

She walked up to the closest uniformed officer she could find. He turned around with his hand on his pistol when he heard her walk up. He wasn't startled, but he was precautious.

"Can I help you?"

"Who is the investigating homicide detective?"

He looked at the Missy in a bizarre way. Then he figured she was a witness with some information. It wasn't typical in his experience for Black people to come forward as open as this. He pointed in the direction of a heavyset white man. The detective had his back to her.

"Just ask to speak to Detective Calhoun."

She walked over to the detective while observing the scene. Parts of the house were burned but it was salvageable. She considered that when she reported everything to her brother. She stopped in her tracks when she thought about Tango. He was already in prison so he was going to really take it hard. She got a hold of her emotions so she could speak to the detective. He turned around a few steps before she reached him. He stared at her with curious observation. He wasn't expecting a thirty something Black woman to be approaching him so he was caught off guard.

"How can I help you ma'am?"

"Are you Calhoun?"

"Yes I'm Calhoun." He acknowledged the officer and nodded.

"Well I'm Missy Davenport and the two victims you pulled out of the house are my sister in law and niece."

"Okay?" Calhoun pulled out his notepad.

"My daughter was there hiding in the cupboard when everything happened. She will need to have a little time to recover from the shock, but she will tell you what happened from what she heard." Missy explained.

"What is her name and how old is she?"

"She is sixteen and her name is Melanie Davenport. She told me that they raped my thirteen year old niece before they killed her." Missy started sobbing.

"Here is my card Ms. Davenport. You call me when you feel your daughter is ready to sit down with us." Calhoun handed her a card.

Missy walked back to the car and nodded at the uniformed cop. She reached the car glancing inside before getting in she seen that Melanie was still in shock. Once she was in the driver's seat she realized that Melanie was mumbling to herself.

"They were Crips because I heard someone say cuz." She mumbled.

Missy glanced at her then started up the car. This was going to be a hard thing to break to Tango. Her brother Kevin was a stable kind of man but things like this could push him over the edge.

Drew Dog and Shook sat back in the garage relaxing while puffing on weed. They also had a couple of bottle of Boone's Farm celebrating the work they put in a couple of days ago.

"You know they found that car we did that move in cuz. But Tidbit must have cleaned that muthafucka up good because they ain't said anything to anyone around here." Shook commented.

"They could have just towed it as an abandoned car after seeing it parked for a few days." Drew Dog considered.

It might not even be considered as part of the crime if no one even seen the car. They were sitting on over two hundred grand but Drew Dog thought it be wise to sit on it for awhile.

"So how much did you give Tidbit?" Shook asked.

"I gave her ass thirty five grand and sent her on her way. She was happy as fuck to get that much. Even though she went to the door we was the ones that had to put down the 187. She's gon' have a good time with that and it will be gone in about two months. We gon' cop some yayo with our money and be straight." Drew Dog dragged on the Entica weed.

He started coughing uncontrollably from trying to hold in the smoke. Shook started laughing.

"Cuz, you can't hold in skunk weed. That shit is way too potent for that kind of shit. But it is a real good high that I can get used to."

They both laughed while swigging the cheap wine they were drinking. They relaxed, listening to oldies in Drew Dog's garage. Drew Dog wasn't about to let anyone mess up his high.

"We did that shit gangster the way we ran up in that house and didn't leave any witnesses. That's how you do that shit." Shook commented.

"Yeah but yo horny ass had to fuck the little broad." Drew Dog snickered.

They were both shaken out of their slumber when a hard knock sounded off at the garage door. Drew Dog looked at Shook with a bizarre expression on his face. He grabbed his pistol and cocked back the hammer.

"If it's the police we're going out with a bang cuz." Drew Dog firmly stated.

"Open the door ya'll its Tidbit."

Drew Dog sighed in relief then got up to answer the door. He peeked out of the little window inside the door then opened it up. She walked in smelling the weed and quickly wanted a hit.

"Damn I want some of that weed." Tidbit reached for the joint.

Shook handed her the weed and she took a few puffs before saying anything. Drew Dog handed her a half empty bottle of Boone's Farm when she passed him the marijuana.

"Somebody else might have been in that house besides his wife and daughter."

"You bullshitting!" Drew Dog leaped from his chair.

"She might have been hiding somewhere in the house. Ya'll niggas didn't search the entire house to see if anyone else was inside?" Tidbit asked.

"Hell nah, we went after the money and once we found it we got rid of who we knew was there. Who else was up in that muthafucka and did they see us?" Drew Dog frowned.

"I don't know just yet. I'm about to find out as much as I can, but the car might not be the last thing we got to worry about." Tidbit shook her head.

"Fuck it cuz, whatever comes we gon' have to deal with that shit. We can't be one hundred percent on everything." Shook commented.

"Yeah, but if some shit comes to light it might backfire on everything we trying to build. Tidbit you need to find out who this is and how we can get at them." Drew Dog replied.

"I think it's Tango's niece or some shit like that. But that is all I know. I don't know if she seen some shit or even if she was there for sure but I think she was." Tidbit frowned.

Drew Dog got up from his chair and paced the floor. He began racking his brain about how to handle this. If anything went wrong it could all blow up in his face. All his plotting and planning could go down the drain in one swoop.

"You don't know where the niece lives or anything like that?"

Tidbit looked at him in disbelief. She tried to hide her feelings from her cousin because when he became nervous he could fly off the handle.

"I just found out she existed." Tidbit replied.

"Fuck it then cuz, try to find out where she lives and if not then we just got to wait for the hammer to drop." Drew Dog sighed.

"But if she's talking to the police you better believe that she gon' have a thousand muthafuckas protecting her. It would still be hard to get at her cuz." Shook added.

"Yeah I figured that much too. We gon' just have to be low key with our shit. Don't get to splurging on shit Tidbit. Hang back for a little while so we can give things time to cool down." Drew Dog continued to pace.

The Boone's Farm bottle was still in his hand so he took a few swigs. They just had to wait until the hammer dropped.

"No matter what; that nigga Tango is probably going to be looking at some time." Shook stated.

Both Tidbit and Drew Dog nodded.

7

KILLER

Injuring all of a man's ten fingers is not as effective as chopping off one!

Mao Tse-tung

Present day:
The crack of the window let the sun shine in. It barely reached Tango's bed, shining brightly on a plant near the bed. It didn't disturb his deep sleep. He was having one of those rests where he was basically dead to the world. The phone ringing was what slowly awoke him from his deep slumber. He shook violently before coming into reality. When he lifted his head he was met by a ray of sunlight that instantly hurt his eyes. Scrambling for the phone he reached for the closest dresser next to the bed. On the third ring he was able to grab the phone.

"Hello?" Tango's raspy voice echoed.

"Was you asleep? This is Leonard."

"Yeah my man been working pretty hard as of lately. I got this new job." Tango yawned.

"You should come down to L.A. and hang out with ya boy or I come out yo way." Leonard suggested.

"What time you talking because I want to get some more sleep?"

"Whenever you wake up call me and we can link up then." Leonard replied.

Tango thought on it for a moment. He was still half asleep but he was able to come up with a tangible answer.

"I'll hit you around eleven." He replied.

"Cool. We can hit up this little Mexican restaurant you might like."

Tango hung up the phone with the intention of going back to sleep. It was difficult since the light of the sun had penetrated a large part of the bedroom. He tossed and turned until he grudgingly climbed out of bed. He hadn't seen Leonard in a few weeks and may have talked on the phone with him twice before. His life was different now, so he didn't have time to run around Los Angeles like when he was a high roller. He decided to light up a scented candle Melanie had put him onto. He wasn't going to meet up with his girlfriend, Colleen, until the weekend. She was his mistress before he went to prison. Now that he was out he was able to resume their relationship. Colleen was so naïve when they first met because she never suspected that he had a wife. If she did she pretended not to know.

Tango finally built up enough energy to turn on the shower. It was nice and hot when he got inside. He took his time getting dressed because he wasn't looking forward to the drive down to Los Angeles. It would be about thirty minutes before he would decide to get out. There were two messages from calls he missed while in the shower. One was from his niece, Melanie, and the other was from Colleen. He promised himself that he would make sure to call them when he got back from hanging with Leonard.

He had a while to think about things on the 10 Freeway. The lunch traffic had picked up when he reached the city of Azusa, but he slowly kept pushing. It wasn't until one-thirty when he showed up to the Mexican restaurant.

Tango was out the game but he still thought like he was still in it. He sat in his car observing the scenery. He actually parked across the street from the restaurant in a way where he could see the restaurant before he walked in. After what happened many years ago he learned to be…extremely careful. It wasn't necessarily that he distrusted Leonard either. It was more of him understanding Leonard's environment and what came along with it. He made a few more glances at the area and decided to slowly walk in on one of the side doors. Leonard didn't see him until he turned a corner. They both smiled as Tango pointed at him to acknowledge him.

"My man, what's the word big bird?" Tango sat across from him.

"Taking it day by day. I always got my mind on the grind. I'm trying to put together a few things for some cash, you know how it is."

Tango nodded, not really having a response. He grabbed the menu from off the table near the side of the window.

"Have you ordered yet?" Tango asked.

"Nah, I told the waitress that I was waiting on a friend. With her little fine ass." Leonard replied.

That was when the Hispanic waitress with pretty eyes and a cute shape came walking up to the table. Tango silently admitted that she was truly good looking.

"Are you ready for me to take your order?" Her accent softly asked.

"I'll have a wet burrito with no onions and no tomatoes." Leonard replied.

"You know what I'll have the same as him but with a medium lemonade as well."

"Would you like anything to drink as well sir?" She glanced at Leonard.

"I'll have a beer."

After taking the menus the waitress scrambled off to place their orders. All four eyes sitting at the table watched her body walk off behind the counter. Leonard turned face forward to talk to his old friend.

"You know that little broad Tidbit got killed the other night?" Leonard commented.

"Who?"

"Tidbit. You know the little Crippette girl from around where Cisco used to live. Her cousin stays a few blocks from where I live, over in that neighborhood."

"Not really. But I wonder whatever happened to Lazy who always kept his thirty-eight under his belt when hanging with Cisco."

"That nigga was never the same after Cisco died. He moved away after awhile and that was the last I heard of him." Leonard replied.

"Yeah he was a cold soldier and loyal too." Tango replied.

The waitress returned with the lemonade and beer so Leonard didn't quickly respond. He sipped on his beer before continuing.

"Yeah but he just disappeared and now the young Crip niggas Drew Dog and Shook are running things. If Lazy would have stuck around he might have gotten killed or something."

"Why do you say that? He might be one of the top dog's calling shots nowadays if he would have stuck with the game." Tango replied.

"I doubt it. He had the muscle but he didn't have the disposition of being the top dog. Some niggas got it and some don't and that muthafucka became a recluse after Cisco passed." Leonard said matter-of-factly.

Tango chuckled after he said that. It startled Leonard because he wasn't used to Tango laughing a lot.

"What's so funny?" Leonard began laughing

"You called that nigga a recluse...So how did the young girl come up missing? She was caught up in a drive-by or some crazy gangbanging shit like that." Tango asked not really caring.

"Nah, she was found dead in her own house. The killer cut off one of her fingers before killing her. I don't know what the fuck made him do that but that's what he did. It probably has something to do with karma coming back on that little broad." Leonard said nonchalantly.

"Was she doing dirt like that?" Tango asked, seeming somewhat stunned.

"You don't think she had anything to do with Cisco coming up missing or anything way out shit like that?" Leonard asked.

"I never even thought about that. My mind is way different than it was way back then. I wanted to kill whoever I thought meant my family harm. I'm an older man now with plans for the future. Though the past hurts me I have to live for today because I really don't know how much time I have left." Tango admitted.

"That's sounds like Kevin not Tango."

"Well maybe that's what it's about nowadays for me. I'm an old man and I have to worry about being Kevin instead the once hustler known as Tango. My niece calls me Uncle Kevin not Uncle Tango."

"How is Melanie, anyway? Where is she nowadays?"

"She is doing pretty good. She had a son now and was once married. For the most part she is taking care of herself." Tango replied.

Once their meal came they talked for awhile about plans for the future. Leonard had opened a few businesses and was concentrating on paying his house note. They promised to keep in touch and hang out at least twice a month. Leonard wasn't ever really attached to the game of hustling but they went to high school together. He kept his ear to the street and was always willing to pass it on to Tango. For awhile Leonard was the only one sending him letters and money for his commissary. Melanie always did after her mother passed but it was a rough patch where she wasn't able to send much money. They were the two people that looked out for him.

When he left the restaurant he decided to visit Colleen. She was always a sight for sore eyes. He told himself that it wasn't supposed to be until the weekend but something made him feel he couldn't wait that long. He called her and she was delighted that he decided to come through before the weekend. It took him about thirty minutes to reach her house from where he was at. When he pulled up in front of her house he sat in his car for a moment. Tango quickly realized that he had to prepare himself for human interaction these days. He was probably what Leonard meant by being a recluse. He had spent four years in the hole with no contact with the outside world. When he finally returned to general population he was a different man. He had to dig deep inside of himself to find any type of sanity. The books he was allowed to have could only sustain him for so long. He sighed as he noticed the clouds trying to creep up in the middle of the day. It was one of those deceptive L.A. weather days where it's hot in the day but at some point it begins to rain.

He finally climbed out of the car. He walked up the stairs eager to see the woman he had once again grown to love. He rang the doorbell twice then sat back and waited. He could hear her footsteps as she walked toward the door. She didn't bother asking who it was. She opened the door and her face lit up when she saw him. Her pretty chocolate complexion was shining in her elegant lingerie. Tango took note that she was well prepared to give him what he came to get. She gently kissed him on the lips with long and sensual consideration. Then she walked away towards the kitchen.

"Would you like something to drink?"

"Whatever you have will be fine." He replied.

Colleen walked around in the high heels like she was born with them on. His eyes observed her frame and wanted her. She came back in with warm tea and sat it in front of him while he sat on the couch. Her living room was a pleasant mixture of brown and beige coloring. Even the frames of the artist WAK or other African art blended in with the décor. The couch and the loveseat were both a rust color brown that offset the beige carpet. The multi-color throw rug that lay under the coffee table matched the couches. She had a peaceful organic scenery in her house that Tango took to. Now he wanted the beautiful woman.

After she sat the tea cups down he grabbed her arm before she could sit down. He pulled her in front of him and began to kiss on her belly button. His hands found its way around her firm supple ass as he made his way downward. With ease he slipped her thongs off to taste her. His lips and tongue began to explore inside of her. She moaned grabbing the top of his head. He pulled her body close to the couch then spread her legs so he can fully indulge in her juices. His tongue darted mercilessly inside of her sliding wet and hard across her clitoris. Her hands stayed planted on his head while her grip became tighter.

"I missed you so much Kevin." She purred.

His lips grabbed a hold of her clit and tugged at it. She gave out a brief yelp as he continued to explore. When she couldn't take it anymore she pulled him up to her. He quickly disrobed then slowly and steadily slid inside of her. Moaning loudly she grabbed his back while he had grabbed a hold of her legs by the thighs. His feet were still touching the ground so with leverage he was able to go deep inside.

"Oooh!" She belted out.

Tango was in rare form as he developed a rhythm with long hard strokes. He knew he couldn't take too much more of this. He finally lifted her up and bent her over the couch. He pushed the end table out of the way and bent her over the arm rest. Her face was in one of the pillows as he penetrated from the back.

"Oooh shit Kevin!" She yelled.

He kept pushing inside of her with passion, sweat dripping from his chest. He couldn't stop giving her the high hard one until finally…He came. He slid both of his hands with his fingers down her back until he reached her ass. She purred as he relaxed her even more. After pushing inside of her with his final gusts of energy he backed off. She turned around to face him so that she could wrap her arms around his broad body. Colleen could not imagine being with any other man. He completed her. He made her feel like a real woman. Her head lay gently on his chest.

"We didn't even make it to the bedroom." She commented.

"Let's go in there now. Let's grab this tea before it gets cold and lie down together." Tango suggested.

They went into the room and sipped on their tea at the edge of the bed. Colleen had kept the color scheme the same in her bedroom so the décor was almost the same. There were slight differences because she had an oak wood king sized bed with cream colored curtains surrounding it. She had three matching oak wood drawers blending in with everything. Tango felt like he was home whenever he came to her house.

"You are a beautiful woman." He commented.

"And you are a beautiful man."

Tango smiled as they finished their tea. He felt complete when he was with her. They laid down on the bed and held each other until they both fell asleep.

Shook decided that it would be best to hook up with his Latina woman another day. He would have to drive way out to Alhambra during traffic hours. It would be easier for him to see her if she was at her cousin's Shorty's house who stayed nearby. She had been giving him the loving for quite awhile and he considered making her his girl. He called her up to cancel because Drew Dog was going through a few things. He had just lost his little cousin Tidbit so he was paranoid and fired up. Only problem that shook him to the core was he didn't have a target to retaliate on. Shook tried to keep calm but since his best friend was suffering it was difficult to relax.

"Hello?" The sweet Latina's voice echoed through the phone.

"What's up Rosie? This is Shook." He replied.

"I know who this is culetto."

"Who are you calling an asshole?" He snickered.

"Well at least you are learning the curse words. Now if I can get you to form sentences than we will be straight." She laughed.

"Yeah, you are trying to turn me into a Mexican." He replied.

"How many times I have to tell you that I'm from Venezuela, fool? She replied. Why do people think that just because we're Latina we are all from Mexico?"

"Damn Rosie, that's my bad. You know what I mean."

"So when are you coming?"

"That's what I was calling about. You know I told you about Drew Dog losing his cousin the other day. He thinks it has something to do with those slob niggas she was fucking with. I got to see what's up with him and make sure he is alright. The funeral was yesterday and he was all fucked up behind that shit… I was thinking that I should come see you tomorrow."

"You did tell me that he was going through some things. Well okay baby, but if you get a chance know that I'm waiting for you." Rosie seductively suggested.

"Fa'sho! If I get a chance to holla at you I will."

Shook jumped in his Coup Deville to roll around the corner and talk with Drew Dog. When he walked up to the door he saw Drew Dog sitting next to the window. His eyes were wandering off somewhere in the sky when Shook tapped on the glass. It brought Drew Dog back down to reality. He lifted up from the chair to almost drop the nine-millimeter he had sitting on his lap. When Drew Dog opened the front door Shook could tell that he had been crying. He must have been really hurt behind Tidbit because he couldn't recall his homeboy crying about anything. He's known his road dog for over twenty years and never seen a sign of hurt. That just wasn't really the make-up of Drew Dog. Shook can think of several times he showed fear but not hurt. When homeboys from the neighborhood died he would attend the funeral but tears would never fall. Shook didn't know how to handle this new revelation. He slowly walked inside the house while Drew Dog stood slightly behind the door.

"What's up cuz?" Shook began.

"I'm just thinking about Tidbit. I loved her crazy ass. We shouldn't have ever cut her out of that money three ways like we did. I mean…she was my family. And I bet you it had something to do with those slob niggas cuz." He lamented.

"You think that it was some shit they got tied up in and she was a witness or some shit?" Shook inquired.

"Everybody knows that Tidbit ain't a snitch. It was some niggas trying to hurt Big Red and Lavelle so Tidbit got caught in the mix." Drew Dog replied.

"You think it got anything to do with what we did years ago, cuz?" Shook considered.

"That Tango shit cuz? Nah, if that was the case they would have got at us first. That nigga probably locked up and if he ain't why would he fuck with Tidbit? That muthafucka had all kinds of charges against him and he had a public defender. He doesn't have any ties to the street like that. I think those niggas tried to do a lick and got caught and my cousin got caught up with them. That's why I feel bad about not cutting her in on a third of the money. She was still doing shit on the side with those slob niggas." Drew Dog lowered his head.

He was visibly hurt. Shook could go ride on anybody if it came down to it. But he never knew anything about comforting a saddened homeboy. He felt bad for his comrade but that was all he could do. They didn't have a target to exact revenge because everything was a mystery.

"So we got some killers on the loose." Shook commented.

"It could be one killer? But it is a muthafucka that doesn't give a fuck about torturing a female. Man I'll kill the people that touched my family, cuz!" Drew Dog said bitterly.

"You want me to start looking around so we can find out who we gon' serve?"

"Nah cuz, we gon' deal with that shit once I regroup. I need to sit down and think about some things. But why don't you pick up the money from the niggas that need to re-cop?"

"I can do that. You want me to bring it back here tonight, it might be a little late but I can bring it back tonight?" Shook replied.

"Just hold on to that shit until tomorrow." Drew Dog shook his head.

That was Shook's cue to leave. His road dog needed time alone. He nodded his head then walked out the door. This was perfect he considered, he could go see Rosie after doing his runs. Once in his car the breeze from the night air hit his face. It would be best to take care of business then holler at Rosie.

It took less than an hour to make all the runs. Everyone wasn't ready to re-cop which he assumed would happen anyway. The Damu they were serving that went by the name of Brazy Bee was just now getting the spot hot. It was expected that he would take a little longer to re-cop because he just got put on. That was the last little business that Tidbit was able to take care of before she was killed. Thoughts of Tidbit made him realize that she was no longer alive. One lone tear fell from Shook's face

"She didn't deserve that shit cuz." Shook said out loud.

When he got home he quickly jumped into the shower. He was thinking about having Rosie come live with him. She was someone he could build some shit with. She stayed by herself, but if they got a place together everything would be even better. His shower was long because the hot water felt so good. He climbed out of the shower and took his time drying off. He wrapped his towel around his waist and walked into the living room. He shivered briefly from the cold air that was coming from a half opened window. After dialing Rosie's number she picked up on the third ring.

"Damn baby I thought you wasn't about to answer."

"I had just jumped out of the tub when I heard the phone ring. So you were able to make some time for me chivala?"

"You better watch who you're calling a punk. I'm gon' show yo ass who's the punk when I get over there."

"You ain't said nothing but a word?" Rosie snapped back.

"I'm gon' wear that big booty out and make you think about what you're saying. Then you gon' see who is the real chivala." Shook playfully replied.

"Whatever!"

They talked for a few more moments then he finally hung up the phone. He told her he would be through in another hour. He had to make sure he was looking good for her when he arrived. He had broken out his Musk for men cologne. Then he laid out his white Puma tennis shoes. He already had a fresh pair of 501 Levis starched so thick that they probably would have stood up in a corner without anything holding them up. Then he pulled out his button down Navy blue shirt that he had just gotten out of the cleaners. Everything was laid out on his bed so now all he had to do was clean his jewelry. The last time he had bought a pinky ring the Asian man at the swap meet offered him jewelry cleaning solution. It would give his rings and his Turkish gold chain the extra shine that he wanted.

He allowed his jewelry to soak in the solution while he played some oldies.

"I'm gon' fuck the shit out of Rosie tonight." He said aloud.

The slow jam by Marvin Gaye 'Let's get it on' was blasting through his stereo when he heard a noise in the kitchen. At least he thought it came from the kitchen. Something could have broken so he rushed into the other room. Once he stepped into the living room he heard another noise that sounded sharp and fast. Suddenly he felt a pain that ran through his ankle so bad that all he could do was moan loudly. His eyes watered quickly before he stumbled to the ground. When he was finally coherent enough to look down at his feet he realized that he had been shot in the ankle. Before he could belt out anything else his mouth was covered by someone. Whoever the man was, he had lifted him up and slammed him down into a chair. Shook was still delirious from the pain so there was no way he could fight when the man began tying him up. Once the man felt that Shook was securely tied down he faced Shook. Shook didn't immediately open his eyes because he was still letting tears fall from the excruciating pain. When he finally opened his eyes he stared at the man with shock and horror.

"You?"

"All the dirt you've done I would never think that you would leave your window open."

"Fuck you cuz." Shook cried.

"You were always tougher than that nigga Andrew but he was always smarter."

"So you are the killer. So you take care of Tidbit and those slob niggas huh?" Shook asked.

The butt of the man's pistol crashed into Shook's mouth. Shook could feel his teeth loosen. Now there was pain coming from his head and from the bottom of his feet. The pain was almost too much for him to bear. Tears fell down his face profusely. The killer didn't blink an eye as the two men stared at each other with intense hatred.

"Which one of you raped Samantha?"

"Ah, I don't know what the fuck you talking about. I was in the other room trying to get the money. I don't know anything about a rape." Shook lied.

"You think I'm just gon' cut off your finger?" The Killer asked in disbelief.

"I'm telling you cuz I don't know anything about any rape." Shook adamantly denied.

"She would be twenty three right now if she was alive. I wonder how she would look and act as a grown woman. We will never know." The killer replied.

"Fuck it, I know you gon' kill me so let's just get this over with." Shook pleaded.

"Come on OG Shook, you are a big time gangster Crip. Have some dignity when you die. How can I make this quick and easy when you didn't make Samantha's death quick and easy. And she was an innocent thirteen year old girl."

"Nobody is innocent." Shook sobbed.

"That little girl was innocent. But you had to take the girls virginity before you killed her. Do you honestly believe you deserve any mercy?"

Shook lowered his head in defeat. He was young, wild and stupid when he committed that act. He thought that he was a changed man after all these years. Some things never leave you. They are connected to your aura forever because the spirit of the people you harmed still emanate around you. Shook knew this to be true deep down but couldn't grasp the concept of that until this very moment. He was defeated and had finally come to that resolve. He didn't deserve any mercy.

"Well, I won't shoot you anymore."

The killer pulled out his machete. He easily stripped the towel from around Shook's waist and discarded it. There was something that Shook noticed about the killer. He wore a black thin tight scuba diving suit from head to toe. He had on comfortable black running or bicycle riding tennis shoes. He even wore thin black gloves. The killer's face was covered except for his eyes and Shook knew whose eyes they were. He started violently shaking as the killer brought the blade of the machete closer to him. This was going to be a gruesome act. The Killer picked up a block of wood he must have carried inside the house. He began to shove the thick plywood between Shook's legs. Shook knew what was coming so the tears fell hard. Marvin Gaye and Tammi Terrell's song 'Nothing like the real thing' was playing loudly in the background. It appeared as though the killer was making every move to the beat of the song. He even hummed to the tune as the blade got closer. Then with one swoop after lifting his dick up with a small stick the blade came down. Shook was not only castrated but he was also demoralized. This was definitely a slow and painful death. He dropped his head and watched the blood flow from his groin. His hands tied behind his back and his manhood lying on the floor he was momentarily in shock.

The killer smacked him in the face a few times to bring him back to his senses. There was no mercy in the man's eyes. But did he really deserve any? Shook knew as well as the killer did that he was in no moral position to ask for mercy. Yet it still came.

"I will put you out of your misery if you tell me everyone that cops from Drew Dog. If I find out you are lying to me I will kill your baby's mother and your son. That is how far I'm willing to go."

"Who says you won't do that anyway?" Shook sobbed.

"Who says, but I don't really want to bother with them but know that if I don't get what I want from you then I will bother with them." The killer assured him.

"Its three niggas and an essay he's serving. The Crip nigga from our set is called Toothpick. The Crip nigga from the other set is called Big Boy. The slob nigga is called Brazy Bee in the lingo of Damus. The Mexican fool they call him Shorty but he is a cold ass Cholo and you don't want to fuck with him." Shook warned.

"Maybe you are saying that because he is related to your girlfriend Rosie." The Killer replied.

Shook didn't respond he just lowered his head and closed his eyes. The killer believed what he was saying and took note of the names he would have to take care of. Drew Dog had to lose his support system before he could make a move on the gangster. The killer lifted Shook's head up and they made brief eye contact. Shortly thereafter Shook's eyes fell and he was passing out from the pain. With one solid swing the machete cut his neck almost to the spinal cord. OG Shook was now just a memory.

8

THE FALL OF A REIGN

To go too far is as bad as to fall short!
Confucius

Past ten years ago

"See things are changing nowadays cuz. I mean you always were a down ass nigga and I know you couldn't prevent that shit from happening to Fat Rat and Cisco. I know you wanted to protect them just like me but some things just ends up fucked up. You come be a part of this shit we putting together and you still will bring in dough like you were when you were fucking with Cisco." Drew Dog explained

"Yeah I'm still a little fucked up over what happened to those two niggas. Who do you think could have pulled that shit off cuz?" Lazy replied.

"Ain't no telling. We got a lot of niggas that want to war with our hood and they just found a way to come up in the process. Me and that nigga Shook was talking about that shit the other day. We need to find out who did this shit to our homeboys, but until we find out who it is; let's get this paper."

"Yeah it would be good to start making some real money again. That nigga Cisco took care of the homies when he was alive." Lazy reminisced.

"Yeah but the reign of Tango and Cisco has ended and we got to make do with what we got. I'm telling you cuz, once this shit is put together right we all can be rolling nice ass cars with gold Dayton's on them." Drew Dog passionately replied.

They strolled down the street to see Shook talking with a bunch of young homies a generation under them. One of the youngsters was a rider by the name of Toothpick. He always kept a toothpick in his mouth trying to be cool. Many of the homies said he didn't have good hands when it came to fighting but he built a reputation from his trigger game. He wasn't necessarily a skinny gangster but in fact a little chubby so the nickname was ironic. Drew Dog didn't give a damn about his fist fighting skills because he liked the little soldier. Not only that, Toothpick looked up to him and Drew Dog knew that he could talk him into doing dirt for him if need be. Toothpick didn't have any problem doing a murder for the big homie. So naturally he was the prime candidate for Drew Dog to put on, once he started serving dope in the hood. It was about six of the little homies following behind Shook and hanging onto his every word.

"What's happening cuz, I was just telling the little homies about how our hood got started." Shook said after embracing Drew Dog and Lazy.

"Yeah cuz, Raymond Washington came over to our hood and personally recruited the OGs. Our set was small at first but then we got bigger and bigger. We ain't as big as the Hoover's and the East Coast niggas but we got deep in our generation." Drew Dog expounded on Shook's comments.

"Have any of you niggas ever met Raymond Washington or Tookie?" Toothpick asked.

"Yeah me and the dead homeboy Cisco met Raymond Washington and Tookie back in the day. Them niggas used to meet up at the park before different sets started breaking off. At first it was just East Side and West Side Crips. Raymond ran the East Side and Tookie ran the West Side." Lazy added.

Lazy didn't notice the venomous look that Drew Dog gave him. This nigga can't get this shit out of his head that those niggas ain't around anymore, Drew Dog thought. He felt an overwhelming wave that suggested that Lazy was trying to upstage he and Shook. None of the other OGs that were older than them was willing to go against them or they were locked up for something. So by right, Drew Dog felt that he and Shook should be calling the shots for the hood.

"This nigga can't adjust to the change of things." He thought.

"Let me holler at you a minute." Drew Dog said to Shook and Toothpick.

As they walked off Lazy talked to all the little homies. He knew which ones were fighters and which ones were shooters. Just like he always knew that Shook was a fighter and Drew Dog was more of a shooter. Cisco was the type of gangster that had skills in both. He remembered Raymond Washington saying that Cisco was what Crips were supposed to be made of. He missed his dead homie and thought about him often. The young gangsters were too busy preparing to slap box to notice his wandering thoughts. Their loud rants didn't distract him from his reminiscing.

"Now Fat Rat is gone too." He said aloud.

The young homies would never get to experience the barbecues that Cisco and Fat Rat would throw. His eyes watered as he considered what they would be missing. He had to make sure that he schooled them on the code of the streets. No snitching would be at the top of the list. Right now wasn't really a good time because he was still dwelling on other things.

"I'm gon' holler at you young niggas later cuz." Lazy walked off.

It stopped the little homies that were slap boxing for a brief moment. After realizing he was gone they went back to slap boxing again.

Lazy was considering what Drew Dog was saying but he had to get himself together. It was still kind of hard to swallow but he wasn't bitch made by far. What ate him up the most; he didn't know who killed his homies. When he got inside the house he decided to just go to sleep. He still needed time to sleep his sorrow away.

He didn't wake up until he heard the phone ringing several times. His mother yelled into the room for him to pick up the phone. Rubbing his eyes he answered the phone near his bed while still yawning.

"Damn Shawn, you live up to that nickname Lazy. It's only eight o'clock and you are already asleep." A sweet voice said.

"Aw shit cuz, I didn't know that I slept for three hours." Lazy glanced at the clock.

"I thought you were coming to see me tonight."

"I'm coming to see you. I just came home for a little bit and fell asleep. Let me get dressed then we can talk."

After getting dressed he called his girl to let her know he was on his way. Lazy wasn't like the young gangsters that was coming up. Everyone he knew were getting wet Jheri Curls but he preferred an afro or braids. Since his girl was planning to braid his hair the next day he sported the afro. He slipped on a hairnet then put on a blue golf hat. His blue khakis laid over his blue Chuck Taylor's All Stars matching his blue button down Honcho. After spraying on some cologne he was ready to hit the door.

"Damn boy, if you put on any more cologne its gon' seem like you bathed in it." His mother yelled behind him.

He chuckled to himself and closed the door behind him. It was pretty dark outside by now but he was sharp. That nap had done him some good. He climbed in his car holding on tightly to his brand new nine-millimeter glock he just purchased. His girl stayed in Crip territory but her neighborhood would set trip from time to time. If need be he didn't have any problem peeling someone's cap.

Once inside his car he fired up the engine then let the O'Jays blast in his sound system. He leaned all the way back while pulling off from the curb in front of his house. He felt good about being a gangster. His dark tan complexion offset his droopy eyes and his sideburns and afro. His eyes are what earned him the nickname Lazy. He could have been a lady's man if he wanted, but he chose to be a gangster. Why not get the women and get respect in the street, was his motto? He looked around the neighborhood as he began to turn the corner. It seemed relatively quiet considering just several hours ago the little homies were hanging out. He wasn't going to pay it any mind because he was going to see his girl. His thoughts wandered for a brief moment.

"I'm gon' fuck the…"

Blah, Blah, Blah were sounds that interrupted his thoughts. Glass had shattered everywhere inside of his car. Startled, it took him a moment to grab his gun. He leaned away from the driver's side and pulled out his pistol and fired outside of his car window. The pistol was held in his right hand while letting the bullets fly. Someone yelled but he couldn't comprehend what was going on. The car went out of control while still rolling and kept going top speed until he crashed into a pick-up truck. He tried to lift himself up with his left hand to only realize that he had been shot in the arm.

"FUCK!"

He slid over to the passenger side then struggled with the gun in hand to open the passenger door. He stumbled to the ground on his back while keeping his pistol in position to shoot. After rolling over he was able to get a hold of some ground and gain his feet. He looked around, but there was no one in sight. He was in pain but he couldn't hold his arm in the fear that he wouldn't be able to shoot back if someone shot at him. It was wise of him to think it might not be over. Whoever wanted him dead might come back for round two. His pistol was lowered to his side as he walked extremely fast. It was almost a slow jog, but he didn't want to bring that much attention to himself.

The vehicle was registered in his name so he knew that the accident would be traced back to him. There was bigger fish to fry then to worry about the police cracking him for a hit and run. Somebody just tried to kill him. His mind raced while he strolled down the street. He couldn't think straight. The arm wound began to throb.

Suddenly another car rolled by with its window rolled down. Before his pursuers could get the drop on him he fired off his gun. Bullets flew in the direction of the passenger riding shotgun.

"Ah shit, I'm hit!"

The driver swerved in another direction. Even though in pain, Lazy pulled out the clip he had slid in his pocket out. He quickly reloaded his gun and chased after his pursuers. His trigger finger felt free as he pulled it back with relative ease.

"I'm OG Lazy Loco, cuz!" He screamed.

The driver did a three way turn as fast as possible. The bullets flying from Lazy's gun was a terrifying distraction. The driver managed to get the car in the opposite direction but his back window and side windows were busted out. Lazy wouldn't stop shooting until his clip was empty. As the driver punched on the gas Lazy followed in pursuit, hearing screeching tires. Before long the car was a safe distance away. Lazy lowered his weapon in frustration. He needed to know who tried to kill him because they probably had something to do with Cisco and Fat Rat. His thoughts wandered as he walked off. If the police weren't already in the neighborhood they were on their way. If he could he would definitely try to avoid jail. The pistol he was carrying was tightly wrapped in his hands. He focused on the moment and concentrated on a sound escape. The adrenalin rush distracted him from the pain of his arm. In a matter of minutes he was feeling the gunshot wound again. He heard a car driving top speed around the corner. From the reflections of the houses across the street he was able to see the blue and red lights.

"One time!" He mumbled.

He didn't have the energy to run like before. He opted to hide behind an old station wagon. He wasn't ready to toss the gun even though there weren't any bullets left. He cursed letting off all those shots without having a clear target.

"I was caught in the moment." He pondered.

After waiting for a while, lying on the grass next to the station wagon he made sure he didn't see any more red and blue lights. He tucked his gun away instantly realizing that it was still warm. He walked to one of the major streets until he reached the bus stop. A minute or two later he noticed a bus coming a couple of stops from him. He pulled out a five dollar bill and patiently waited to climb on. When the bus driver opened the doors his mouth dropped. Lazy's mind was so disoriented that he didn't pay any attention to the facial expression of the bus driver.

"I don't know if it is safe to let you on this bus sir." The bus driver began.

"What the fuck are you talking about cuz? I just got shot and I don't have any other way to get to the hospital. Here is the fucking fare." Lazy barked.

The bus driver nodded and closed the slide doors. As the bus continued down the street more police cars swarmed past them. The chubby middle aged bus driver glanced at Lazy through the rearview mirror.

"Damn cuz; keep yo eyes on the road. I'm the one that got shot." Lazy clarified.

That was obvious to the nosy Black man. Reluctantly he did as he was told and kept driving the bus. Lazy tried to doze off as a way to ignore the pain but it was no use. The chaos of the entire situation had him somewhat drained. The bus driver anxiously announced the closest stop to the nearest hospital. Lazy struggled to get up from the seat as he trekked toward the emergency room. By now the pain was so excruciating tears fell from his face. He had a good half a block to walk before he reached the emergency room.

When he reached the emergency room he was in half a nod trying to stay coherent. He was basically surviving off of pure heart and determination. His darted around in confusion until he noticed a woman standing behind a small podium in the hallway. He reached her with his head lowered.

"I need a doctor." He firmly stated.

"Do you have medical insurance because…"

He stumbled to the ground and passed out before she could finish her sentence. When he awoke several hours later he was lying down handcuffed to the bed. He reached over to grab his arm and realized that it was bandaged. He took a long breath after noticing his clothes sitting in a chair close to his bed. Looking down at his body he suddenly realized that his gun was missing.

"That's why I'm handcuffed." He openly acknowledged.

Two white men filed in after hearing some noise come from his room. They both wore suits and ties. They walked up a few inches from his bed without speaking. They stared at him and he stared back. He knew right away that they were detectives. He closed his eyes until the detective with dark hair bumped his bed. When Lazy opened his eyes the same detective was holding a clear plastic bag with his gun inside. Lazy glared at him and noticed the obvious smirk on his face.

The blond detective spoke: "I'm Detective Gates and this is Detective Ward. We have your gun with your fingerprints on it. The hospital staff found your weapon. Gunpowder was also found on your hand. We also have your car in tow with the windshield and the driver's window busted out. Not to mention you fled a scene of a car accident. You don't have that many options Mr. Douglas."

Lazy didn't respond to him. He looked at both officers then closed his eyes again. He tried to go back to sleep but the dark haired Detective Ward began bumping his bed again.

"Did you understand what I just told you?" Detective Gates asked.

"I don't have shit to say to you." Lazy replied.

"We haven't read you your rights yet so everything can be negotiated. I know you at least want to get the people that did this to you. Give us some information on them and we can maybe reduce some of the time you're facing." Detective Gates pried.

"I don't have shit to say to you." Lazy shrugged.

Both detectives walked out of the hospital room frustrated. Lazy glanced up at the ceiling then down near his clothes. Even if he wanted to talk to the police, he didn't have a clue to who tried to kill him. It wasn't a typical drive-by because they came back to get him. One of the shooters had gotten shot as well. If the police found out who was shot that same night they might find out who shot him. It didn't matter at this point because he knew he was on his way to prison. It would be several years before he had a chance to exact revenge on whoever pulled this. He began to calculate the time he would get for his crimes. He would have to swallow the gun charge automatically. He wasn't the registered owner. The hit and run charge he might be able to beat because he was being shot at. Five years if he played his cards right.

"I can do that standing on my head." He said aloud.

He wondered if they were going to let his mother come see him. It would be good to see her and his girl before he was hauled off to prison. Water welled up in his eyes because he knew it was all related to what happened to his peoples Cisco and Fat Rat. At this point he felt helpless and that was not a good position for a gangster. In an attempt to blink away the tears he kept closing his eyes until he fell asleep.

Shook and Drew Dog sat at the table counting up money from the first drop offs of the crack they were now hustling. Drew Dog was in the best of spirit but there was one thing bothering him. Shook knew his road dog like the back of his hand and though he was jovial, something underneath had gotten to him.

"You know I sent those niggas to blast on Lazy." Drew Dog admitted.

"Is that why something is fucking with you? Why didn't you tell me you was gon' have that nigga killed?" Shook asked.

"I thought you would try to talk me out of it." Drew Dog replied.

"Well why you want to smoke that nigga? He wasn't any type of threat to what we were trying to do. He was just real fucked up behind what happened to Cisco and Fat Rat." Shook didn't understand the logic.

"That's all the nigga kept talking about though. Cisco this, Fat Rat that, and at some point a nigga got to thinking he might be a problem later on. You know the first thing I'm gon' want to do is get rid of a problem, cuz." Drew Dog nodded.

"You got them niggas from the other set to put in the work?"

"Yeah, because I figured that he might recognize one of the homies. I told Big Boy that if he wanted to start getting dope at a good price then he needs to prove something to me. They put in the work but didn't kill the nigga. What kind of shit is that, cuz?"

"You think Lazy knows who sent them or who it was that was trying to kill him?" Shook showed serious concern.

"I don't know." Drew Dog admitted.

"You my nigga and you know that. But sometimes cuz, you can go too far. Lazy is the type of nigga that if you win him over to yo side he will die committed to that shit. Now everything is up in the air." Shook warned.

"I know I fucked up in more ways than one. If I'm gon' kill the nigga I should have made sure it was done right. But truthfully he was probably best left alone. He didn't have a clue that we had anything to do with Fat Rat and Cisco. I was just on some paranoid shit, cuz."

"If we go to the hospital to see how he's doing then it might throw any suspicion he has off of us." Shook suggested.

"Nah, he already has police posted upstairs in his room at the hospital. I sent Tidbit up to the hospital when Big Boy told me they didn't kill him. The cold thing about it is that they lost one of their homeboys. Big Boy had one of his little homeboys with him that Lazy picked off." Drew Dog smirked.

"That muthafucka Lazy is a soldier. It would be better if he was on our team. Lazy's probably looking at some jail time for that pistol he had. So he's gon' be gone for a few years. What did Big Boy and those niggas do with the body."

"Trip this shit out, they buried the body so he could just be missing. They went out to an open field that night and buried him. No funeral or anything." Drew Dog shook his head.

Shook needed time to process what was going on. At least with the youngster buried somewhere they didn't have to worry about someone coming back on them. Drew Dog was letting some of those things run through his mind as well. It was a whole bunch of unnecessary shit that might get tied back to them. He would have to be mindful of things like this from now on.

"Yeah Shook, this was too much trouble and still could be trouble. I might have gone too far."

"All we can do is wait and see."

Shook continued counting the money but pondering on the recent events. He worried about some of Drew Dog's impulsive decisions.

Missy strolled into the waiting room to visit her brother Kevin. Only the privileged people in Tango's family were allowed to call him Kevin. Everyone knew to call him by his nickname. It took her awhile to visit because the authorities kept telling her he was in the hole. He didn't take losing his wife and daughter too well. He almost assaulted a correctional officer and could have caught a new case. He needed time to be alone. After two months in the hole he finally came out of his depression. When he reached his cell word got back to him quickly that his sister had came to visit him. Missy would usually come visit him with Loretta. She didn't have the courage to tell him his family had been killed so she told Melanie to write him. She tried to visit him a few weeks after the letter had arrived only to find out he was in the box. She knew it might drive him crazy and she wasn't prepared to see his reaction.

Now she sat at the window waiting for him to arrive. Her only brother finally walked into the room and sat at the window and picked up the phone. He always had a stern look but this was one was more defined. It appeared as though he had aged by ten years. She even noticed small speckles of gray in his hair and beard. He also looked pale and suffered from malnutrition. The whites of his eyes were more like a dark tan color. He looked drained. This brought tears to her eyes to see Tango in this state. She reluctantly picked up the phone and put it to her ear.

"Kevin, honey I am so sorry." Missy began.

"What do you need to be sorry about?" He asked, shaking his head.

"It was just too hard for me to tell you in person. I felt for you and I knew it would break my heart to see your expression. You've gone through a lot in the last few months but what don't kill you can only makes you stronger." Missy dredged up a smile.

"You know what fucks me up the most? It was times that I wasn't right by that woman and she gets killed behind some shit I'm caught up in." Tango replied.

A tear had fallen down his cheek. He lowered his head trying to regain his composure. Missy touched the glass with the palm of her hand. If she could only give him a hug.

"You know I go to trial next week. I still got some money stashed away. For some reason I prepared for this day like I knew it would always happen. They got this punk ass public defender but we can get a better one before the trial if you follow what I tell you to do."

Missy caught on that he didn't really want to talk about it. She hesitated before replying.

"I'll do whatever I can but I need to tell you something."

"What's up big sis?" Tango looked up.

"There isn't any easy way to say this, I don't want to keep being the bearer of bad news and ..."

"I can handle it, Missy." Tango interrupted her.

"Okay, I have cancer and I might not be around too long."

She couldn't look him in the eye. Tango lowered his head and banged it on the slab of metal in front of him. When he lifted his head his entire face was dripping with tears.

"What about Melanie?" He managed to blurt out.

"I'm going to have her stay with some of her daddy's family. But whatever I'm not able to do Melanie can get someone to do for you. I go into the hospital a couple of weeks from now. I'll try to get you that lawyer before I start chemotherapy." Missy explained.

"Never mind all of that. You just get better so that I can see more of you. You are the only sister I got. They say that cancer is some kind of killer." Tango sighed.

"Listen here, Kevin, don't be giving up on me and don't be giving up on yourself. We can pull through all of this we just got to have faith." Missy replied.

"I'm losing faith, Missy. Too many bad things have happened that I can't see a way out of. Get that key from out of the house that I wrote you about. Hold onto it as long as possible. If anything happens to you, the only person I want to know about it is Melanie."

"Kevin, everything is gon' be alright. We just got to stay strong because we are the last of the family." She cried.

Tango touched the glass with his palm as she did the same. It was only the two of them after their parents passed away. They were all they had. At that very moment Tango realized it was the dawn of a new day. He would have to go through a period of pain and purification.

9

STRIKING AGAIN

There is no fate worse than being continuously under guard, for it means you are always afraid.
Julius Caesar

Present day:
Drew Dog began packing his things to start laying low for awhile. He, Kelly and his children had just attended Shook's funeral. To say the least he was devastated. Now he understood that it could be someone personally out to get him and his people. They had gotten two of the most important people to him outside his immediate family. He was going to send Kelly and the kids with her mother while he found different spots to hide out. He had several women he could post up with in different cities in Los Angeles and San Bernardino Counties. He had a good idea who the culprit might be but he wasn't for sure. Besides, he didn't know where the man could be. When he really thought about it, there were a lot of people he crossed at one time or another. Or it could be someone that wanted his spot and his money. He was supplying dope to different hoods and was able to makes moves in Blood, Crip and Mexican hoods. He had hidden enemies as much as he had open ones. Kelly was moving a little too slow for him as he observed her through his peripheral.

"Andrew, I don't understand why we can't just go with you. If some shit hits the fan don't you want to be there to protect us? I mean, you are just running out on yo family." She complained.

"Would you shut the fuck up? Bitch, I got someone killing people that are closest to me. I have to draw them out so that they can come after me. If you are with me and they are able to get the drop on me they will have to kill you too. They can't let ya'll live. But if he wants me and I'm away from ya'll then it's either he gets me or I get him."

"But he still might come after us even if we are not with you. Then what are we supposed to do?"

"This muthafucka wants *me*. Tidbit and Shook done some things with me so naturally they went after them as well. But he wouldn't get any joy out of getting to you and not being able to get at me. Just listen to what I'm saying. This is a fucked up time to be bitching." Drew Dog waived her away.

She grudgingly got her things together for her mother's house. He piled everyone up in his Monte Carlo. Kelly moved around the passenger seat restless and annoyed. Drew Dog attempted to ignore her but he knew something was coming out her mouth.

"How will we know that you are okay? How will we know how to contact you?" She belted out.

"I will give you a number once I'm set up. I know your mother's number; so don't even trip. I don't have anyone on my team right now, but you, so I got to be able to trust you." He calmly explained.

"I've always been here for you Andrew I just haven't seen you scared like this before. You were always the one that had people scared of you. It's just something new to me, that's all."

"Let's get some shit straight, I ain't scared of shit. I'm just trying to protect ya'll. Just shut the fuck up." Drew Dog growled.

He was actually scared but wouldn't dare admit it to her. He glared at her and she turned around trying to avoid eye contact. She still displayed a slight disposition of contempt. It was underlying but Drew Dog was able to spot it.

"Bitch, don't make me beat yo ass."

She didn't take the time to look back at the children hanging on their every word. Kelly laid back in the chair and tried to go to sleep. Sometimes Andrew could be a rotten muthafucka, she thought. It bothered her that he was willing to do that in front of the kids. He was stressed out right now, she considered.

Drew Dog pulled out a joint and blazed it as he headed for the freeway. He rolled down the window slightly but the marijuana smoke quickly filled the car. There was no thought to putting it out until he heard his daughter coughing in the back seat. That was his little girl so he decided to deal with his stress some other way. When he looked over at Kelly she was sound asleep. Both kids were asleep as well so his mind wandered. There were so many enemies that might go after him. But there were only two people who knew the ins and outs of his hood. What bothered him more was the fact that the two Damus he was fucking with were dead as well. Everything pointed toward that nigga Tango. He didn't have a clue if the nigga was around or still in prison. Things weren't right based on what was going on. It was mind boggling Lazy could have been behind all this shit as well. He was the only one that could get at Shook like that. He didn't know how to plan for this shit. There was no telling when the killer would strike again. He damn near had to be a detective.

Pulling in front of his mother in law's house he looked through the rearview mirror. He had to make sure after every so many miles that no one was following him. He blew on the horn until his family woke up. His eyes were red and hurting from so much lack of sleep. The family took its time getting out the car and grabbing their things. He wanted to hurry them but he knew that would be fruitless. Instead he grabbed what he could and walked up the walkway. Once everyone was settled in he pulled his son outside for a moment.

"You gon' have to be the man of the family for a time. Just until I put some things together. Listen to what yo mother and grandmother say and I'll come to scoop you soon."

"When are you coming back?"

"I'll be back to see you next weekend. You are a soldier, right?"

"Fa'sho cuz."

Drew Dog chuckled after hearing him say that. They embraced one last time before Kelly stepped on the porch. She slowly walked down the stairs while their daughter came running into his arms.

"You know daddy loves you, right?"

His daughter nodded after he lifted her up. She wrapped her arms around his neck and kissed him on the cheek. By that time Kelly was within a yard of both of them. She was still supposed to be mad at him but she had to say her goodbyes. He looked over at her then put his daughter down. She held on to his leg for a moment.

"Drew Jr. take yo little sister in the house with you." Drew Dog smoothly said.

Kelly was standing in front of him by then. He gently picked up her hand and pulled her closer to him. He wrapped his arms around her waist as they kissed. He couldn't stay mad at her for too long and neither could she at him. They were kissing while staring into each other's eyes.

"You be sure to call me once you get settled."

"I will."

They slowly loosened their embrace and he walked back to the car. She stood there watching him drive off in the Monte Carlo. No matter what problems they had he was still her man.

Drew Dog drove off with his thoughts running. He blazed up the weed he had put out earlier and let the smoke fill the car. He had to meet up with Toothpick a little later. He wanted him to personally drive the El Dorado up to Kelly so that she could have a vehicle. He would instruct him to bring his girlfriend so that only a minimum amount of people knew where Kelly lived. Toothpick was a real reliable nigga but nowadays he felt like anyone could turn on him. The thing that kept Toothpick from being any kind of threat was that fact that he was getting fed off of Drew Dog's table. Since he copped from Drew Dog there was no reason for him to cross any lines. Drew Dog knew this to be true and didn't worry about him crossing his family but he still refused to let Toothpick know where he was laying his head now. He now had to think of everyone as a potential enemy, someone that could be used to hurt him.

He called Toothpick that morning and told him where to meet at two o'clock in a restaurant in Hollywood. Drew Dog was so nervous he didn't want to be anywhere near the neighborhood. Toothpick pulled up in his 1964 Chevy Impala. It was a royal blue color with three wheel motion and hydraulics. Drew Dog hated that he rolled up there in that because he thought it was too flamboyant. He was trying to be discreet and Toothpick drove up in a ride that brought nothing but attention. It even brought attention from the police. He pulled up next to Drew Dog in the parking of the restaurant. He lowered his ride then climbed out. Drew Dog had an obvious look of contempt on his face.

"What's wrong cuz?" Toothpick asked stupidly.

"I tell you that I want to meet up way in Hollywood so that I can be low key and you show up flossing the 64' Chevy, cuz." Drew Dog angrily replied.

"Felicia had boned out in the Crown Victoria so I had no choice. She has problems with the Chevy so she always drives the Crown Vic. I thought that bitch was gon' be back before I left but she wasn't." Toothpick explained.

"You supposed to be getting that yayo from me and you gon' drive all the way back to L.A. dirty driving this muthafucka." Drew Dog pointed at the Impala.

"Everything is legal cuz. I got my driver's license, insurance and everything. If they pull me over the most they gon' give me is a ticket. And I don't plan on going that fast in this ride so they won't have any reason to pull me over." Toothpick said with conviction.

Drew Dog laughed at the naivety of the young soldier. He couldn't believe his ears. That didn't even sound like a nigga that was born and raised in L.A. He lowered his head trying to remain cool but irritated right under the surface.

"Alright cuz, you are hard headed. You act like the L.A.P.D. got to have a reason to pull someone over. They will do that shit because they want to. You don't grab that shit until you are about to leave, you hear me?"

Toothpick nodded grudgingly thinking that Drew Dog was making it bigger than what it was. He had respect for his big homie but sometimes he thought that nigga was too paranoid.

They went into the restaurant and ordered something to eat. While eating he explained how he wanted Felicia to drive the El Dorado while he followed behind in the Crown Victoria. That way, he figured if someone started following them they would follow the Crown Victoria instead of the El Dorado.

"So how am I going to pick up Felicia?" Toothpick asked.

"You tell Felicia to have Kelly drop her off at a liquor store or something nearby. She goes into the store while Kelly leaves. After she gets out of the store she gets in the car with you and everything will be straight." Drew Dog explained.

Toothpick sighed after hearing the plan. He thought that he was doing too much but nodded nevertheless.

"Why are you breathing so muthafuckin hard, cuz? You act like you got some kind of problem with what I'm telling you."

"Nah, big homie it ain't like that. I just think we are going too far about this shit. But if that's the way you want to do it then that's the way we'll do it." Toothpick replied.

After he loaded the dope deep inside of his trunk he took off toward the neighborhood. Drew Dog had contacted another female that he was planning to live with for awhile. She stayed out in Arcadia, a city east of Los Angeles off the 10 Freeway. That way he could be close enough to watch what was going on without having to be in the city. She wasn't that complicated to please as long as he paid her rent and gave her the high hard one from time to time. Toothpick on the other hand was headed straight for the hood. He wasn't comfortable living outside of the hood even though his girl Felicia tried to get him to move out the city. She had a cousin that stayed in Long Beach where apartments were much cheaper.

Toothpick made his way home as quickly as possible. He still had to bag up the dope; and no matter how paranoid he thought Drew Dog was, he wasn't going to ride around dirty for too long. He jumped on the 101 Hollywood Freeway to the 110 Freeway then took the street back towards the east side.

He hadn't gotten too far on the street when he noticed a car driving up beside him. He glanced at the driver then suddenly the Buick ran right into his Impala. He was infuriated but he stashed his gun deep in the seats thinking if he gets pulled over they won't find it. He regretted that decision because out of the Buick, the driver pulled out an all black long nosed six-shooter. As Toothpick glanced at the weapon he quickly realized that it was a 357. He knew that it would put holes through him and his car. The first shot went into the front tire. Toothpick tried to gain control of the Impala but there was no use.

"Ain't this a bitch?" He yelled.

The Buick suddenly hit the brakes, allowing the Impala to swerve out of control. Toothpick swerved around then crashed right into a wall. Since he didn't have on his seatbelt he slammed into the windshield. It took him several minutes for him to regain his composure. When he did, there was no Buick in sight. The face of the man was covered by a handkerchief except for his eyes. The eyes looked familiar but he couldn't place where. He could only remember that the familiar man was around when he first got put on the set. He was practically an OG by now but this was when he was still putting in work. He thought about some of the Damus he might have got at and the face still didn't ring a bell.

"Nah, those eyes was from somebody I knew over in the hood back in the day. Who from the hood would want to kill me?"

He tried to rack his brain but had drawn a blank. Then he thought about how scandalous Drew Dog could be. Was this a set up by his big homie? He quickly abandoned that idea considering the dope he had gotten was from Drew Dog. He was one of the few people Drew Dog trusted enough to give him dope on consignment. It would have to be something he would figure out later.

He climbed out of his battered Impala and staggered from it. He knew the police were close behind the accident but the Buick couldn't be found. That was even more bizarre because he could have put holes in him with the 357. That is when it dawned on Toothpick that the culprit wasn't trying to kill him. He glanced at his ride and cursed. His frustration quickly turned into a headache because the collision was still fresh. He grabbed the top of his head then looked up to find a tow truck passing by. With all the strength he could muster he waved for the tow truck driver to pull over. The Hispanic looked over at the accident and quickly jumped at the opportunity.

"What the hell happened to you homes?"

"Someone ran me off the road by shooting at my front tire. I lost control of the wheel like a muthafucka and crashed into this wall." Toothpick bitterly explained.

"You need me to tow this to the junkyard or what?"

Toothpick shook his head without telling him where he wanted him to take it. They had to wait for the police anyway. There was a big dent in the wall and it had to be explained. Toothpick glanced at the Hispanic man and could tell he was an American born Chicano. He still had the accent but he spoke English fluent enough to tell he went to school out here.

"I'm gon' have you take it to my house on the East Side near Central Boulevard."

"That will be eighty dollars, homes."

"Eighty dollars?" Toothpick asked incredulously.

"Yeah homes, you have to consider that I'm pulling that shit from out of the wall. Then after that I have to load it on the flatbed. That shit is work and I ain't even talking about the gas."

"Alright fuck it cuz." Toothpick wasn't in the mood.

He peeled off a C-note then leaned on his Impala. While the tow truck driver was setting everything up the police pulled up. He hadn't got the tow truck driver's name but noticed his name on the tag of his shirt.

"Ay Giovanni let the police take a report first before you pull the car out the wall. I got insurance for this muthafucka so they need to know it ain't my fault."

Giovanni nodded nonchalantly as though he was expecting to hear that. There were two police that showed up on the scene. One was a Black man and the other was a white man. Toothpick felt a little nervous because in situations like this the Black cop would show his alliance to the white cop.

"Is this your vehicle?" The white cop asked.

Toothpick nodded without speaking but holding his head in pain. The Black officer walked around to the front of the Impala without saying anything. He was observing the entire scenery but never spoke. Toothpick felt uneasy but kept his eyes on the white cop.

"Do you have a driver's license, registration and insurance?"

"Yeah they are in the car. You want me to get them for you?"

"Yeah that would be good. Would you also be willing to take a test to see if you are drunk?"

"I haven't been drinking, someone ran me off the road. If you look at the front tire you can tell that my front tire was shot out." Toothpick replied.

"The man didn't ask you that. He asked you if you were willing to take a test to see if you are drunk." The Black cop finally spoke.

"I have a headache but yeah I can take a test."

After they tested him and wrote down all his information they gave him a copy of the police report. He was a little irritated but he kept his calm because of what he had in the trunk of his car. Why ruffle feathers he considered.

There wasn't much to say to Giovanni on his way back to the house. He looked around wondering if he could find the Buick following closely behind somewhere. He couldn't wrap his fingers around the situation. They could have killed him but chose to scare him instead. What was this all about?

Kelly paced up and down the house after her children were asleep. She couldn't stand being away from L.A. where everything was cracking. Her homegirls would usually hang out tonight, getting drunk and talking about their trifling men. She was the only one that had a man with some real money. Most of her homegirls were dating guys that were working 9 to 5 jobs or slanging dope just above curb serving. But the fun they would have would get her through the week sometimes. Now her man Andrew had gotten caught up in some shit and she was the one lying low.

She kept glancing out at the El Dorado wondering where she could go.

"Just go ahead and leave because you know you want to. My grandbabies are asleep so I'm not worried about you." Her mother interrupted her thoughts.

"Yeah I was thinking about taking the El Dorado out for a spin. Andrew was talking about I should lay low and only use the car for local use. But I ain't used to this shit mama."

"Girl, I listened to a man tell me what to do for ten years and he couldn't keep his dick out of other women. You act like you ain't grown. This is the best time if any while those babies are in there asleep."

Kelly thought on her mother's words and decided she was right. First thing she would do was get out of the house so that she could buy some Night Train. She had been craving something strong to drink. She quickly hopped into the El Dorado, letting the music from Morris Day and the 'Time' flow into in her ears.

"Jungle love,"

She drove to the nearest liquor store and grabbed a bottle of Night Train. She pulled out a pack of Kool cigarettes and lit up a square. She was standing right next to a phone booth.

"Fuck it, I got some spare change, I'm calling up Tammy and see what that Crazy bitch is doing," She laughed to herself.

The phone rang several times before Tammy picked up. Kelly could tell already that Tammy was already drunk. Her inebriated voice loudly spoke through the phone.

"Girl you done fell off the face of the earth over that nigga Andrew. Girl, this is Kelly's crazy ass on the phone." Tammy yelled.

"Damn bitch, you don't have to put it out there like that. What ya'll doing?"

"Shantrice is fucking with this new nigga who she says has a little dick. She was saying how he was trying to knock the bottom out but didn't have shit to do it with." Tammy replied. Kelly could hear laughter in the background.

"You know what, I'm coming down there. Ya'll bitches keep the liquor coming and I'll be there in about thirty to forty minutes."

"Okay girl and you know Chante got some bomb ass weed. This shit is real good."

"Don't smoke all that shit up before I get down there because I'm on my way."

Kelly hopped off the phone and slowly walked to her car. She was finishing the last remnants of her cigarette and she didn't want the smell in the El Dorado. She wasn't a heavy smoker but she smoked occasionally. She only smoked weed when she was in social circles. She could never see herself buying some weed. After dragging on her cigarette for the last few times she climbed into her car.

The engine roared as she turned the key. She glanced at her rearview then her side mirrors so that she could back up. Before she could put the car in reverse she felt a cold piece of steel at her neck.

"This can be cool or it can be a problem. I don't have any problem with leaving you dead in this here parking lot."

"Who the fuck are you?" Kelly's voice trembled.

"Don't worry about who I am. Go ahead and back up then drive off slowly. If you pick up any speed I will shoot you. If you make any signals to any other cars I will kill you. If you don't do exactly what I say, I will kill you. Now nod your head if you understand."

She nodded her head, trying to hold back the tears. Andrew warned her that this was no time to go against what he said. Now she wished she would have listened to him.

"Are you going to kill me?" She asked out of panic.

"Maybe."

They drove about two or three blocks before he directed her to turn. They pulled onto a street that was next to a park. The park was empty and that made her really nervous. She slowed the car down almost to a snail's pace.

"Pull into the parking area."

She did as she was told but the tears began to fall. The man sat in the back seat for a few moments after instructing her to turn off the engine. He opened the back door but kept his pistol pointed at her.

"Now open up your door."

She tried to relax for a moment, considering that he might just want to steal her car. A carjack wasn't shit to her. Her man Andrew would be able to get her a car in no time. When she climbed out of the car the man was dressed in all black. He even had black gloves and a black mask covering his face except for his eyes. The eyes looked familiar to her. That was when panic set in again. She realized that it might be more than a carjack.

"This has something to do with Andrew, huh?" She asked, hoping it was just a carjack.

"Yep!"

He pulled out some handcuffs and quickly put her in them. Then he covered her eyes with a handkerchief. He took the keys to the car, while heading for the trunk. After popping the trunk, he carefully placed her inside and closed it. They drove for about twenty minutes before Kelly heard him cut off the engine. She could hear him unlocking the trunk. He forcefully lifted her from the trunk and escorted through a few rooms. She could tell that it was an empty warehouse or office. Her legs went weak with anxiety wondering if she would die tonight. Suddenly she was lifted back to her feet then sat down at a table.

"Page him 9-1-1"

He lifted the covering from her eyes and she began paging him repeatedly. She stared at the phone hoping that he called back.

Drew Dog had just finished fucking his Arcadia girl. He was laying on top of her when his pager began to go off violently. He climbed off the girl to check the number. It wasn't a familiar number but it had 9-1-1 attached to it. He considered not calling the number back until he received another 9-1-1 page. Then another one came after that. If someone was calling it must be something serious. He wasn't too fond of talking on the phone about business but all of his people knew better.

"I got to go."

"Damn Derrick, where are you going?"

"I'll be back in a minute."

He always had to remember that he gave her a bogus name when they met. It still took a little getting used to. He threw on his sweat suit and headed for the liquor store. He kept staring at the number trying to get an idea who was calling him. Suddenly his pager went off again.

"Damn cuz."

He pulled into the parking lot of the closest liquor store he could find. He didn't want to talk at the house so that his Arcadia girl could eavesdrop. He dipped into the liquor store to get some change but the Asian man wouldn't give it to him unless he bought something. Irritated he bought a beer then went to use the phone. Before the first ring could go through a woman picked up the phone.

"Andrew?"

"Who is this? Kelly?"

"Yeah this is me. I just got kidnapped and the man wants three hundred grand or he's going to kill me." Kelly quickly replied.

"Get the fuck out of here. Quit bullshitting."

"Do it sound like I'm bullshitting?

Drew Dog lowered his head finally understanding the circumstances. He wanted to go off but didn't know who to go off on.

"Fuck!"

"What's up Andrew?" Kelly sounded concerned.

He could pull together the money but he had to seriously consider if Kelly was worth that much. She asked him several times what was up but he didn't respond. He thought about his children being without their mother. He thought about having to face her mother after she was killed. He still might kill her, he considered.

"Tell that muthafucka I got a hundred grand." He calmly replied.

"This ain't a negotiation Andrew what the fuck." She snapped.

He didn't reply. This muthafucka doesn't plan on killing me, he plans on tormenting me. I can't live like this.

"Andrew, muthafucka I'm the mother of your children." She reminded him.

"Alright damn, tell him I got it."

"You shouldn't have had to think about it." She cried.

He could tell she was crying. He closed his eyes and shook his head. He had to find a way to get to whoever this was that kept fucking with him.

"This is war muthafucka, this is war." He mumbled.

10
A CONVICT'S TEARS

A rapid, powerful transition to the attack- the glinting sword of vengeance- is the most brilliant moment of the defense.
Carl von Clausewitz

Past five years ago

The dreaded letter finally came. He hadn't heard from Missy in a while so he expected the worse. The correctional officer called his name to receive his mail. One was his court records from his lawyer. The other one was from his niece Melanie. Missy was a soldier, but he could tell on those last visits that the cancer was getting to her. Chemotherapy just wasn't working and she was feeling drained every time she went through the procedure. As people say, "she fought the good fight." He stared at the envelope not wanting to open it. He wanted to hear from his niece Melanie, but he didn't want to hear the bad news he was pretty sure she would tell him. The last few visits Melanie would come to visit him with Missy. She had grown up to be a very pretty young woman with impeccable intelligence. She was definitely a diamond in the rough. He climbed on top of his bunk with the letter in hand. He was fighting back his tears because for some reason he felt that it would be harder to read the words. The penitentiary wasn't really a place where you should be seen crying. But Tango made a name for himself that he was not to be played with.

He tore open the letter and slowly began to read. Melanie started off slow letting him know that she was doing well. She had enough money to support herself and now she was living in the dorms at Cal State Fullerton. She was majoring in business and her minor was education. Tango smiled at the thought of his niece becoming a school teacher. She always had a way of teaching his daughter Samantha different things. That would be a fitting job for Melanie, he considered. Where Missy was hard at the edges Melanie was refined. Missy raised her to be more lady like than she was. For that brief moment he wondered if Missy always wanted to be that way but circumstances wouldn't allow it. The letter let him know that Melanie was away from any sort of drama and she was enjoying her best years. Then the bomb dropped. She hated that she would be having her best years without her mother. The few tears fell from his face. He would never get to see his sister alive again. She was the toughest person he knew.

He had to take a few moments to contemplate what he knew to be true. He breathed out to calm himself. There wasn't a sense of panic but more like an inner turmoil. He couldn't let some of the people in here see his pain. Some people will antagonize you if they see a weakness. Even the guards at the prison could be cruel and aggressive. He looked around his cell then glanced outside into the hallway. Sometimes the four walls were your best friend.

Now his thoughts went back to the letter. She promised to keep in touch with him and every intention on keeping the lawyer satisfied. Her mother had given her clear instructions on what to do concerning his appeal. Melanie assured him that she would stay on top of it even though she was in college. He sat back and smiled, remembering how sweet his niece could be. He could only look forward to her letters. He had pain for his sister's death but at least her daughter was alive and well. She ended her letter by explaining how much she loved him in hopes that the lawyer did his job.

He smiled after reading the letter. He knew the news of his sister was coming but she wrote in a way that he still had some form of comfort. He laid the letter on his bed then stared at the wall for a moment. He was lost in thought when he heard his name called.

"Davenport!"

"Davenport!"

It startled him momentarily as he rose from his bed. His cell door slid open as he walked outside.

"Your lawyer is here." A familiar correctional officer announced.

Tango walked down to the aisle on his way to where visitors were. He kept his head up and face straight ahead. He had been known as a stand up guy among the many convicts. He started to see the emergence of the Crips and Bloods as well as the still standing Black Guerilla Family. All of them were trying to get his attention and he knew eventually he would have to choose sides. Even though his cousin Cisco was an original Crip he didn't want to go that route. He was more in line with the Black Guerilla Family because of their long standing organization. Both the Crips and the Black Guerilla Family was courting him but he wasn't quite sure. He had been a hustler for a long time and hadn't turned snitch or burned anyone. There weren't too many criminals that could lay claim to that. One of the top soldiers from the BGF acknowledged him with a slight nod and he did the same. He focused on his objective but paid attention to his surroundings. If he joined the Crips then he naturally had the Bloods and the United Blood Nation against him. If he joined the Black Guerilla Family he would have the Mexican Mafia against him. That wasn't so bad when considering they weren't cool with him just for being Black in the first place. He needed allies and that was for sure. He would have to make a decision soon.

He walked into the solitary room so that he could have a private conversation with his lawyer. The Jewish guy stood up and firmly shook his hand. He sat down at the same time Tango was pulling his chair out to sit.

"So Mr. Davenport, your case looks good. They didn't have probable cause to search you. They physically assaulted you and they cannot produce the informant that tipped them. I received the money from your niece…Right?"

Tango nodded not really having anything to say. The lawyer jotted down some information then continued.

"I am Hyman Steinberg and I will walk you through every step. The public defender didn't really pay attention to your case. It is hard to believe that he let you take this many years without a fight."

"Well you know how public defenders can be. They only want to get through the case as quickly as possible. He never had any intentions on doing the research that it would take to get my case truly heard." Tango replied.

"All of that will change after today Mr. Davenport. My team works hard for our clients and it will be no exception with you. Your niece informed me that her mother recently passed and she was your sister. I know that you are going through a painful time in your life and we will keep that in consideration.

"I have my pain but a convict's tears must stay hidden. This is a world that preys on the weak so I have to keep my hurt concealed." Tango replied.

He walked back to his cell pondering on his good news. On his way back he noticed the man he had acknowledged earlier from BGF. The man walked up to him to give him the greetings in Swahili. Tango attempted to respond in the same tongue but he was relatively new to the language. The man came in arms distance and spoke to him slowly and calmly.

"Word is out about your loss. I'm sending out my condolences to you and your family. We need to talk real soon about a few things."

"Yeah we do. I'm prepared to do what it takes." Tango replied.

"Well then meet me in the yard when we have yard time after lunch tomorrow. I'll give you all the details later."

They didn't bother to shake hands but casually walked away. Tango went back to his cell pretty sure what was expected of him. He climbed in his bunk and laid back so he could ponder on his decision. If things went well he might be released in a short period of time. He wondered if it would be wise to shake the boat when his appeal was looking so promising.

"I still got to live in here while fighting my appeal." He said to himself.

The following day he met up with the man and they once again greeted each other in Swahili. They walked away from the weight area and decided to talk near the walls. He passed Tango a cigarette and began his explanation.

"We got paperwork on a nigga that supposed to be affiliated with the Crips. He doesn't really have any representation as a shot caller. Some niggas did some dirt with the nigga and he started cooperating with the law. You handle this and you gon' be alright with us. Its best you make sure he's dead."

"What about the Crip niggas? How are they gon' act when one of theirs gets got?" Tango asked.

"They are the ones that are paying out for us to take care of the shit. They don't want it done by someone with them because it will set a bad precedent. They didn't want any of the Bloods to do it because it would only start a riot. They want to pretend that it is a mystery. You were given the assignment."

"Okay, how are we gon' make this happen? What's the plan?" Tango dragged on a cigarette.

"He has kitchen duty so after chow we are going to send you back there to take care of that shit."

With that said, they talked about other things briefly then they went their separate ways. Later that night, Tango was shown a way into the mess hall kitchen. He was handed a shank right before he went into the kitchen. Someone he knew as part of the BGF pointed in the direction of this empty room. Inside the room were bags and boxes of the different foods like bags of rice and potatoes. It had shelves stacked with various items as well as big pots and pans. Tango relaxed for a minute pondering the kill. He squatted down in the corner with the lights out. He pulled the shank out when he heard footsteps coming closer to the room. He could tell when the man spoke that he was the target. The man was obviously complaining about having to get something out of the dark room. To Tango it felt like he was taking a thousand years before making it to the room. When the door finally swung open the man paused before entering. He began mumbling to himself about the lights being out. In a flash, Tango attacked. He swung the shank several time aiming for the heart and stomach until the man collapsed. When he walked out of the room the man that pointed towards the room was there to greet him. Tango handed him the shank inside of a towel he had ready for him. The man walked away while Tango quickly slid out the other way. In a matter of moments he was back cleaning up his cell. Before he made it to his cell he went to the bathroom to wash his hands. He was lying on his bed later that night when he heard the siren go off. He knew exactly what the loud noise was about.

The following afternoon he met up with the man in the yard. Once again they greeted each other in Swahili and leaned against the wall. The body of the snitch wasn't found until roll call later that night. Everyone in the kitchen was questioned but everyone knew to keep silent. The warden considered locking down the prison but it wouldn't have gotten any further in the case. Tango had grown numb to the entire ordeal. His pain was an inner turmoil that damn near consumed him. The man looked at Tango and could tell the man was going through some things.

"You will be able to meet with some of our people. I know this is a hard period in your life but you are a soldier." He commented.

"Yeah I got a few things fucking with me. But I will do what I got to do." Tango replied.

"Remember more than anything that killers don't talk. Anyone can murder a muthafucka and go about things in a stupid way. But killers don't talk. We dispose of people that need to be disposed of; nothing more and nothing less. When handling someone we don't allow our emotions to get involved. We do what's needed to be done and move on to other business." The man explained.

"Even if its revenge?" Tango asked.

"Especially if it is revenge. That work you did was business and it was easy to do because you didn't have any emotional attachments. It might come a time when you have to kill someone that you have emotional attachments to. You will have to put your emotions to the side and handle your business if you want to accomplish yo goal. Soldiers are given missions so they don't get emotional about the mission. Be passionate about getting done what you need to get done and that's about it."

"That sounds different from being human. I'm not taking a man's money I'm taking a man's life, in which he will never get back. How can you not have some kind of emotional reaction? Isn't that what separates us from the animals?" Tango asked.

"What separates us from the animals is the awareness of our existence. When you fit into a roll in life there comes a time when a man has to acknowledge who he is. He has to understand this is a path he has chosen so he has to accept what comes with that path. Look around at the young gangbangers saying I'm a

Blood or I'm a Crip. They believe in it like it is a religion. But at their stage of development they only get emotional when they kill their enemy. That's why so many of them are coming in here in droves. They do it for the name and reputation when they should accept their cause and act on that without getting emotional. Some of them are starting to know the difference. They learn to understand that if someone has to go the best way to carry it out is to not get emotionally involved." The man continued to explain.

"What about serial killers and shit like that? You got mass murderers that kill people skillfully and they get emotional. Some even go as far as keeping the body parts of their victims." Tango replied.

"Don't mistake insanity with the objective. Those that are killers for sport don't operate under the same rules as us. They have an insatiable appetite that they themselves cannot control. They're not functioning as we are." The man passed Tango a cigarette.

They both puffed on their cigarettes while Tango pondered on his words. In a matter of years he lost his entire family with the exception of his niece. It was difficult not to deal with things emotionally. That would be something he would have to work on and master.

"I've lost my entire family so it won't be easy to kill without emotions." Tango remarked.

"Do you think they deserved to die?" The man nonchalantly asked.

"Hell nah, I don't think they deserved it." Tango replied incredulously.

"Yet and still they were dealt that hand. Fate wasn't emotional about the tragedy that happened to your family. It was swift and merciless. We as men and women have the ability to make fate. So when you exact your revenge you have to be as efficient as fate was towards your family."

That fell on Tango like a ton of bricks. He never put two and two together until that very moment. It was a moment of clarity. Tango dragged on his cigarette and slightly chuckled. The man didn't take the time to look and see what Tango was laughing about. He just puffed on his cigarette and stared out into the yard.

"Killers Don't Talk!" Tango replied.

"Killers Don't Talk!" The man reiterated.

Drew Dog sat on his porch puffing on some Entica and sipping on Night Train. His road dog/best friend Shook were enjoying the fruits of their labor. They had been serving dope to four different neighborhoods now.

"I'm gon' ending up fucking Rosie, Shorty's little cousin." Shook commented.

"You know I got major love for you nigga but yo ass is a molester. She is only about fourteen or fifteen. Just like when we had to handle that business with that one nigga's family. You had to fuck his daughter." Drew Dog chuckled.

"If she's got hair down there she's old enough to get fucked." Shook replied.

"See nigga, how would you feel if someone fucked yo daughter like that?"

"I'm expecting that one day they will." Shook laughed.

Drew Dog laughed right along with him as he stood up to leave the porch. Shook followed closely behind him until they got to front of the yard. His girl Kelly was inside the house and he didn't want her to hear anything important.

"Didn't I tell you that the plan would work? All we had to do was get rid of Cisco and Tango and everything would fall into place. I know that nigga Fat Rat was a casualty but we just got to chalk that up to the game." Drew Dog began.

"You also got to think about that nigga Lazy. He ain't out the picture yet. He just fell off the face of the earth right now." Shook replied.

"Yeah but that nigga don't know if we had anything to do with what happened to him. I think he has a warrant out for his arrest anyway for that hit and run." Drew Dog brushed it off.

"I'm telling you though my nigga he would have been a cool nigga to have on the team." Shook commented.

"Yeah I fucked up with that one. I didn't think the nigga could get past the fact that Cisco was dead."

"Well this is this nigga's hood so he will eventually resurface." Shook replied.

"Tidbit is on her way over here, she's been fucking with that slob nigga Big Red and I think she's getting feelings. Other than that everything is good because that nigga Tango sitting on a whole bunch of years."

"Yeah and he don't know how everything went bad for him. He has plenty of time to think about it though." Shook replied.

"Yeah but by the time that nigga sees daylight he will be too old to do anything about it. He's a convict nigga with plenty of time for tattoo tears."

Big Red and Tidbit were posted on the porch of Big Red's house. His pockets are fat and he is loving the new arrangement. He thought about making Tidbit his girl but he always thinks about her people being from the other side.

"I'd marry yo ass if you wasn't a crab bitch." Big Red commented.

"Whatever nigga! You know my cousin is waiting on me so you might want to give me that money for you to re-cop." Tidbit replied.

"Yeah I got that fifteen even right here. Lavelle and I should sell out by the end of today. So what's up, you said you wanted to talk to me? Here I am."

"I'm pregnant." Tidbit bluntly replied.

"And what do you want me to do about it?"

"You are the daddy, nigga." Tidbit retorted.

"You sure you ain't pregnant by one of the crab niggas over in your relative's hood? Are you sure you want to have a baby by a Damu nigga?" Big Red teased.

"Fuck you nigga, you know I ain't been fucking no one but yo ass." Tidbit slapped him on his chest.

"I'm just making sure I don't know how the other side works. I want to be able to trust you."

"You can trust me, why would you think you can't?" Tidbit replied.

"Okay if I can trust you, who was the nigga that we smoked up in that house you tipped us on to? You know the nigga that had all the yayo." Big Red asked.

"Okay, Okay, it was this nigga named Cisco from our neighborhood. He was holding out on making money with the homies so they thought he had to go." Tidbit admitted.

"That shit is crazy, those crab niggas will smoke they own homie. B-Dogs have a code but ya'll erickets don't have a code about shit." Big Red said with disgust.

"It's so many Crips that they eventually turn on each other. Ya'll Blood niggas ain't got a lot of people so ya'll have to stick together." Tidbit replied.

"Okay, what about his people? Is it somebody that is gon' come back on us because of what happened to that nigga? Has he got any killers in his family?" Big Red continued to pry.

"He has a cousin that just got a whole bunch of jail time. He won't be seeing daylight for awhile. By the time he gets out he will be too old to do shit. Besides, he doesn't know who did that shit to Cisco. All he knows is that his family got caught slipping in one of the dope spots. You ain't got shit to worry about."

Big Red nodded but was still somewhat skeptical. He didn't know if he was being set up for the fall or what. He let his thoughts wander for a minute.

"Well give me the money so I can give it to my cousin." Tidbit said.

"Why didn't yo people put in the work and take care of that shit. They wouldn't have had to share any of the money with us." Big Red pried.

"Because my people had to have an alibi when all the shit went down. The nigga that got smoked was the one holding out on them so the first person they gon' think did it is them. So they just got rid of him and let ya'll keep the money while they set it up to make money in the long run." Tidbit explained.

"Yo peoples is slick." Big Red commented.

Tidbit took the money Big Red handed to her and drove off. When she pulled up in front of Drew Dog's house they were already standing out front. She gathered everything that she had to hand to him first. Her cousin was real stiff about how his money was handled. She knew to get down to business with him first. She climbed out of the car with everything in hand. He smiled when she handed him the money.

"It's all of it for a whole bird." She said.

"I see the little slob nigga got some things on the ball. He must be moving weight over there nowadays. What about that other thing?"

"Yeah, she's alive and she was more than likely there when that shit went down."

"What's her name?"

"Melody or Melanie; some shit like that. She's disappeared off the face of the earth like that nigga Lazy." Tidbit replied.

"Besides that nigga Tango she's the only one left in their family, huh? She shouldn't be a problem because she couldn't see how we looked or anything." Drew Dog considered.

"Yeah, probably so but what was funny was that nigga Big Red was asking me about that shit he did to that nigga Cisco."

"What was he asking you?"

"Why didn't ya'll put in the work? He was worried about that shit coming back on him like we were trying to set him up. I let him know that we had to have an alibi that was why we had him do it." Tidbit explained.

"Why didn't you just keep yo mouth shut? You see Shook, that's the reason why you can't do shit with females. They don't know when to keep their mouth shut." Drew Dog pointed at his cousin.

"It wasn't even like that. He wanted to see if I trusted him so he asked me a question to see if I would honestly answer him." Tidbit shrugged.

"What the fuck does it matter if he trusts you or not? He's making money off the shit we linked him to so that should be enough. I don't know about you Tidbit; you might buckle if the police get you in the interrogation room." Drew Dog commented.

"That's bullshit Andrew. I ain't ever been a snitch. I'm pregnant by that nigga so he has to believe that he can trust me." Tidbit protested.

"Damn Tidbit, I was just fucking with you. Now you are about to have this nigga's baby? I didn't know it was that serious." Drew Dog replied.

"That was why I was answering all his bullshit questions." Tidbit explained.

"Well he doesn't have shit to worry about because that nigga is locked up for a long time. If and when he gets out he doesn't know what happened to him and who did what. The little bitch might be a problem but if she was she would have been one by now." Shook commented.

"Yeah I think so too." Drew Dog added.

11
BLOOD LUST

In war-time, truth is so precious that she should always be attended by a bodyguard of lies!
Winston Churchill

Present

Brazy Bee posted up in front of his baby mama's house snacking on sunflower seeds. It was a cold California breeze that promised to get colder when darkness struck. He could see the curb servers hustling that yayo and it was selling like hot cakes. He would be able to re-cop from that nigga Drew Dog any day now. He didn't personally like dealing with him and it wasn't just because he was a Crip.

"Something ain't right with that Crab nigga." He would say.

Drew Dog didn't quite rub him right but he had the best deals for that raw Columbian Cocaine. He had to make his money the only way he knew how. It was crazy to him because the police were hot from time to time but not because of dope. Boston was on the run for smoking Lavelle. Brazy Bee was an OG just like Lavelle but he understood why Boston had to peel his cap. You ain't ever supposed to pull a gun on a nigga and don't use it. He watched some of the hustlers from his neighborhood post up and serve. It was the fifteenth of the month so everyone had their county checks. He loved his hood and the people that lived in it. He happened to notice this crack head he went to high school with. Her name was Teneshia but everyone called her Tu-Tu. He somewhat lamented for her because in her prime she was really fine. She turned heads to the point where the high rollers were all trying to get at her. The high roller she chose got her into smoking crack and within a few years she had lost everything. Brazy Bee remembered having a crush on her when he was younger. She still would be considered attractive but she was only a shell to what she used to be.

"What's up with you Tu-Tu?" He yelled over to her.

"Damn Corey, how have you been? You look like you got things going good for you nowadays." She commented while crossing the street.

"Just doing my thing. What's been up with you?"

"Same ole shit. You know that nigga Deuce got fifteen years for attempted murder. I'm out here on my own nowadays…You think that young nigga Mookie will give me a twenty piece for sixteen dollars?" She lowered her head in shame.

"You ain't got to beg that nigga for a twenty piece. You could just come to me and I'll hook you up." Brazy Bee replied.

"Damn Corey, you got it like that. If you able to do all that, why don't you break a bitch off with a twenty-five piece?"

"What you gon' do for me?" Brazy Bee sharply replied.

Tu-Tu shrugged her shoulders with an expression of taking suggestions. He smirked a little then waived for her to get in the car. She followed him knowing exactly what he expected. Brazy Bee saw his baby's mama walk outside through his peripheral but he ignored her. He cut the engine on fast to his 62' Impala and turned the music up. He quickly rolled out before she could yell for him. He knew she was going to ask a bunch of questions but he wasn't in the mood. He had wanted to fuck Tu-Tu for years. He rolled around the corner to the hang out shack where some of the young homies took hoodrats they were trying to fuck. He hopped out of his ride with Tu-Tu following right behind him. He was relieved to open the garage and find no one inside. He sat down on some raggedy couches the homies had put inside the shack. It was really a back house that the homie had that was part of another house in the front. It had been the kick it spot for years. He made sure to lock the door before he sat down. Tu-Tu stood at the door then slowly joined him on the couch. She wasn't reluctant but she was unsure about what he wanted.

"Come over here and suck my dick."

She got on her hands and knees then pulled him out. She slowly wrapped her lips around his manhood. She did a deep throat that made him moan loudly. She kept stroking him while her lips traveled up and down his the shaft down to his balls. She was putting in work that he truly could appreciate. His baby mama was too stuck up to give him head. He laid his head back and let her do wonders with her mouth. Further she got into it the faster she went until finally he exploded in her mouth.

"Damn Tu-Tu you did yo thing. We gon' have to link up more often for this kind of shit. How did you learn how to suck a dick like that?"

Tu-Tu just laughed and asked him how she could rinse out her mouth. He pointed to a sink over in the corner. He waited by the door while she rinsed out her mouth. When she walked over toward the door he handed her a thirty piece of crack for her troubles.

"You keep giving head like that we gon' be cool." He commented.

She smiled then pulled out a stick of gum and put it in her mouth. They walked outside of the shack making small talk. When Brazy Bee turned around he bumped right into someone. He turned around to see Boston staring at him with a smirk on his face.

"What that Bee like Blood?" Boston stated.

"What that Bee like nigga? So this is where the fuck you been hiding Blood?" Brazy Bee commented.

"Yeah here and there. One of the neighbors must be snitching Blood...What's up Tu-Tu?" Boston acknowledge her.

"Where the fuck is Rocky?" Brazy Bee asked but didn't really care.

"That nigga is out hustling. He leaves the back door open so that I can take showers in the house while his moms is gone to work."

"Okay then Blood you Bee up and I'll holla at you soon." Brazy Bee replied.

Tu-Tu followed closely behind Brazy Bee and hopped in on the passenger side. She wouldn't look in Boston's direction and was relieved that they had made it to the car.

"I heard that nigga smoked Lavelle over an argument. It ain't one of the neighbors snitching that shit is all over the east side." Tu-Tu commented.

"I don't know because I don't speak on murders. Where you want me to take you? It would be good if it was somewhere away from my baby mama's spot because she's gon' talk shit."

"Nah, I was going around the corner to blaze this shit up. This is some right shit you did for a bitch. I won't forget that. So how can I get at you if I need a little taste?" She smiled.

"I'll give my beeper number so you can hit me up any time. But don't be paging me after ten o'clock or its gon' start some shit." Brazy Bee replied.

She nodded then directed him to her destination. He hit about three or four corners before he arrived at her spot. He put the car in park so that they could play catch up for a minute. She was one of the baddest bitches he knew, back in the day.

"My homegirl is letting me crash on her couch for awhile. I try to keep this shit away from her so she won't kick my ass out." Tu-Tu chuckled.

"Yeah well we gon' have to talk from time to time and see what's up with you." Brazy Bee smiled.

He kept eyeing her down wondering how he would hit the ass the next time they linked up. Unbeknownst to him a Black pick-up truck was pulling up to the side of him. It slowed down long enough to allow the passenger to throw a cocktail in the backseat of Brazy Bee's car. The broken glass instantly startled him and Tu-Tu. The fire set ablaze quickly and before he knew it the inside of his car was in flames. He was able to push himself out of the car. He glanced back into the car to see that Tu-Tu was struggling to get out the car. He had parked too close to the curb for her to open the car all the way. She screamed as he climbed back inside from the passenger side to pull her out. She struggled with him a little because she was hysterical and on fire. He pulled her out finally and made her roll on the ground. Within minutes the flames that had caught on to her was out and she was gasping for breath. Once he realized that she was safe he noticed the burn marks on her body and felt bad. At that very moment he heard the glass break inside of his car. He turned around and shook his head in fury as his vehicle went up in flames. Within ten to fifteen minutes the fire truck came and began putting out the blaze.

Brazy Bee and Tu-Tu sat on the curb watching the flames go down while in their own thoughts. Brazy Bee didn't know what to think or who could have done this to him. His thoughts raced as he tried to put the pieces together. Tu-Tu received some bandages but refused to be taken to the hospital.

"If it wasn't for bad luck I wouldn't have any luck at all." She reflected.

"Somebody did this shit to me. It was a nigga trying to get back at me about some shit." Brazy Bee replied.

"It could be over some gangbanging shit because one of those niggas had on a blue rag. He was wearing over his head Aunt Jemima style. I caught a glimpse of that shit right before the flames got big."

"Are you for real?" Brazy Bee snapped.

Tu-Tu nodded her head confirming what she seen. Brazy Bee pounded the palms of his hands against his forehead. He couldn't remember being disrespected like that. Certain niggas knew who to fuck with and who not to fuck with. If this was over gangbanging he was going to show them gangbanging.

"They want to get some shit started. I'm telling you Blood that was some punk shit those niggas pulled."

He stood up then looked down at Tu-Tu to see if she was following. She got up from the curb but had plans to go in another direction. She pointed toward the opposite direction he was going so he nodded.

"Ain't you gon' check on what's gon' happen to yo car?" Tu-Tu asked out of curiosity.

"I ain't worried about that car because I got insurance on that shit anyway. When I fixed it up I got insurance on that shit just in case I wrecked it. But I'm about to bounce so I can handle some shit." He sharply replied.

"Okay then, I will talk to you later." Tu-Tu waved.

Brazy Bee was preparing to rally the troops. Drew Dog previously tried to avoid wars because of money reasons but Brazy Bee had a feeling he let that shit go down. It would have been easier to swallow if they would have tried to shoot him. Instead it was as if he was getting some kind of warning for something. The more he thought about it the more he was pissed off. It had to be behind some personal shit.

"We about to serve these crab ass niggas." He mumbled loudly.

He strolled down the street watching his back every so often because he wasn't strapped. He had left his 40 Cal at his baby mama's house. He was walking back to her house to pick it up. He knew that she would start bitching because she seen him drive off with Tu-Tu. He was going to check her at the door before she got started.

It took him fifteen minutes to make it around the corner and down two blocks. He opened the screen and his baby's mama started in on him.

"That's some fucked up shit Corey; you drive off with that bitch when you heard me calling you. You heard me when I was calling you." She began.

"Would you shut the fuck up? Somebody just firebombed my car and you worried about who the fuck is in it."

She looked at him in disbelief then noticed that the car wasn't parked out front. He went into the room and went under the bed to grab a shoe box. Within a matter of minutes he had his gun under his waist band. He stepped past her and walked outside without saying a word. She knew this wasn't a good time to talk shit so she let him go. He crossed the street and went near the vacant house to find a few of the homies in the backyard. A few were serving in the same spot he seen Tu-Tu walking up to earlier.

"What's happening Blood?" He announced.

"What that Bee like?" One of the little homies replied.

"We gon' rally against these crab ass niggas Blood." Brazy Bee announced.

The few remaining homies in the front made their way to the backyard. In the backyard a few of the homies were slap boxing and drinking.

"What's up OG Brazy Bee?" Someone announced.

"Soowooop!" Brazy Bee replied.

The homies gathered around him when he yelled out the Damu call. Within seconds he had everyone's undivided attention. Once they were was settled in he gave out his orders.

"Look here Blood, these crab niggas is starting to set trip so ya'll need to load up. By the time we through they gon' know not to fuck with us." Brazy Bee declared.

In an instant, guns started popping up out of everywhere. Brazy Bee smiled devilishly as his mind began to plan on how to ride on the Crips.

"We about to do rotation on these crabs."

"If you knew where Boston was we could have that nigga get in on this." A little homie suggested.

"Get everything ready to ride tonight right when dark hits. I'll find Boston while ya'll niggas gather all the guns you can."

He walked out of the backyard and back across the street to his baby mama's house. She was still looking out the window when he made it back to the porch. She stared at him in awe without saying a word.

"Give me the keys to the Toyota."

"For what? Don't put in work in that car because you lost yours." She blurted out.

He gave her a look that pierced through her and she knew not to say another word. She glanced at her purse on the dining room table. He quickly grabbed the keys from out of her purse and strolled out the door. He hopped into the Toyota and quickly drove around the corner. He went right back to the shack and noticed the door was unlocked. When he opened the door he saw Boston staring at him with a 38' snub nose pointed at the door. Brazy Bee stopped in his tracks after seeing the weapon.

"Aw Blood, I thought you were the police. I heard a whole bunch of sirens and I didn't know what the fuck was going on." Boston sighed in relief.

"Blood, you are a muthafuckin trip. You were gon' blast on the police?"

Boston nodded without making a remark. Brazy Bee sat down across from the young killer to talk.

"I know you on the run right now; but are you down to put in work against these crabs?" Brazy Bee began.

"I'm always down to put in work on these crabs. This is crab killer until I die Blood." Boston sharply replied.

"Alright then, grab yo heat and we gon' meet up with the homies tonight and start doing rotation on these niggas." Brazy Bee replied.

"Yeah I'm with that." Boston replied. His lust for blood was evident.

Later that night Brazy Bee had it set up for them to steal two cars. They were going to give their enemies problems on both sides. Brazy Bee made sure that he was able to drive one of the cars. He was driving a car with Boston and another young Damu rider. Some of youngsters knew where the Crips were hanging out. A second car was set up to catch them when they ran in the opposite direction. There was also three of his homies rolling in the second car.

In a matter of minutes they had rolled over into Crip territory. Boston spotted a bunch of Crips hanging out in front of a house.

"Cut off yo lights Blood." Boston announced.

They crept up slow as Boston and the young rider poked their heads out the window. Before anyone could notice the car, Boston and the young rider had began shooting into the crowd. Boston had quickly learned how to be a good shot. So he picked off his enemies with fierce efficiency. The youngster wasn't precise but he was able to let off with the 45' he was brandishing. Bodies began to fall as Brazy Bee sped off into the night. The Crips that were able to escape ran off into the direction Brazy Bee had planned. The homies in the second car came in just in time to catch the remaining gangsters that had escaped the first assault. Bullets flew in their direction as they ran right into the ambush. Some were able to dodge the shots and hide in neighboring yards. The second car sped off into the night.

Like always when one puts in work, they dumped the stolen car near the neighborhood wearing brownie gloves so the car couldn't be traced back. They all decided to meet back up at the shack. The group that was in the second car was greeted by Boston and Brazy Bee once they walked in the door.

"Now that's how you put in work." Brazy Bee said while embracing the homies.

"Yeah, we let them crab niggas have it." Another homie announced.

For the last week or two the Damus had been riding on the Crips. It was becoming a problem because the homies were coming up missing. Brazy Bee was a shot caller from the other side and he wasn't returning Drew Dog's pages. Drew Dog didn't like the fact that the homies were getting shot and killed. But what bothered him more was that money wasn't flowing because of the war. He understood that Bloods and Crips have wars, but it seemed as though there was some vendetta. He racked his brain trying to figure out how to get at Brazy Bee to calm shit down. He was still in hiding because of the war. There were some issues he had to address before he could really feel comfortable. Drew Dog figured the best way to get at Brazy Bee was to holla at Toothpick. Toothpick was locked up with a Damu that he was actually cool with. According to Toothpick they were distant cousins through marriage or something like that. He called Toothpick but he felt a little uneasy. Toothpick didn't seem the same after their last meeting when he wrecked the Impala. Drew Dog felt like the young OG was somehow blaming him for the shit. He had bigger fish to fry and the money coming from Brazy Bee was needed. The phone rang several times before someone picked it up.

"Hello?" A deep voice answered.

"What's Up Cuz, this is Drew Dog?"

"Ay what's up Cuz?"

"I need you to get at that slob homeboy you got that's related to you somehow. Let him know that you need to meet up with Brazy Bee on some money shit. I'm gon' give you the number, once he's set it up then ya'll talk." Drew Dog explained.

"Why can't you get at that slob nigga? He knows you way better than I do." Toothpick subtly protested.

"I'm out of pocket Cuz. Besides, that nigga hasn't been answering my pages. So get at the nigga to see what's up so that we can stop this bullshit war." Drew Dog replied.

"I should just smoke that slob nigga and end the war right there."

"Hell nah, if you do that shit then that is only gon' make the war get worse. Trust me on this shit Cuz, if you see what's up then maybe we can calm this shit down. Tell him that I'll be letting those birds go for thirteen-five if the nigga listens." Drew Dog explained.

"Damn Cuz, you ain't hooking the homies up like that." Toothpick said in disbelief.

"If you make this shit happen and stop the war I'll give it to you for the same amount." Drew Dog quickly replied.

"Alright then Cuz."

After taking down the pager number Drew Dog gave to him, Toothpick contemplated on how to do this. He hated having to back deal with the slob nigga that was blasting on his homies. He was having a hard time swallowing Drew Dog asking him to trust him. He must really be desperate, he considered. He was letting a kilo of cocaine go for thirteen-five and he was using the word trust. That was like a blasphemous word to Drew Dog. He began making the necessary phone calls and within a few hours the meeting was set a couple of days later. Toothpick knew the only reason Drew Dog didn't like his suggestion of smoking Brazy Bee was because that would take money out of his pocket. It was always about the money to Drew Dog.

It was a California cold day in the afternoon when Toothpick and Brazy Bee met up. His distant family member attended and made the informal introduction. They sat across from each other inside of a Winchell's Donut shop. Both soldiers possessed what was known as the thousand-yard-stare. They were both alumni from the school of hard knocks. They sat down across from each other at a restaurant booth.

"I used to go to elementary school with you. We had Mr. Hubbard in the third grade and Mrs. Davis in the fourth." Toothpick remembered.

"Yeah that's right. When we didn't play kickball you and I used to play marbles. You got that nigga Kenny for damn near a whole bag of marbles." Brazy Bee replied.

"Yep and you beat up Marcus for fucking with that girl Sharon, yo name is Corey something." Toothpick nodded.

"Yeah, and yo name was Jason Mosley. So now we are on two different sides of a war. You used to be a bool ass nigga back in the day when we were kids. It's a shame it done came down to this." Brazy Bee replied.

"Look here, I know you a down ass Damu and you know that I'm a down ass Crip. But we can put that bullshit to the side to make this money. Yo homeboys started blasting us and we took it like ya'll just wanted to go to war." Toothpick explained.

"Nah, somebody threw a cocktail into my ride. My whole fucking car caught on fire. The niggas that did that shit was wearing a blue rag over their head. We started riding on ya'll niggas because of that." Brazy Bee replied.

"I'm a shot caller and no one ever gave the okay to firebomb somebody's car. That's on everything I love I didn't know shit about that." Toothpick passionately explained.

"I don't think it was you. I think yo homeboy Drew Dog is a foul ass nigga. I know he from yo hood and everything, but he scandalous."

Toothpick didn't really want to respond. He agreed with the Damu even though he was supposed to be his enemy. He looked around trying not to look so obvious that he agreed with him. Brazy Bee caught the facial expression in a glance. In that instant Brazy Bee had to respect the Crip. He had his loyalties but it appeared as though he shared the same sentiment.

"Look here gangsta, it seems like you are on the same page as I am. You know yo homeboy is into some shady shit. You might know more than me. That was why I didn't know the other day if he was trying to set me up for some reason or what. Fuck that gangbanging shit for a minute and let's talk real." Brazy Bee stressed.

"Okay, I think the nigga is scandalous but he is from my hood. So I truthfully don't know if he was behind that shit that happened to yo car, but I wouldn't put it past him." Toothpick frowned.

"Yeah I figured that much." Brazy Bee also frowned.

"But check this out here. That nigga told me that he will let a whole bird go for thirteen-five. Thirteen-five is a deal you can't beat anywhere. All he asks is that you stop the war. You stop putting in work against my homies then we will make that shit happen."

"Alright then but I want to just deal with you. You always been a cool nigga we just from different hoods. I want to get my raw from you."

"I don't know if he gon' want to roll with that but I will find out. But if you stop the war you gon' get that thirteen-five deal for sure."

"Alright then, that ain't a problem. I'll tell the young riders to chill out. But I ain't gon' bullshit you, if I get another connect going all the way up to fifteen-five I'm fucking with them." Brazy Bee nodded.

"You get a connect like that just let me know and we will both stop fucking with that nigga." Toothpick shrugged.

"Fa'sho! Slide me yo pager number and we'll connect."

Brazy Bee stood up from the booth and shook the man's hand. Toothpick shook hands with him and stayed seated in the booth after he left. Brazy Bee walked into the parking lot and climbed into his new black Cadillac. He drove off with everything on his mind. He made it back to his neighborhood in about ten minutes. He wondered if Toothpick was sincere about not trusting Drew Dog.

"The nigga could have just made the offer for thirteen-five and not mentioned his distrust." He said aloud.

He wanted to make a stopover at the shack to holler at Boston. Boston would be the first person he would have to get at about stopping the war. When he pulled up on the block he noticed police lights flashing everywhere. He had already turned so he couldn't stop at this point. He decided to not roll past the blockade but just park the car several houses from the shack and observe what was going on. By the time he parked he realized that the police were parked near the shack.

"Those muthafuckas is looking for Boston." He blurted out.

Within seconds after his revelation he heard the sound of gunfire. The police were jumping out of squad cars filing into the back towards the shack. The gunshots were coming from inside the shack as well as being fired into the shack. Boston was having a shootout with the police. Brazy Bee just sat back in astonishment as he seen more police rushing in. As far as he knew there were a few guns stashed inside of the shack. He knew in his heart that Boston had every intention of using every one. Tears came down Brazy Bee's face because he knew there wasn't any escape for his young homie.

The standoff and shootout continued as it was well into thirty minutes now. He thought about walking over there to tell

Boston to surrender. But he knew what kind of soldier he was. If he didn't want to go to jail then he wasn't going to jail. Boston was going to fight until his last breath. He was a soldier to the bitter end.

Finally S.W.A.T arrived and that was when Brazy Bee knew it was over. The uniformed cops slowly backed away. The S.W.A.T. team moved in quickly securing the area for no escape. The moment that Boston heard the shots had stopped firing he reloaded his clip and stepped out of the shack. When he came outside he was instantly greeted by members of the S.W.A.T. team. He fired off a few shots to the head of one knocking him back but not killing him. He ran a few feet and caught a shot to the chest. The gunshot wound didn't knock Boston down but it dazed him for a moment. His gun had fallen from his hands so he grabbed his piece tucked in his waist. He wasn't able to get a shot off when he was caught several times in the head from behind. He body dropped to the floor as the team moved in to surround the body. After realizing he was dead they barged into the shack to find no one else inside. They checked every possible hiding place to find that he was doing all that shooting alone. It took awhile for everyone to clear out. Once they did the coroner came and put the body on a gurney. They rolled the body out covered in a white sheet from head to toe. Brazy Bee stared at the gurney coming out of the yard and into the paramedic's truck. He put his face in the palm of his hands and wept for his young homie.

12

APPEALS

*Make the enemy believe that support is lacking…cut off, flank, turn,
in a thousand ways make his men believe themselves isolated.
Isolate in like manner his squadron, battalions, brigades and
divisions; and victory is yours.*

Colonel Ardant du Picq

Drew Dog finally had a little breathing room now that the
war was over. He had one person he wanted to talk to first and
foremost. That way he could get some of his questions answered.
He called her up and she picked up on the second ring.

"Hello?"

"What's up Debbie, I need to talk to you as soon as
possible." Drew Dog demanded.

"Well I'm about to run an errand then I'll be back home in
about an hour. Is that cool." She replied.

"Yeah that's cool. I'll see you at yo house."

Drew Dog waited forty-five minutes after he was off the
phone with Debbie. He parked in front of her house because it
only took him five minutes to drive over. He noticed that she had
already made it home. He casually walked up to the house and
banged on the door. Drew Dog could hear her walking towards the
door. His foot kept tapping on the porch as he anticipated his
conversation with her. They both smiled when she opened the
door.

"What's up Debbie?" Drew Dog said lightheartedly.

"It's been a long time since I've seen you, Andrew, how have you been?"

"I need to know where that nigga Leonard lays his head." Drew Dog got straight to the point.

"That nigga picks me up then he takes me to a room or on a date. I've never been to his house before." Debbie replied.

"You've never been to his house. What did I tell you about fucking a nigga and you don't know where he rests his head." He calmly replied.

It was a little too calm for Debbie's taste. She was actually surprised that he just accepted that she didn't know where he lived. She had to move along with the lie.

"I know, but that was how we did things. He is doing certain things so I never thought about asking because I don't want to have anything to do with his business." She replied.

"Are you getting feelings for the nigga? You can be honest with me." Drew Dog smiled.

"What…Not like that, but he is fun to kick it with from time to time."

"I see that yo moms done moved the furniture around. It's been you, her and yo little sister for some time now huh? Let me see if you still keep yo room junkie like you used to do." Drew Dog walked towards her room.

"Wait a minute Andrew. I've made some changes in that room but it is mostly clean…"

Drew Dog had made his way back to her room and noticed some changes. He looked around to observe his surroundings and realized a lot had changed. He then walked over to the closet to find that it was empty with a few exceptions. There weren't any clothes in the closet like it used to be.

"I remember when you and I used to fuck like jackrabbits when yo mama would go to work." He commented.

"Yeah those days were crazy."

Debbie didn't notice the pistol Drew Dog had pulled out by now. She was trying to ease out of the room. Before she could make it all the way out of the room he had the barrel of cold steel touching her neck. She jumped for a brief moment, being startled from the cold metal.

"Look here bitch I don't know when you got it in yo heart to think lying to me is healthy. I done lost a lot of good people in recent times so bitch you better get to talking or you gon' find a bullet in yo brain."

"Come on now Andrew, you don't have to do this." She pleaded.

"How do you know what the fuck I have to do? I know you are living with that nigga but you don't want to tell me where. I got questions that he can only answer and I need to know where he lives." Drew Dog's lips curled when he spoke.

"How about I tell him to come over here?" Debbie offered.

"Not good enough. If you don't give me an address soon I'm laying you out here for yo family to find you." He snarled.

"Okay, we live not too far from yo neighborhood off of Central. He's been laying in the cut for some time so what do you want from him." She sniffled.

"Bitch you forgot the arrangement? You supposed to be watching that nigga for anything that was suspect or shady. Right when you found out where he lived you was supposed to tell me." Drew Dog pushed the gun harder against her neck.

"He ain't been doing anything out of the ordinary. He's been on the up and up handling his business. Look Andrew, I care about the nigga, but not to the point where if I see him doing something way out I won't tell you." She cried.

Drew Dog looked at her with tears falling down her face. He didn't have any mercy in his heart for her, but he put the pistol away anyway. He knew that any smart nigga would know to keep shit from his woman. He suspected Leonard was the same. He was an old school hustler so he would be careful about his shit more than most.

"You gon' take me to his house, where you living at right now."

She looked at him briefly as if she wanted to disagree but nodded instead. He walked over to her and grabbed her by the arm. They walked outside and he directed her towards her car.

"I want you to drive so if he's at home he will think it's you pulling up."

It didn't take her too long to get to Leonard's house. Drew Dog let the seat down so that he couldn't be seen when she pulled up. Leonard must have heard her car pull up because he had stepped on the porch. She jumped out with a bizarre look on her face. He seen fear but couldn't quite make out what was going on. Since she drove into the driveway it was hard for him to notice Drew Dog getting out of the passenger side. He closed the door the same time she did. He made sure to be down low enough so that Leonard couldn't see him. He crept from the other side of the car and by the time Drew Dog had shown himself it was too late. Drew Dog walked up to the porch with his pistol drawn. Leonard angrily glanced at Debbie and he could see it in her eyes that she was sorry. He focused on Drew Dog walking up swiftly with his pistol pointed at his chest.

"Now Leonard, you know that I ain't the type of nigga that pulls out a gun and don't plan on using it. You give me what I want and we will be okay. I can go my merry little way and I won't bother with you."

"Debbie go in the house while I talk to this man." Leonard sharply said.

"Yeah Debbie you go inside." Drew Dog smiled.

By now Drew Dog had walked onto the porch and sat down on one of the porch chairs. His pistol was still drawn and pointing at Leonard. They made sure that Debbie was out of ear's reach before they started talking.

"Shook is dead, Tidbit is dead and someone has kidnapped my girl Kelly. Now I'm only going to ask you this once, did that nigga Tango get out of jail?"

"Tango? Trust and believe if he would have gotten out of jail he would be too old to do the shit you are talking about." Leonard said in disbelief.

"I told you I was going to only ask you once. Now don't think for a moment that I won't peel yo cap right on yo own porch." Drew Dog growled.

"I'm not in the business of getting shot so there is no reason to lie to you."

"When was the last time you talked to him?"

"About three weeks ago."

"What pen is he at?"

"San Quentin." Leonard quickly replied.

"Show me a recent letter from that nigga with the new postmark." Drew Dog demanded.

"I can show you a letter with him being in San Quentin but it's not a recent one. He ain't that big on writing letters but he will call collect from time to time. I don't have anything to gain by lying to you. If he was out I would tell you he's out. That nigga done found religion since he's been locked up." Leonard lied with ease.

"Cuz, you keep lying to me." Drew Dog snapped.

"What benefit would that do for me?" Leonard flatly asked.

"I don't know just yet." Drew Dog replied.

For a moment they were at a standstill. Drew Dog didn't know what to believe at this point. A whole bunch of people close to him was suffering and Tango was the only one that could have really made sense. Then a flash went through his head as he considered Lazy. That was when the gun he had in his hand fired one shot. He popped Leonard in the foot. Leonard fell to the ground moaning loudly. Debbie's heavy feet came stomping onto the porch to see her man on the ground. Blood was coming out of his foot. Debbie glanced at Drew Dog with contempt in her eyes. Drew Dog squatted down near Leonard and got close enough for only Leonard to hear.

"Look here cuz; you got plenty of reasons to lie to me. So you need to start talking or you gon' have a lot more problems besides a shot in the foot."

"I told you man that he hasn't got out of jail. You done wronged a few people in yo lifetime. You might want to check with everybody." Leonard talked through his clenched teeth trying to endure the pain.

"Alright then fuck it cuz. But if I find out that nigga is out and behind all of this shit, you gon' die first." Drew Dog stood up.

He waived with his pistol for Debbie to hand him the keys to the car. She walked back in the house and came back out to hand them over. He glanced at the keys then walked toward the car.

"You can pick up yo ride at yo mama's house. The keys will be in the glove compartment." Drew Dog frowned.

He hopped in the vehicle and drove off. Leonard was helped up by Debbie. She was going to drive his truck to the hospital. Drew Dog didn't bother himself about either one snitching because they knew better. He could send some shooters over to Leonard's house while he was in jail. Lazy was from the hood so he knew of all the details that a nigga might know to kidnap Kelly. All he had to do was follow Toothpick back to Kelly's mothers' house, he thought. There was no way to get at Lazy so he had to play it by ear. He had to take his mind off all of this bullshit. Once he picked up the money from Shorty, his Mexican hustler, he would be okay. He could use that money to put with the rest he had put aside for Kelly. He still dwelled on the fact that she might not be worth the amount he was paying.

"That bitch don't be listening to what the fuck I have to say. That's why we in this shit now." He said aloud as he pulled up to Debbie's house.

He slid her keys into the glove compartment then hopped into his ride. When he pulled up into Shorty's neighborhood he noticed Shorty hanging outside with his cholo homeboys. There were remnants of six pack Coronas surrounding where they hung. Drew Dog wasn't too comfortable walking up on a pack of Mexican gangsters but this was business. Usually this is what Shook would do because he was fucking with Rosie. Shorty acknowledged him before he got out the car. He walked over to Drew Dog before he had the chance to walk up on the pack. Shorty knew how one of his homies might fly off the handle. He was beginning to question Drew Dog as a man, but he wasn't for sure just yet.

"Pinche Mayates turn on each other which means he might turn on me." He said before reaching Drew Dog.

Drew Dog decided to greet him first. He was able to climb all the way out of his car but not that much away from it.

"What's up Shorty?" They shook hands.

"You came to pick up that money for those birds, essay?" Shorty got to the point.

"Yeah, it's about that time. You know Shook would have done it by now." Drew Dog reflected.

"You know my little cousin was fucking with him right?" Shorty rhetorically asked.

"Yeah I know that." Drew Dog nodded.

"Word is homes, that you was the one that gave the order for him to get smoked. He got killed behind some shit you was caught up in and you let him get his cap peeled." Shorty replied."

180

"Where the fuck did you hear that shit from? It is a nigga trying to get at me but if I could have stopped my homie from getting killed I would have did everything in my power. I loved that nigga like a brother." Drew Dog snapped.

"Calm down essay. My homeboys might think there is a problem. Rosie heard through the grapevine that you had set him up to get killed and castrated, homes."

"Where did Rosie hear that from? That's some hurtful shit just to know people would think some shit like that." Drew Dog lowered his tone.

"She heard it from this Maya… This Black broad that she had seen back in the day."

"Did Rosie tell you her name?"

"She didn't remember. But she knew her from back in the day."

"That's some bullshit Shorty. I had too much love for Shook. The nigga that is trying to get at me was able to get at Shook first. But that nigga's been my road dog since we were toddlers. Somebody is trying to feed you shit to turn you against me."

"Whatever you say homes." Shorty's face showed skepticism.

He handed Drew Dog a plastic bag with money inside. Drew Dog didn't consider counting it. He had to get the fuck away from everything because it was all coming too fast. He had a designated time to drop off the money and he couldn't be late. What bothered him the most was he didn't know if they were going to return Kelly to him. He hated having to give up this money in the first place. If he gave up the money and she still wasn't returned he might go crazy. He chalked the money loss up to the game considering he had been on easy street for some time now. A big loss was inevitable in the dope game but he had just lost his best friend and cousin all around the same time.

He drove off so that he could find a spot to make sure he had the right amount. It took him about an hour to count the money then make the drop. A note was written in the place where he was supposed to drop off the money. Once he dropped off the dough the kidnapper or kidnappers would then let him know where to pick up Kelly...dead or alive. After reading the note then going to the location he waited in his car with his pistol cocked and loaded.

Kelly didn't bother staring at the man because his eyes weren't enough for her to identify him on the street. He only whispered when he needed to ask or tell her something. She was more nervous about Drew Dog coming through with the money. She wanted to look at life in an entirely different way if she was able to survive this ordeal. Strangely enough the man that kidnapped her didn't seem like he meant her any harm. She knew that he wasn't to be crossed, but he made it obvious that his gripe wasn't with her.

"You know it's not about the money." The man began.

"It's always about the money." Kelly sighed.

"Not this time. It's more about the principle. The man you have children by don't have rules to shit he does. He doesn't respect honor amongst thieves."

Kelly knew the man was telling the truth. This was the most the kidnapper had ever said to her since she had been taken hostage. She didn't really have a response so she let him continue.

"By all rights I should slit your throat and send you back to him dead. But instead I plan on letting you go. You better believe he doesn't want to pay the money to set you free." The man continued.

"I know he didn't want to pay and that was why he tried to lower the price. Only reason he would pay it because I'm the mother of his kids. That's the only thing I'm banking on. I know

Andrew has been scandalous for years but I already had babies by his trifling ass." Kelly admitted.

"Well I wanted to show you firsthand how scandalous yo man can get."

The kidnapper lifted Kelly from the chair then opened the trunk of his car. He covered her eyes with some sort of bandage then cleared the trunk. He wanted to make it as comfortable as possible. He took her far out to an unknown city near open trees and forest. He looked around to clear the way for witnesses. After popping the trunk and helping her climb out.

"Here is the key to the handcuffs in your shirt pocket. Don't take off the blindfold for five minutes. If you take them off before then you will realize you shouldn't have."

"When will I know when five minutes is up?" Kelly frantically asked.

The man didn't respond. All she could hear was the engine of the car driving away. She waited about three minutes before she pulled the blindfold off. After looking around she grabbed the keys from her shirt pocket then unlocked her handcuffs. She felt like crying but not because she was kidnapped. She felt like crying because Andrew didn't feel she was worth him coming to get.

"Even after bearing that muthafucka's babies." She cried out.

She didn't reach a phone booth until she had walked a couple of miles. When she finally reached the phone booth she realized the kidnapper had given her a bunch of quarters. The more she thought about it the more she hated Andrew. After dialing the number someone picked up on the second ring.

"Hello?"

"Hello mama, could you come and get me?"

"Kelly? Girl, I was beginning to think you had run off with that boy Andrew and left me with the kids. You have a whole lot of explaining to do. I love my grandbabies but I've raised my children and…"

"Mama, Mama, I'm going to give you directions to come get me. I have a whole lot of explaining to do." Kelly cut her off.

"Okay tell me where you're at and I'm on my way." Her mother caught the tone.

Leonard calmly slept in the hospital bed with his leg in a sling. He had grown accustomed to the pain by now. The antibiotics kept him sleepy so from time to time he would doze off. Debra had just left so he was bored. Twenty minutes into his sleep he opened his eyes to see Tango looking down at him. He jumped for a brief moment being slightly startled.

"What's happening with you comrade?" Tango asked.

"Lying in this bed waiting to be released. They plan on releasing me tomorrow."

"How in the hell did you get shot?" Tango wondered.

"That muthafucka Andrew came by the house looking for you. A whole bunch of shit has been happening to him and he thinks you are the master mind behind it all." Leonard replied.

"Are you serious? Why would he think that I was up to something with him? I barely even knew the young nigga." Tango sighed.

"Yeah I had to lie and tell him that you were locked up still. I think he would have been trying to get me to say where you live. He would have done a lot worse if he thought I was lying about you being free."

"He must have thought you were lying if he shot you in the leg. He's clutching for straws."

"You don't think he had anything to do with the death of yo cousin Cisco?"

"Not really. He was at the party that Fat Rat was throwing when that shit went down. Besides, I always wondered if Fat Rat was playing both sides and working with the law." Tango replied.

"You think the people Fat Rat was double dealing with was the ones that killed him?" Leonard asked.

"Yeah probably so. I've been gone for ten years so that young nigga Drew Dog could have gotten a lot of enemies since then." Tango replied.

"That makes plenty of sense. I guess now that he is the Top Dog in the game he has to check all angles. He shot me because he wanted to see how far I would lie. I was going to stick to my story to the death comrade."

"I know comrade, I know." Tango smiled.

Drew Dog never got a call on where to pick up Kelly. He somewhat lamented on his dilemma. He finally realized that he loved her. His feelings for her were deeper than he really understood until that moment. He wouldn't ever see her again. How was he going to tell her mother? He let the tears build up in his eyes. All he could do was put off seeing Kelly's mother or his kids. He drove back to the drop off point wondering if the money was still left. It wasn't a surprise when the money wasn't there anymore. He lost Kelly and he lost a bunch of money.

"Now I kind of know how that nigga Tango felt." He admitted.

Then it dawned on him to go back Leonard's house. He might be able to get Tango's legal name. He never bothered with that before. He just knew that he had to get rid of the man. He was so frantic and off balance when he went to Leonard's house the first time that he didn't think to ask him for Tango's legal name. He cursed at his stupidity. He would have to post up until Leonard returned from the hospital. He would ask again for the address and information so he could investigate on his own.

When he rolled by the house he realized that neither car was in the driveway. He decided it would be best to come back another day. He swallowed his pride and decided to drive over to Kelly's mother's house. It took him about an hour to get there as he took his time thinking about his dilemma. When he pulled up in front of the house it had gotten dark and he was having second thoughts. He finally climbed out of the car after sitting in the driver's seat for about twenty minutes. He rang the doorbell twice and he heard heavy footsteps walk towards the door. It sounded like Kelly was walking towards the door but he knew better than that. Suddenly the door swung open and his eyes widened in surprise.

"I bet you are surprised to see me standing here. You know what Andrew; I know I'm just yo baby's mama or whatever but to just leave me there to die is fucked up." Kelly began.

"It ain't like that. I made the drop off like he told me to but he never called me back."

"Whatever nigga!" Kelly replied while stepping on the porch.

He observed how she never invited him inside. He stood on the porch sort of relieved that she was still alive. Her cold shoulder was nothing compared to the fact that she was standing in front of him.

"Look Kelly, I paid the man what he asked for but he never came. You got to believe me. I went to the drop off spot and the money was gone. I never received a call about you so I came to yo house." Drew Dog explained.

"You left me out to dry. What's worse than anything is the fact that I was probably kidnapped behind some shit you were into." Kelly dismissed his words.

"What will I need to do to convince you I'm not bullshitting?"

"There is nothing you can say or do right now to make me believe you. You a trifling ass nigga." She replied.

"I'm appealing to yo real side; we got too much history for you to think I left you hanging like that Kelly." Drew Dog practically pleaded.

"You sound pathetic right now. There is nothing appealing about you at this moment. You can come visit yo children but as far as you and me, we are through." She flatly replied.

He looked in her face and could tell that she had had enough. It was a lot of things that would make her want to leave him but this was the one time he wasn't at fault. He lowered his head without saying a word. He tried to think of something to say but he knew it was useless. Though he was a gangster, he couldn't deny the fact that he loved her. He lifted his head trying to find the right words then her mother walked up to the screen door.

"I knew you were a criminal nigga but for you to leave the mother of your children out to dry to kidnappers for money you know you have. You really ain't shit to me Andrew. You don't even have to worry about the children, Kelly and I will make sure they have everything they want or need." Kelly's mother stated firmly.

Drew Dog glanced at the screen door to respond but her statement knocked the wind out of him. Kelly saw the defeat in his face so she turned towards her mother.

"Mama I can handle this."

Her mother reluctantly walked away from the door. Kelly stared at him with contempt so he walked off the porch towards his car. After driving off, Kelly broke out in tears. She had loved that man for a long time.

Drew Dog let the tears fall from his face this time. He couldn't deny he was hurt that she didn't believe him. He had done some scandalous things in the game but he didn't leave her hanging. He only had one lead so he would have to play it out. He figured he would post up near Leonard's house a few days from now. That would give him time to get home from the hospital. Then he would get Tango's legal name and address. There would be some connects that he could link up with in the pen that would let him know what was going on with the man.

He waited a couple of days to post up over Leonard's house but once again the cars were gone. He drove by a second time and noticed that the furniture on the porch was gone as well. After parking about a block away from the house he walked into the yard. When he got close enough he realized that the curtains were down from the windows. He began to curse while walking up to the window to see that the house was totally empty. Using his hand as a visor he scanned the house to make sure. Out of frustration he kicked the wall.

"This nigga Leonard pulled a fast one. That's alright because I know where his girl's mama stays."

He walked out of the yard thinking on vengeance. He felt like his life was falling apart on all sides. For the very first time in his life he felt alone in the world.

"If I fall I won't be the only one... I can guarantee that."

13
FALLING APART

To remain disciplined and calm while waiting for disorder to appear amongst the enemy is the art of self-possession!
Sun-Tzu

Tango stepped out of his brand new Lincoln Town Car with a smile on his face. He would be spending the day with Colleen and they had grown quite close as of late. She eagerly glanced out the window to see her man looking as sharp as he wanted to look. She had seen when he first pulled up and was elated. She had some good news to tell him. She stepped out on the porch while he walked up the walkway. A few nights a week he would spend the night but usually he would go back home. Colleen couldn't deny that she was really in love with the man. Some things bothered her though. She didn't like the fact that he was so secretive. She had been to his house several times but not as much as he had been to her house. Nevertheless she was always excited when she saw him. They quickly embraced as he gently kissed her on the lips then stared into her eyes.

"Do we have the entire day together like you promised?"

"Yeah baby, the whole day belongs to you and me." Tango smiled.

She wrapped her arms around his neck and smiled from ear to ear. Tango had to admit he was smitten with the young woman. He was a hard man though and even smiling was difficult at times. She somewhat understood. Colleen grabbed Tango's hand and escorted him into her house like he had never been there before.

Once they were inside she grabbed her coat and purse then met him at the door.

"I have some good news." She smiled.

"What would that be baby?"

"I'm pregnant. I just found out that I'm six weeks pregnant." Colleen beamed with enthusiasm.

"Ah baby that's beautiful; we should do the family thing and get married after I settle some unfinished business." Tango replied.

"The family thing? What is the unfinished business that you need to take care that is more important than us having a family?"

"It isn't that it is more important it is the fact that I won't be able to give you a hundred percent. And you know I didn't mean anything by saying the family thing. It was just a figure of speech." Tango replied.

"Baby I know you've been through a lot in the last ten years. Some things you will never get back, but we love each other. You do love me, right?"

"With all my heart. You mean the world to me but like you said I lost a lot so there are some things I have to make right before I settle down and relax." He stated firmly.

She glanced up at him, trying to read into anything but his stern face was unreadable. She sighed, realizing that her attempts were futile. Just like any man he was going to do what he wanted in his due time. She knew in her heart that he loved her and his words were sincere. She smiled at him as they walked out the door.

He had an entire day planned for them to enjoy. The first thing he wanted to do was cruise the coast. They would look at the sites then grab something to eat in Malibu. Then he would take her up to Palos Verde's to see a view of the ocean she had never seen before. They walked the hills of Palos Verde's and held hands talking about various things.

"Let's roll up the coastline on the 101 freeway. We can look at the ocean and go to wine country." Tango suggested.

"That would be wonderful, Kevin."

They climbed into the Lincoln and rolled toward the freeway. While checking out the sites he decided to pull over near a phone booth. Colleen patiently waited in the car while he took care of business.

"What are you about to do?"

"I'm about to surprise Colleen by getting married up in northern California."

"Are you serious?"

"I'll holla at you when we get back."

Big Boy walked over to his blue Monte Carlo with his pistol secured in his waist. He wanted to meet up with Toothpick because the fellow Crip had something to drop on him. He drove off top speed hitting a few side streets before he turned Imperial. They had decided to meet up at this hamburger spot they were both familiar with. When he got there Toothpick was already posted up with a nigga that looked like a Blood. He was somewhat reluctant, wondering if it was some kind of set up. He put his hand on his pistol and before he was all the way in the door, Toothpick had stood up with his hand out, gesturing for Big Boy to remain calm. Big Boy glared at the Damu and they made eye contact for a moment.

"What's this shit about cuz?" Big Boy demanded.

"This is Brazy Bee and he is from the other side." Toothpick explained.

"I can see that. What's this nigga doing here? I thought it was supposed to be you and me talking some important shit." Big Boy replied.

"This nigga right here has something to do with the important shit I was talking about. All three of us are niggas that cop from Drew Dog. All I'm saying is let's talk then if you liking what you hear then we can continue." Toothpick continued.

Big Boy reluctantly nodded then sat down. He thought about ordering something to eat but he wasn't too comfortable sitting next to a Blood. He fidgeted in his seat while Toothpick started talking.

"Look here Big Boy, this nigga is a stand up muthafucka that just so happens to be from the other side. We've been talking about what's been going on with Drew Dog. He's been a shady ass nigga and he's from my set. We got an opportunity to cop from a nigga that ain't as shady as that nigga."

"I don't know about that Toothpick. That nigga ain't really been shady with me and I'm not in the habit of buying dope from anyone. These young niggas are snitching nowadays."

"So this nigga Drew Dog ain't ever did anything shady to you?" Toothpick asked sarcastically.

"Are you talking about that little stupid ass broad Neicy? Fuck that little bitch cuz. If she belonged to me then she would come back to me, that's how I look at it." Big Boy stubbornly replied.

"Come on now Big Boy, me and you have both talked about how shady that nigga can be and now you are playing crazy, cuz." Toothpick snapped.

There was an uncomfortable silence as Big Boy glanced at Brazy Bee. He wasn't comfortable talking about a Crip while a Blood was present.

"Look here, I know you ain't too bool...Cool with me being here with you. But this shit we're talking about is some shit that can put more money in yo pocket and clear out all the bullshit." Brazy Bee explained.

"So you say." Big Boy replied.

"So we both say. This nigga's hood and my hood was going to war and we put a stop to that shit for business sake. You might get something good out of this shit because Drew Dog's days are numbered, cuz." Toothpick passionately explained.

"But if you down with a nigga you down with a nigga. All of us might get our turn but real niggas is gon' stand with you and not break camp when they sense some bad shit is about to go down." Big Boy sighed.

"This ain't a loyalty thing as you might think. This nigga Drew ain't been loyal to anyone but his own pockets. I heard through the grapevine that his girl Kelly got kidnapped and he didn't do shit about it." Toothpick explained.

"Is she dead?" Big Boy asked.

"Nah, she is alive, but she was still kidnapped.

"So where did you hear that she was kidnapped and that he didn't do shit about it if she's alive?" Big Boy skeptically asked.

"My girl is her homegirl, cuz. She was telling my girl all about it. The kidnapper didn't even trip off the money, he just wanted to show how scandalous that nigga can be. Come on now Big Boy that's his baby mama." Toothpick reasoned.

"I don't know, you know how women gossip. She could be pissed at the nigga then start spreading rumors."

"Alright fuck it then. We warned the nigga so let him do what he wants to." Brazy Bee sighed.

"That's right CUZ, I'm gon' do what I want to."

"What you trying to say BLOOD? I see you got a strap but I'm strapped too." Brazy Bee stood up in a confrontational stance.

"Nah, let's squash that gangbanging shit for a minute. If you ain't trying to hear us that's on you Big Boy." Toothpick stepped in between the two.

"Yeah, I'm sticking with the nigga that put me on. I never thought a rider like you, Toothpick, would side with a Damu." Big Boy remarked while leaving.

"You just don't get it do you...I used to do anything that nigga asked me to do? Some niggas ain't right even if they Crip or Blood." Toothpick shook his head.

With that being said Big Boy walked out the door. In his heart he figured they were probably right. He just couldn't wrap around his finger that he would side with a slob over a Crip. He climbed in his car with what they were saying heavy on his mind.

He had to run a few errands before he went to his dope spot. Big Boy had become a shot caller a long time ago but his money was long just recently. He set up a dope spot at this crack head homegirl of his. He provided her with a high and she let him use her spot. She had a couple of kids but they were too little to know what was going on. He didn't feel bad about the arrangement because she was turning tricks before he made her the offer. His baby mama was the one that Drew Dog went after. Big Boy loved the girl, but he couldn't show hurt when Drew Dog moved in. He was the nigga supplying her and they was still fucking but not officially together. It always bothered him but he chalked it up as her not really belonging to him.

When he finally pulled up to the house it seemed quieter than usual. Most people came there to cop ounces who more than likely was curb serving. He always had lookouts just in case the police were lurking somewhere. No one was outside which was kind of strange. He didn't pay it any mind because he would just have to set some niggas straight. He had the keys so he opened the door then walked in the house. Before he could look around the house he was hit across the head and he passed out.

It would be several hours before he finally awoke. He looked around and saw that he was tied up at the hands. Whoever tied him up must have been in a hurry because they didn't do a good job. He walked around the house then opened the door to see his friend and her children sitting on the bed frightened.

"What happened?" Big Boy barked.

194

"Some niggas came in here knowing where everything was at. Some of the homies went to the store and when they were gone this nigga rushed in. I thought it was the homies knocking on the door because he knocked right after they left."

"Where are the homies?"

"He got them tied up somewhere in the house. What was crazy, he was by himself."

"Let's look for these niggas and see if they are still alive."

After looking around the entire house they couldn't find anything or anyone. His homegirl finally remembered she had a small basement that had an entrance in the back. That was where the water heater was at. Her and Big Boy rushed in the back and opened the basement door to find two of the homies tied up. Big Boy rushed down the small cellar door and quickly untied them. One of his little homies had been shot in the leg. He helped carry him upstairs.

"I'm about to take you to the hospital young nigga. They can bandage you up there, cuz."

Big Boy glanced at his little homeboy whimpering in pain. He ran upstairs to the stash and as he expected the dope was gone. He cursed loudly trying to think how he would pay Drew Dog for the re-cop. He had some of the money but he didn't have it all. He thought about the meeting he had earlier today. He ran straight to the phone.

"Ay cuz, did you rob me for my stash trying to make a point?" Big Boy barked through the phone.

"Nigga what!?! I don't even know where yo stash is. You need to find out who knows where yo stash is at, cuz before you get to accusing muthafuckas." Toothpick replied.

"We gon' need to talk." Big Boy added.

"That's what I've been trying to tell you cuz. Someone took off with yo shit and that probably means it is someone close to you. If anything I bet you that nigga Drew has something to do with it." Toothpick continued.

"I was just a little leery because you had that slob nigga with you." Big Boy replied.

"Yeah nigga, but you got to put that kind of shit behind you." Toothpick sighed.

"Alright then, I'll meet up with you in a couple of hours...Just you though. I got to take my little homie to the hospital."

After he arrived at the hospital he went to the closest phone booth. It would be a good time to page Drew Dog. If he can tell him what happened maybe he would work with him to work it off. It took about ten minutes before Drew Dog called him back.

"What's happening cuz?"

"This is Big Boy cuz. I had a little problem in my hood...Some nigga ran up in the stash and got me for everything." Big Boy explained.

"What the fuck you want me to do? You just copped from me, cuz."

"Work with a nigga Drew. I'm good for some consignment shit until I even up with you, cuz." Big Boy pleaded.

"Work with you? If I started giving you shit on consignment then everyone that copping from me gon' want the same. I was serving to you because I thought you were a hustler, nigga. You gon' have to scrape together money to at least get a half a bird, then we can talk."

"They got everything cuz...Everything." Big Boy snapped.

"Watch how you coming at me cuz. Who in the fuck told you to put yo shit in one stash anyway? If you wasn't putting all yo money in that Monte Carlo you would have enough to at least cop a bird." Drew Dog viciously replied.

"Alright cuz, but you and the little homies were the only ones that knew where the spot was at." Big Boy nonchalantly warned.

"Then you need to look at yo little homies or that bitch whose house you been using. Get at me nigga when you get yo paper up." Drew Dog hung up the phone.

Big Boy held the phone to his ear listening to the dial tone. He was pissed off at this point. Drew Dog made it easier to fuck with Toothpick and hear what he was talking about. But he didn't even know if they had someone else to cop from. Then he had to consider that he didn't have any money to cop even if they did. He paced the hospital hallway contemplating his next move. Once he glanced at his watch he raced off to meet up with Toothpick. They met at the same place they had met earlier. Big Boy noticed that Toothpick was in there by himself this time.

"What's up cuz?" Big Boy greeted.

Toothpick pointed to the chair for him to sit down. Toothpick kept his mouth shut for several seconds.

"Are you ready to know some real shit?"

"Talk to me."

"That nigga Drew Dog has been shady for years. I found out that he had something to do with two OGs from my hood getting smoked. He had the OG homeboy Cisco robbed and killed then set up the homie Fat Rat. That Damu that was here earlier swears that Drew Dog tried to start a war with our hoods so he could have power over both of us. Then the nigga sent another muthafucka to crash my Impala while I had birds in the car. His baby mama says that she got kidnapped and he didn't put up the money for her0.. to get released. She also told me that he sells to this cholo named Shorty. I plan on getting at him about this shit too."

"That's all fine and good but we been knowing that Drew Dog was scandalous but he always had that raw. Where would we get that raw from if we don't cop from him?"

"I already put some shit in motion for that. We all can be copping birds for less than what Drew Dog was charging and it's the raw. We ain't got to fuck with that nigga again, cuz."

"Yeah that's cool. But I just got robbed; I don't have the bread to cop a whole kilo right now. I got to work my way up from the ground." Big Boy complained.

"You ain't got to worry about that."

14

CONNECTIONS

The forces of a powerful ally can be useful and good to those who have recourse to them...but are perilous to those who become dependent on them!
Niccolo Machiavelli

Drew Dog sat on the couch somewhat perplexed. He hit up Toothpick and Brazy Bee and neither had called him back. He knew that he couldn't depend on Big Boy right now because he had just gotten robbed. He would have to come up with someone else he could put on over in that neighborhood. Big Boy had a few young homies that were probably hungry enough to take his spot. He considered how the young generation couldn't take doing time so he suddenly decided he would have to stick with Big Boy. It had only been several days since he talked to him. He was pretty sure that he wasn't going to have the money for a half kilo by now. He didn't want to look soft but he needed some money to be turned over because all he had was product. He decided to page Big Boy to see what he had to put on the dope. He had a little bit of money but he didn't want to spend that. He only went into his stash when he really needed it. After losing all that money from the Kelly kidnapping his money was tighter than before. Drew Dog hurriedly paged Big Boy 911 to see what was going on with the man.

After several hours he realized that he wasn't getting a call from any of his workers. They couldn't have all got arrested at the same time. He decided to switch up cars and take a cruise around the neighborhoods. He didn't want anyone to notice him so he switched up cars completely. He was able to get a hold of a Cadillac with tinted windows. He was able to secure the Black vehicle from a family member of the girl he was staying with. It was a simple trade in cars so there wasn't much fuss.

Drew Dog took his time cruising the streets hoping to see what was going on. His senses weren't reading as well as they normally did; but he still knew something wasn't right. The best thing for him to do, he considered, was to go by Brazy Bee's hood so that he could get through the Blood neighborhood first. When he rolled past one of Brazy Bee's dope spots he realized that it was buzzing like always. The crack heads were rushing the curb servers like routine. He took a mental note of this considering that Brazy Bee might have tried to find someone else ever since the war. A few of the young Damus walked by the Cadillac he was in, while he was scoping everything; but they didn't notice him. He had taken off his blue L.A. Dodgers baseball cap before he drove into their territory. Right when he was about to start the engine Brazy Bee came walking across the street. In a simple exchange the young curb server slid him a wad of money. They made conversation for awhile.

Drew Dog decided to bring his mobile phone so he paged Brazy Bee to see what kind of response he would get. Brazy Bee looked down at his pager when it went off but waved his hand as if to dismiss the call. Drew Dog knew at that moment that he had lost that connection. If worse came to worse he might have to put the police on Brazy Bee and replace him. That was a nice chunk of money coming out of his pocket. This was also a bad time to be losing that money. Drew Dog turned on the engine and tried to creep off as quietly as possible. Brazy Bee glanced up, noticing the Cadillac but the windows were rolled up and tinted so he didn't pay it any mind.

His next stop was over in Big Boy's neighborhood. He drove around for about ten minutes and nothing was going on. In fact it seemed kind of quiet considering it was the middle of the month. Big Boy wasn't stupid enough to set up his dope spot in the same place but Drew Dog had to make sure. When he rolled by the dope spot he noticed that there was nothing there as well. He had run out of ideas so he drove out of Big Boy's hood. As he was leaving he noticed a little activity on a side street. Quickly he made a wide turn to reach the street and drive by. From his observation it appeared as though some activity was going on. He saw a couple of curb servers working a dead end street. There was only one way in and only one way out. Even though he was playing it low key Drew Dog always had a sharp eye for the hustlers. He knew that it would be too obvious to actually roll down the street unless he was about to cop dope. His best bet would be to roll around the block and come around to park across the street from the dead end street. That way he could see everyone coming in and out.

He wasn't there long when he noticed Toothpick roll up. Drew Dog sat up in his seat as he observed the familiar vehicle. That bothered him because more than likely since Big Boy couldn't get what he wanted from him he went to Toothpick. If he had lost Toothpick's loyalty then there was a serious problem. Suddenly it fell on him like a ton of bricks. Toothpick was probably behind the kidnapping and everything. His ego had blinded him into thinking that Toothpick admired him too much to cross him. He briefly remembered looking up to Cisco before he set him up to be robbed and killed.

"But I'm smart enough to do something about it." He said aloud.

He started up the engine and slowly drove off. He was lost in his thoughts so he didn't notice that there was a car following him. He hopped on the freeway so that he could return the

Cadillac back to its owner. He was contemplating how he would fix Toothpick, Big Boy and Brazy Bee. He cursed himself for not checking on Shorty to see if the cholo had changed sides as well. It would be best, he considered; that he found out where Shorty stood with the rest of them. He changed lanes from the fast lane and attempted to change again but the car next to him wasn't allowing him to do so. He glanced over to see three gangsters and two of them had their pistols drawn.

"Ain't this a bitch, a fucking set up?" He muttered.

He reached under his seat as bullets began to riddle the Cadillac. He was barely able to pry the gun from under his seat. Before he could get a shot off more bullets pierced the windows. He rolled down the window with the automatic window button on the driver's side and started shooting.

The driver of the opposite vehicle swerved out of the way. Drew Dog's pistol had some kick to it so he momentarily lost control of the steering wheel. The Cadillac brushed up against their car.

"Fuck!!! Toothpick must have spotted me, cuz." Drew Dog blurted out.

He decided to speed up but was matched in speed by the other driver. Bullets once again started flying into the Cadillac putting holes into the passenger side. He decided to ram the Cadillac into their car. It made them veer over to the right just to gain control so Drew Dog punched on the gas. His pursuers regained control and followed behind him shooting out the side windows. Unbeknownst to either car a California Highway Patrol car was parked on the side of the freeway. The highway patrolman woke up out of his slumber and instantly cut on his lights. He went after the vehicle with the three gangsters inside. When Drew Dog heard the sirens he glanced through the rearview mirror to notice they hadn't slowed down. He had to stay in top speed.

Before long they began to shoot at the highway patrolman. In that split second Drew Dog slowed down and let his pistol finger go. The fire pierced their windshield as they lost control. The CHP officer couldn't continue to give chase. It appeared as though he was calling for back up. That was Drew Dog's cue to slide off the freeway. He veered quickly over to the exit quick enough to catch the exit. The gangsters that were following him weren't so lucky. They tried to jump off but missed the exit so they swerved on to the grass of the off ramp.

Drew Dog quickly exited the freeway then hit two corners before he found a residential area. He climbed out the Cadillac looking in every direction. Lifting his legs from out the car he realized that he had been shot. The fear must have made him not notice the pain. It wasn't anything more than a flesh wound but it was enough pain to make him limp.

"Toothpick is behind all this shit cuz." He mumbled.

He made sure to grab his mobile phone but he didn't know who to call. He stashed his pistol behind his back and limped to the closest intersection. After several blocks he was out of breath and tired. He crossed the street and walked into the closest fast food restaurant. He walked past the counter and went directly into the dining area. He had to think and he needed a place to do it. He posted up hoping no one would notice that blood was leaking from his pants leg. As he thought about getting something to drink he heard the sirens of three police cars roll by the restaurant. He figured they were either looking for his black Cadillac or they were going to help arrest the niggas that went after him. He stood up and went to order some food to maybe calm him down and settle his stomach. He stared at the menu for a moment wondering what he might order.

"Sir…do you know that you're bleeding?"

Another woman started screaming as if she had seen someone killed. He looked around and realized that he was in a white community. He hurriedly walked out the door glancing back at the white people staring at him. After going to the closest phone booth he found a close by taxi service that could pick him up. His mobile phone had went dead by now. He puffed on a cigarette waiting nervously for the taxi to come. In a matter of minutes the taxi arrived. He smiled then quickly hopped inside. He slid down in the seat while handing the driver a twenty dollar bill.

"Where are we going?"

"Just hop on the freeway and I will tell you where to go from there." Drew Dog mumbled.

Just as the driver was turning the block to get on the freeway, a police car pulled into the parking lot of the fast food restaurant. Drew Dog breathed a sigh of relief after catching a quick glimpse of the cop car. For a moment there was a slight traffic jam once they entered the freeway. He tried to lay low but he had to peek out of the side window to see what was holding up traffic. As they pushed forward he noticed the red lights. Over on the side of the road was a busted up CHP vehicle. A tow truck was pulling another vehicle from out of a side ditch that it had fallen in. The vehicle was familiar to Drew Dog. He glanced toward the ground and seen two body bags with bodies inside. There were two CHP vehicles behind the tow truck and with someone in the back seat of the first squad car. The prisoner in the back seat of the squad car made eye contact with Drew Dog for a brief moment. Drew Dog slightly grinned as the taxi drove past.

"Some guys trying to fight the police." The taxi driver commented.

Drew Dog ignored his comment and slid back down in the seat. He made him drive far out until he came across a hotel he knew would be out of dodge. He tipped the driver pretty good then paid for a room. He would have to post up for a few days and map out how he was going to get at everybody. It was payback time but he had to do the shit right.

After settling in his room and patching up his flesh wound he decided to get supplies. He stepped out into the cold air and walked down the block. He gathered a bunch of quarters and called up Shorty. It was later so he was hoping to catch him inside for a minute.

"Hello?" A female voice answered.

"Is Shorty there?"

"Can I ask who is calling?"

"Tell him his Mayate homeboy Melvin."

"Melvin?" The female questioned.

"Yeah."

He heard her sit down the phone. It took about two to three minutes before he came to the phone. Drew Dog could tell that the man was irritated once he picked up the phone.

"Who is this, homes?"

"Ay Shorty, this is Drew Dog. This was the only way I could holler at you and I didn't know who was picking up the phone."

"Aw hell nah homes. I can't fuck with you anymore, essay."

"You are leaving me high and dry like everyone else?"

"Word on the street is that you smoked yo own homeboys. Not only did you kill Shook, but you killed some Mayate named Fat Rat and Cisco from your own neighborhood. Everybody is saying not to fuck with you because you are scandalous. All yo connections is dried up."

"I can always get new connections but whoever told you that bullshit is lying. I had love for all those niggas but somebody is trying to frame me. I'm starting to think it's that young nigga Toothpick."

"I don't know who to believe homes. Right now on the street everyone believes that you did a lot of people in. I even heard that there is a price on yo head essay." Shorty continued.

"For how much?"

"One hundred large."

"The nigga that is putting that out is the same muthafucka that kidnapped my baby mama." Drew Dog vented.

"If I were you homes I would count my losses and move out of town. You can pretty much say you are through in L.A."

"Yeah maybe you're right. So that means you ain't fucking with me anymore either?"

"What do you think? If I fuck with you then I might have all the fucking pinche Mayates coming after me on the east side. Like I said homes, you are on yo own." Shorty replied.

Drew Dog didn't really have much to say after that. He didn't bother with saying goodbye. He rolled up some weed after having picked up Zig Zags papers from the liquor store. After eating, smoking weed and drinking on Boone's Farm he laid down on the bed. It was time to put together a reply against the niggas that turned on him.

"They declare war on me so I'm declaring war on them. Now it's my turn."

He dozed off in a matter of seconds with the empty Boone's Farm bottle still in his hand.

15
NO SAFETY NETS

When the vanes are removed from an arrow, even though the shaft and tip remain it is difficult for the arrow to penetrate deeply!

Chieh Hsuan

Toothpick glanced at the man that he had grown to respect and admire in recent times. It was an unusually rainy day so they were talking on the porch of a vacant house in the neighborhood.

"We got a price on the nigga's head but he can't be found. That muthafucka just fell off the face of the earth." Toothpick shrugged.

"Nah, somebody tipped that nigga." The man bluntly replied.

"I don't know who would do that shit. We made sure the word got out that he had been scandalous to his own homeboys. He might pop up suddenly after some years like you did." Toothpick commented.

"Yeah but we gon' have to be ready for him when he does. In fact, we have to find a way to hunt that nigga down. If we cut off all his safety nets the nigga might come out of hiding." The man explained.

"His back is against the wall cuz. Any desperate man will fight until his last drop because he doesn't have anything else to lose. Besides, he can lay low for awhile because he has a little money saved up."

"His money will be running out sooner than you might think. Gather everyone and give them the run down and I'll check into some things. You might not see me for a week or two but that's okay, you can still page me if you need some work." The man walked down the porch stairs.

"Yeah, okay."

He remembered respecting the man when he grew up back in the day. Toothpick watched the man climb into his Thunderbird and drive off.

"He wants that nigga Drew real bad." He said aloud.

Toothpick covered his head with newspaper then rushed out into the rain to his car. It had been a month since a group of niggas went after Drew Dog when he was noticed parked in a black Cadillac.

Toothpick started up the engine pondering on that day. It was Brazy Bee that had spotted him first. It would have been smart for Drew Dog to cruise the neighborhoods in an unknown car if they weren't already waiting on him. That should have been a clear hit.

"Those dumb niggas tried to get him on the freeway instead of waiting until he posted up somewhere. Dumb ass niggas!" Toothpick vented.

He went to the local phone booth and paged everyone. After getting calls back everyone agreed to meet up in a couple of hours. Brazy Bee was there before everyone. Toothpick walked up shortly thereafter. Even though they were from opposite sides of the color bar they had developed a rapport. The Mexican homeboy Shorty walked in third then followed Big Boy. After everyone order their food Toothpick got straight to the point.

"Look here, my man is really trying to catch up with Drew. Now he gave us the raw on consignment and then knocked two grand off of each brick from what we were originally paying. That muthafucka wants some results." Toothpick firmly began.

"I'm telling you homes he fell off the face of the earth. No one knows where he went to or anyone he's connected with." Shorty explained.

"He hasn't called you since that one day?"

Shorty shook his head then glanced at everyone else. It was quiet at the table for a few minutes.

"Everybody is on the hunt, but what you want niggas to do if he can't be found?" Brazy Bee asked.

"Ya'll not looking at the big picture. If we don't catch up with him soon he might be trying to catch up with us." Toothpick replied.

"I think we're looking at the big picture it's just we can't get at the nigga. Once we find someone that can connect us to the nigga then we're good." Big Boy commented.

"Well we need to do something soon. We have to cut off any safety nets he might have." Toothpick replied.

That was all he had to say to them so everyone was in and out. Toothpick thought it was best that he have a meeting to let them know the urgency. He drove back to his neighborhood, dwelling on his recent dilemma. He parked in front of the new dope spot and sat inside the car to think. It was a smoother set up than before. He only kept a certain amount of dope at the spot. The crack heads had to go through the backyard of the vacant house to cop their high. All those years he had worked for Drew Dog he had never been so organized. He always felt at edge with the man honestly. Drew Dog was scandalous in little ways and until recently he was nervous about crossing him.

After sitting in his car for about twenty minutes he finally climbed out. As he closed the driver's side door he heard a car pulling up slow. He was a little worried about the police so he glanced up without looking too paranoid. It was a blue Monte Carlo pulling up on him. He wanted to ignore the car but something inside of him was sensing danger. He tried to glance in the car but there wasn't enough time. He had left his glock in the car under the seat. He cursed his foolishness then quickly walked toward the other side. Toothpick and the driver made eye contact briefly before Toothpick realized who it was. Before he could react fire from an automatic pistol came right at him. He ducked but caught one in the shoulder.

"Aw shit."

He ran towards the yard, but it had a small fence. By then Drew Dog had put the Monte Carlo in park and was firing from two guns. His bullets wouldn't stop coming as Toothpick tried to get through the fence while trying to dodge the shots.

"You gon' back door a real muthafuckin' gangster, cuz? You ain't seen shit about doing niggas in. I put yo punk ass on, and you gon' try to do me like this?" Drew Dog spat.

Toothpick took a few shots in the upper body but was able to make it in the yard and towards the backyard. Drew Dog didn't follow him inside the gate. He headed towards the Monte Carlo and sped off. One of Toothpick's workers came running out of the backyard blazing away with a thirty-eight. A few shots picked off the Monte Carlo, but not enough to make a difference. Drew Dog had hit two corners in a heartbeat and headed towards the freeway.

The young worker ran toward the backyard to check on Toothpick. By then he was laid out on the grass breathing hard.

"Ay young cuz, get me to the hospital." Toothpick coughed.

"Ay homes, be looking out for a blue Monte Carlo or anything else that might look crazy." Shorty announced to his workers.

All of his workers nodded then went into their places. It had been four days since Drew Dog put Toothpick in the hospital. It disrupted a few things because Toothpick was the one everyone meshed with. He was the peacekeeper in a time of war. Shorty was starting to regret choosing the side of Toothpick because there wasn't any safety net. Only problem was that there was no turning back. He didn't take Drew Dog to be the forgiving type. And if he was on the hunt he could ride on anyone at anytime. He knew where everyone else was at, but no one knew where he was. Shorty puffed on his Camel cigarette while listening to oldies on his boom box. The oldie station was playing 'You are everything!' from the Stylistics. His pistol was sitting right next to him on the small brick wall he sat upon. He brandished a black forty-five and was ready for anything.

The day went smooth for Shorty as he wrapped up his corner. He figured he would get some drink before the liquor store closed. He made sure that everything was running smooth before he headed up to the store. Before he could hop in his car his little cousin Rosie came walking up.

"How is everything at the spot?" She asked, more out of curiosity.

"We've been moving real good today. I'm about to call it a night but I'm going to pick up some Budweiser from the store." He replied.

"Can I roll with you?"

"I don't know Rosie, you know that guy Toothpick was shot up real bad by that pinche Mayate Drew. He might be on the hunt and I can't watch yo back while I'm watching mine. I could understand if you were a shooter then I would know you can watch your own back."

"Aw come on primo Shorty. You are just running to the store and that's it." She pleaded.

"Alright but you are staying in the car." He surrendered.

They pulled up into the liquor store and he parked. He fumbled with a few things trying to get his money together.

"Get me a tall can of Old English." Rosie asked.

He glanced at her and smiled. She started drinking what Shook would drink when he was alive and now she was hooked. Shorty was a Budweiser man. He climbed out of the car while sliding the money in his pocket. He had to remember to get some

Zig Zag papers so that he could roll up some Angel Dust a little later. Within seconds Rosie saw him disappear into the liquor store. He left the keys in the car so she moved her head to the oldies that were playing. She was tempted to turn it to KDAY but she knew how sensitive her cousin was about his radio. She fondled around his car just because she was bored. She noticed that his big black gun he always carried was sitting in the driver's seat. She glanced up for a moment to see her cousin walking out with a bag full of beer. She smiled as he slid a fresh pack of Camel cigarettes in his pocket. He was a down ass Cholo and she loved her primo for that. He paused at the door as she looked on with admiration. Then she noticed that he was looking at something in shock. She followed his eyes and saw a man standing in front of him with a hoodie on. She noticed the glock that the man was holding and she let out a quick yelp. She covered her mouth in disbelief as the bullets began to riddle the body of her beloved cousin. The brown grocery bag filled with beer fell to the ground. Shorty's body fell backwards into the liquor store. Rosie began to scream uncontrollably until she noticed the gun pointing in her direction. She gasped for breath but couldn't move a limb on her body. The assailant ran off into the night. Rosie started hyperventilating while still glued to the car seat. After taking several deep breaths she climbed out of the car slowly with her hand over her mouth. She took baby steps toward her cousin. Trembling, she reached his body and looked down at him to see he was clearly dead. His body was filled with holes, his mouth was wide open. She began to sob uncontrollably while the store clerk was rising from behind the counter. He approached the grief stricken girl and the dead body cautiously.

"I call the paramedics." The store clerk suggested.

"He needs a coroner." She screamed.

The store clerk went back into the store to call the police. He remained in the back until the paramedics and police arrived.

Rosie continued to sob over the body of her cousin until the police and paramedics pulled her away. Two detectives eventually arrived and began their investigation. She sat on the passenger side of her cousin's car until one of the detectives approached her.

"Are you the girlfriend of Ronald Hernandez? He is also a gang member known as Shorty." The detective sounded redundant.

"He was my primo, my fucking primo."

"Calm down young lady. Since you are related to him maybe you can give us some information to who would want to do this to him?"

"It was that pinche Mayate Andrew that did this to my cousin. You find that motherfucker then you will find the killer." She screamed

"Do you have a last name of this Andrew? Do you have a residents or address where we can find him? Did you see the man in question shoot your cousin?"

"He wore something over his face. But he was the only one that would want my cousin dead." She replied.

"So you wouldn't be able to identify the suspect?"

"I know how Andrew looks when I see him." She snapped.

"But can you identify him as the shooter tonight. It might have been him and he might have had a motive but did you actually see him pull the trigger?"

She lowered her head in disgust. She was so frightened after seeing Shorty shot and killed she had lost all her senses when the gun was pointed at her. She didn't even think of looking the man in the face. She just stared down the barrel of his gun. After a momentary silence she shook her head indicating that she couldn't positively identify the shooter. The detective continued scribbling in his pad. He looked at her for a moment then walked off to report to his partner. Rosie started sobbing, knowing that she would never see her cousin alive again. She would have to be the one to tell his mother and her own mother.

Big Boy and Brazy Bee had decided to bury the hatchet and visit Toothpick in the hospital. They were supposed to be enemies but they began to realize that they had a bigger enemy to worry about. They strolled into the intensive care unit to visit the comrade that they had both grown to respect. It was earth shattering to see tubes sticking out of his body. It was an emotional moment as Toothpick slowly opened his eyes.

"Aw cuz, ya'll two niggas startled the shit out of me. How the fuck ya'll know where I was at?"

"One of yo little homies told us that that nigga Drew Dog did what he did," Big Boy replied.

"Yeah that muthafucka did a number on me. The doctors are saying that I'm paralyzed for the rest of my life. That muthafucka Drew Dog has always been kind of scandalous, but I never thought the nigga would leave me like this." Toothpick said.

"You know he touched the Cholo homeboy Shorty. That muthafucka is deader than a doorknob. He filled him up with a bunch of holes right in front of his cousin Rosie." Brazy Bee commented.

"Are you bullshitting? We supposed to be hunting that nigga but he's hunting us instead. You never really had any safety nets with Drew Dog. He always had you hanging out on a limb so that he could have one up on you. That's just how he worked." Toothpick sighed.

"We got niggas on the street trying to hunt this nigga. Anybody looking suspicious is getting blasted on. No one has seen anything though." Big Boy commented.

"Yeah, well tell yo peoples to back off on the hunt. I had visits from some people and we gon' have to chill out." Toothpick explained.

"After what that nigga did to you and Shorty, you want us to chill?" Brazy Bee asked.

"Yeah, I want ya'll to chill. The man I'm fucking with told me personally that he would have to take care of it. Then the police came in the other day trying to get me to start snitching. It's getting hot on the street right now so we got to keep things cool for a minute. Don't get me wrong; watch ya back, but stop being on the hunt." Toothpick continued.

"Whatever you say but we not gon' have much dope in a few days. What are we supposed to do for supply?" Big Boy asked.

"I'm gon' connect ya'll with my man because I'm gon' be out of pocket for a minute. I've had time to reflect on some of the shit I've done in the past. I'm just getting back what I done to other muthafuckas." Toothpick explained.

"What about all the dirt that nigga Drew has done? When is a nigga like that gon' get payback for shit he's done to people. That's one of the most scandalous niggas I know so when is the shit gon' come back around on him?" Brazy Bee passionately replied.

"I don't know." Toothpick shrugged.

"I don't believe in that shit; what goes around comes around. It's niggas that didn't deserve some of the shit they got and they dead as fuck. Then it's niggas like Drew that walk around forever that did major dirt. A nigga just got to watch his own and never get caught slipping." Big Boy stated.

"Well it seems to me homie that all the dirt I did came back on me. The only thing worse than being dead is being in a fucking wheelchair. I'm just tired of this game and what comes with it. But I will connect ya'll with the man so ya'll can get what ya'll need."

16
NO REMORSE

As dripping water wears through rock, so the weak and yielding can subdue the firm and strong!
Sun Haichen

Drew Dog swigged the bottle of 'Night Train' as he sat on the edge of the bed in his hotel room. He had to be a little more meticulous when it was time to go after Brazy Bee and Big Boy. They would be expecting him to attack them the same way he got Shorty and Toothpick. Both of them were dead as far as he was concerned.

"It'll teach niggas not to cross OG Drew Dog." He arrogantly said aloud.

He swallowed another gulp of strong alcohol, pondering on his dilemma. His name had become dirt in the street. Everyone that would listen believed that he was this scandalous nigga. He knew that he had done some things to get on top, but that was about all he could think of.

"I was hungry back then so I did some things that I wouldn't do today." He spoke aloud again.

He fell back on his bed trying to think of a way to get back in. If he was able to get rid of his last two obstacles he could push up on a young up and coming. There was no room to be hasty and reckless but his money was running low. One thing he knew from his own experiences, that there was always young hungry gangsters ready to replace their big homies. It was always one or two that didn't have loyalty to anyone but the dollar bill. He could provide the product that could get them the dollar bill. The liquor was starting to get to him. He staggered to the side of the bed so that he could put the pistol on top of his dresser. His hotel room was in the city of Azusa, which was far enough from L.A. but close enough for him to commute for his missions. After sitting the almost empty bottle next to the pistol on the dresser his head touched the pillow. In a matter of minutes he was in a deep sleep, snoring loudly.

He didn't wake up until he heard his pager go off. He glanced at the dresser and reached for his beeper. The number was familiar but it was hard for him to believe she was calling. He couldn't trust anyone nowadays so he figured she was either calling for money or she was up to something. He picked up the phone, wondering what he would say to her.

"Hello?"

"Is Kelly there?"

"This is she. How have you been Andrew?"

"I'm alive, in case you wanted to know."

"Well, that's good to know. The babies have been asking where is they daddy. You might want to come see them." Kelly softly suggested.

"I thought you were through with me. I thought you didn't want anything else to do with me."

"I didn't at first but I honestly started to miss you. Then the kids wanted to know what was going on with you so I decided to give you a call."

"You want some money from me right now or what? Keep it real with a nigga; I don't have time for you to be beating around the bush. Times is hard right now and my back is against the wall." Drew Dog firmly replied.

"I can always use some more money but I'm holding up nowadays. I really miss you Andrew."

"If you trying to set me up or some shit like that you gon' regret that shit I promise you." He snapped.

"Who am I going to set you up with? Just because you have done all kinds of shit to people doesn't mean that everyone is like you. Yo trifling ass is my babies' daddy and my childhood sweetheart, so don't act like there isn't any love there." She finally snapped.

The phone was silent for a moment. It was the same Kelly he had grown to love through the years. He missed the little things about her. Certain idiosyncrasies that he hadn't got a chance to experience in a while. He smiled without saying anything. It would be good to see her.

"Where is yo mama?"

"She's here, but I was thinking we meet up somewhere because this is nearby where the kidnappers snatched me up."

Drew Dog didn't consider that. In fact, he had forgotten all about the kidnapping for a moment. He thought about his own problems before he spoke.

"You know what? I'll have to come and get you from yo mama's house and watch my back." He decided.

"No, that won't work. Then they will know what kind of car you're driving and everything. I wonder sometimes if they are watching me every day." Kelly protested.

"Well I don't know what to do."

"Why don't you meet me at the bus stop in downtown L.A? We can meet up at Union Station. When I'm down in front of the station I will page you then you roll by to scoop me up. It will be in broad daylight and a thousand witnesses if anything goes down."

Drew Dog thought about it for a moment then decided it was a good idea. His head was throbbing because of the hangover but he was thinking straight.

"That's cool; I'll come to pick you up at eleven in the morning. When you get there just page me and I'll be there. And bring the kids with you."

"Okay."

He laid his head down so that he could rid himself of his headache. Eventually he would have to make his way to the liquor store for some Tylenol. All he could do was reminisce about his times with Kelly. He still had to wonder about her. What if this was just a set up? He was hoping that she sincerely wanted to see him and he wouldn't have to kill her because in the end he wouldn't have any remorse if he had to kill the mother of his kids. Rubbing his forehead he considered all the possibilities.

"I'll be ready for whatever comes."

Early that morning Drew Dog woke up a little after nine; dreaming about spending time with Kelly. He couldn't believe how eager he was to see her. It had been awhile since he had been with a woman so he knew that was part of it. But it was something more to him seeing Kelly than just some pussy. She was his confidant back in the days. He was always careful not to pillow talk with her but she knew when he wasn't feeling his best. She also knew how to comfort him. For some reason he felt like time was running out with her. It was a strange feeling he had. That was why he had to be on his pees and cues. He finally lifted himself from the bed and yawned. He rubbed both of his blood shot red eyes before stretching. He laid out what he would wear for the day then headed for the shower. It took him a little over half an hour before he was dressed and out the door. He hopped on the 10 freeway in a heartbeat headed towards downtown Los Angeles. Traffic wasn't that bad so he was able to make it down there in about forty minutes. He rolled around the Union Station looking for anything that might be suspicious. He was very low key with the air condition on it was hard to look inside his Coup. His money was running real low but he still had a few tricks up his sleeve. He spotted her before she noticed him. He pulled into the parking lot and drove right past her. He had to scan his surroundings before he let her in the car. After scoping the parking lot he pulled next to her while she was walking to the phone booth.

"Get in."

She looked around before she climbed into the ride. She seemed to be just as nervous as he was. He took note of that.

"Where are the kids?"

"I told my mama that I was catching the bus to Union Station and she wasn't trying to hear me taking the kids." She shrugged.

"Did you tell her that I wanted to see my babies?" Drew Dog snapped.

"If I would have told her that she really wouldn't have let me take the kids. In fact, she would have gotten a joy knowing that she kept them from you." Kelly stared at him.

"Yeah that's true, yo mama never did like me. That's why I knew I couldn't stay in her house with you and the kids."

He had already hit two corners before she could reply. All mirrors on his ride were being observed to make sure no one was following.

"My mom is funny like that. It is good to see you Andrew. I must admit I didn't think I would feel that way after you left me hanging with the kidnappers." She admitted.

"I'm trying to tell you I paid that muthafucka; he just released you before I could get at you. He was supposed to call me after I made the drop but he never showed up. I don't have any reason to lie to you." He frowned.

"That's some bullshit in the past. Let's just try to be better than we were before. We can make the moments count from now on." She suggested.

"I'm with that."

The oldie station started playing 'My Girl' from the Temptations. They allowed the music to consume them as they sung along. He was with his girl and she was with her man. Times were harder than before so he or she didn't know how long this would last. The entire time he still kept his eyes on all three mirrors. In about thirty minutes flat he had pulled into the parking lot of the hotel. She climbed out of the car first looking around at her surroundings.

"This is nice Andrew. We never really had a honeymoon or anything like that so we should enjoy the moment we have now." She smiled.

Drew Dog just nodded his head. It had been a long time coming since he had seen his woman and he wanted to make up for lost time. He led her upstairs with his pistol drawn looking for anyone that might have followed them. It seemed pretty clear so they both went upstairs. She sat her purse on the table in the corner of the room. She sat her overnight bag on the floor next to the bed then undressed. Before long she had hopped in the shower. It wasn't long before he joined her.

They began kissing slowly while the water bounced off their bodies. Drew Dog hadn't felt the body of a soft woman in months. He had forgotten how wonderful it could be. He rubbed the palm of his hands on her hard nipples. She moaned as she sucked on his bottom lip. It had been a long time since she had a man. He worked his tongue slowly down her neck sucking hard and gently biting. She had missed the pleasure pain that came with making love to her man. He sucked on her supple titties while she continued to tell him to suck harder. His dick was hard as Chinese arithmetic as their bodies collided in the small shower. His hands began to slide down her ass with his finger slipping through the crack. She wanted his strong hands all over her. She grabbed the cheap hotel soap and began to lather him down. First she started with his chest and arms. Then she worked her way down to his torso and upper groin. She grabbed a hold of his manhood with both of her hands and lathered away in a stroking motion.

"Goddamn that feels so good."

He grabbed the soap from her and worked his way around her breast and arms. Then he slid his hands down her small waist and circled her belly button. She giggled when his finger went in her navel. He had forgotten that she was ticklish down there. His fingers and strong hands worked his way around her plump ass while they continued to kiss.

After finally rinsing off the soap they forgot to take the time to dry off. They were in a locked embrace as he pushed her toward the bed. As she fell backwards onto the bed he kept both his feet on the floor. He grabbed her legs and spread them in opposite directions while penetrating roughly inside her.

"Damn that feels good to me baby." She closed her eyes.

His feet firmly planted on the nappy carpet while he slid inside her long and hard. He had to suck in his saliva as he felt the pleasure of her tight walls. He could feel her getting wet as he plunged inside with force.

"That's it Andrew, go deeper…go deeper." She moaned.

That made him go faster and faster. That made him go harder and harder. Right before he felt that nut about to cum.

"Bend over so I can hit that ass from the back."

He slid out of her and turned her over on her stomach. He had her slightly on the edge of the bed while her plump round ass was in the air. He quickly spread her ass cheeks then pushed inside her throbbing wet walls.

"Yeah that's it right there." He moaned.

She could feel him pushing all his strength inside of her. He began to break out in a cold sweat. It was feeling real good and he couldn't control his pace. It was like his body had a mind of its own. She pushed her ass into his pelvis while squeezing her ass cheeks to his rhythm. Kelly hadn't made him feel this good in a long time. His face was soaking wet as he felt the sensation all over his body. He kept up his speed and force but knew the climax was coming. In a matter of seconds he released inside of her.

"Damn that feel too good." He blurted out.

He tried to push inside her several times after he had released his fluids. He found that his strength had been depleted. He collapsed on top of her and laid there for a moment. They were both breathing hard until he finally mustered enough strength to get off of her.

She climbed on the bed after him and laid her head on his chest. He still hadn't fully caught his breath but he was slowly recovering.

"Damn Kelly that felt really good. You were putting in major work today. You must have really missed a nigga."

"I told you that I missed you." She kissed his cheek.

"We've had some good times together huh?"

"Of course we've had some good times. We are just going through a rough patch because we haven't been together in so long. But we can make up for it today and some of tomorrow." She smiled.

"Yeah, I need to clear up some mess that's been going on in the streets then everything can be better than before."

"Do you ever regret being in this life? I mean… Do you regret doing some of the things that you had to do to be on top for so long?"

"Hell no! I did what any nigga with heart had to do to get what was his. I feel no remorse for niggas that was weaker than me in the game. Only the strong survive on the East Side of South Central L.A. If I wouldn't have done some of the things I did I would have turned out to be another bum ass nigga with nothing to live for. I had to be hard because the hood is hard." He vehemently explained.

He closed his eyes still feeling the aftershocks of the sex. She rubbed his chest thinking on his words.

"Do you think we will ever be a family again? What if things never get right again with what's going on in the street and our family?" She glanced up at him.

He slowly opened his eyes feeling indifferent about her dialog. It was meaningless to him because he knew what he had to do. He sighed trying to say the right words to put her at ease. After all she just performed some really good sex so he owed her some form of explanation.

"We gon' be alright, we just got to stick together until everything gets right. I'm working on that right now, so don't worry." He nodded.

"Like that one song 'Don't worry, Be Happy' is that what you are telling me to do?" She giggled.

"Yeah, now let's get some sleep."

It wasn't until two in the morning before either one woke up. They made love one last time before they were awakened by the eleven o' clock AM wake-up call. The loud phone ring shook both of them out of their slumber. He rolled out of his bed looking around for anything unusual.

"What the hell was that?" Kelly asked.

"That was the wake-up call letting me know I need to pay them for another week up in this bitch."

"Is that cheaper than paying daily?"

"Yeah but not by that much. I'll probably get another room somewhere so that I can always stay on my toes. It's crazy because I just had a dream about Shook and Tidbit tonight. It was good to see them and everything. We were reminiscing about good ole times and…"

His pager started going off. He slid across the bed to Kelly's side to pick up the beeper. He instantly recognized the number. He tried to dial out but quickly realized that he had to pay the hotel clerk first.

"I'll be right back I need to use the pay phone."

"Where is yo mobile phone?"

"The battery is dead."

He slipped on his Levis 501 jeans and his Nike sneakers then dashed out the door. Kelly decided to get in the shower. By the time she got out he had just made it back upstairs.

"What took you so long?" She asked.

"I had to pay the clerk for the week then I was talking to one of my boys that know some people at the parole board. He said that nigga Tango been out of jail for a while now. That nigga Leonard was lying." He shook his head in disbelief.

"Who is Tango?"

"Never mind I was just thinking out loud."

"Well you better jump in the shower so we can go."

"You know what… I'm gon' wait to take a shower when I get back from dropping you off at Union Station." He replied.

She shrugged showing her indifference. He slipped on his tank top and grabbed his car keys. Within minutes they were on the freeway headed back to downtown L.A. When he pulled up to the station they gently kissed on the lips then she climbed out the car. They held hands briefly before she was all the way out the car.

"I'll talk to you later." She said.

"Call me when you've made it home. Just let me know that you are safe by sending 411 to my pager."

She smiled after blowing him a kiss. He checked his rearview and side mirrors then peeled out. He had really enjoyed the time he had with Kelly this time around. He understood why she was always his main girl. He cruised all the way back to Azusa taking his time and letting the air blow inside the car. Periodically he would make sure he wasn't being tailed or followed. When he got off the freeway it was easy to tell if someone was following and as far as he could see the coast was clear.

He collapsed on his bed after making it inside and turned on the television. It was a few stations on but nothing he really wanted to watch. He wished that Kelly could have stayed another day. She had mentioned in a conversation that she had to return in the morning because her mom was tripping. They would get another chance to see each other again. Before long he had dozed off.

His pager had woke him up once again. It was Kelly letting him know that she had made it home. But instead of a 411 at the end it was a 911. He stared at his phone for a moment wondering what that meant. He grabbed a few quarters from out of his pants pocket and went down to the phone booth near the clerk's office. He was still groggy but he moved gracefully down the stairs to the pay phone.

"Damn, why didn't I just use the phone upstairs? Nah, they will charge that shit to the room and using these quarters are cheaper."

He dialed the number after putting the quarters in the phone but all he got was a busy signal. He did it two or three times before he got frustrated and decided to go upstairs. He stepped out of the phone booth and yawned. He heard a sharp noise but couldn't see where it was coming from. His body was in mid air going backwards when he realized that something was wrong. Then he felt the sharp pain in his shoulder once he slammed onto the pavement. Before words could come out of his mouth everything went black.

17
A DISH SERVED COLD

*You must make your opponent acknowledge defeat from the
bottom of his heart!*
Miyamoto Musashi

Slowly and painfully Drew Dog began to open his eyes.
His head was throbbing to the point where it was almost numb.
His eyelids were heavy but he managed to keep them open. Tears
fell down his face as he tried to grasp what was going on. He
looked around, but there was nothing but darkness. His eyes had
to adjust to see that he was in an empty room. He was handcuffed
to a chair. His body was tied in rope that seemed impossible to
untangle. After several attempts he finally surrendered to the fact
that he had been captured. He started to panic because he knew
that it wouldn't be anything quick and easy. Whoever put him in
this predicament could have finished him at the hotel. They
wanted to take their time. He yelled, hoping someone would hear
him. After getting no answer he finally just sat there waiting for
what fate had in store for him. After a couple of hours of
screaming and yelling someone finally walked in.
"YOU!!!"
The man didn't reply. He walked in with a folded table and
a duffel bag. He slowly and carefully pulled out all four legs of the
table. Then he unzipped the duffel bag. He sat a nine millimeter
glock with a silencer on the table. He also sat on the table a

machete and a long knife. Drew Dog's eyes widened because he knew this would be slow and torturous.

After setting down a pair of pliers, he grabbed the pistol. The man didn't look in the direction of Drew Dog but shot him once in the knee cap. It was so fast he jumped for a moment before he even felt the pain. He tried to reach for his knee cap but was quickly brought to reality that he was tied up. He had to suffer the pain of the bullet wound. Tears fell down his face hard as he went into delirious spells. The man waited for him to calm down so that the pain could settle in. The bullet shattered his knee cap but it wasn't a fatal wound. Once Drew Dog stopped hyperventilating the man calmly walked over with the pistol still in hand. With the butt of the gun he slammed it into Drew Dog's nose. He began to bleed profusely as the man stood in front of him quietly.

"Fuck you!" Drew Dog defiantly cried.

All the man did was smile. That was a worse blow than Drew Dog could have ever imagined. It hurt him worse than the gunshot wound to the knee cap and the broken nose. He had been defeated and humiliated by his enemy. This was worse than any torture he could ever imagine. The man studied Drew Dog's face to see the signs of defeat. He wasn't satisfied. Drew Dog had a way of making you think that he was standing tall no matter what. He walked back over to the table and grabbed the pliers. Before the night was over Drew Dog would be begging to be killed. There was a glimmer of hope that disturbed the man. It even appeared that he was silently praying for some form of miracle to happen. He decided to pick up his machete. He gently rubbed his finger on the blade to test its sharpness. He cracked another smile as though he was a villain that had captured a superhero.

"Black muthafuckas don't do this kind of shit cuz. Just finish it already." Drew Dog whimpered.

The man quickly walked over and slid the blade across his chest. Drew yelled out in pain while rocking the chair. He finally managed to make the chair fall on the ground. Bad thing was that it landed on his handcuffed hands. He moaned even louder when his head hit the hard concrete. The man lifted the chair from off the ground.

"Fuck it cuz you won. I'm begging you to get it over with. PLEASE!!!"

That was what the man wanted to hear. He slid the blade across Drew Dog right arm. After waiting for him to calm down he slid the blade down his other arm. It was nothing but torture. Drew Dog went into shock for a moment. He was beginning to grow numb to the pain. The man blazed up a cigarette and waited for him to recover.

A couple of hours later Drew Dog woke from his shock surprised that he was still alive. His body was numb and had grown accustomed to the pain. He stared at the man that had done this to him.

"What the fuck are you waiting for? Finish this!" Drew Dog was exhausted.

The man shook his head then stood up from the chair. This time he grabbed his pliers when he walked toward Drew Dog. Drew Dog began crying, wanting the torture to end.

"Why are you doing this to me?"

The man stared at him in disbelief. It was a bizarre question considering all the dirt he had done. The man went behind the chair and began pulling off Drew Dog's fingernails with the pliers. He cried and moaned as each nail was taken from his fingers. His hands were bleeding as the man went back to the front of the chair to see Drew Dog's facial expression.

"Why in the fuck won't you just kill me?" He pleaded.

The man didn't say a word. He just looked at Drew Dog with a slight smile and contempt. It hurt Drew Dog deep down in his soul. That was the reason he had the dream about seeing Tidbit and Shook. He was on his way to join them.

"I guess if there is such thing as hell, that's where I'm going. Well, you will be right there with me you heartless muthafucka."

The man still didn't say anything as he watched his victim go through different emotions. He walked back over to the table and grabbed the machete. He looked at Drew Dog and lifted his blade. He slowly slid the blade across his neck. Drew Dog coughed up blood while it leaked from his throat. His eyes went heavy as he finally went into cardiac arrest.

The man looked at the dead body making sure that it was over. He went over to the table and grabbed all of his equipment. He placed the equipment in the sink and rinsed everything off. After his thorough cleaning he rolled out a large plastic sheet and laid it on the floor. He untied Drew Dog from the chair and rolled him up in the plastic. He taped and stapled the ends then dragged the body to the trunk of his car. He parked his car at a port next to a boat. He pulled the body into the boat then set the sail. It took about an hour for him to get in a position where he felt comfortable. He wrapped twenty pound weights to the head and the feet of the body. It was difficult lifting the body so he had to first lift the head then the feet. He watched the body sink deep into the Pacific Ocean. It was over and he didn't really know how to feel about that. He puffed on his cigarette while returning the boat back to the harbor.

18
NEW BEGINNING

Beware of sentimental alliances where the consciousness of good deeds is the only compensation for noble sacrifices!
Otto von Bismarck

Tango yawned as he sautéed the meat for his cookout. His wife and newborn son were inside the house with his niece Melanie and her son. He decided to invite Leonard and his girl Debbie up to the new house. It was still hot outside even though it was close to autumn. He breathed out trying to get everything ready for everyone to show up. He lit up the gas grill and started putting the steak on the fire. His beautiful wife stepped outside in the back yard with the baby in her hand.

"Kevin, I just seen Debbie and Leonard pull up."

"Okay baby, I'll be inside in a minute. I got all the meat on the grill I just have to make sure everything is right." Tango smiled.

He cleaned off his hands as best he could then walked inside. Leonard had rung the doorbell a moment after he had walked in from the backyard. His niece Melanie answered the door. Leonard couldn't believe his eyes because he hadn't seen her since she was a little girl. They both embraced then Leonard introduced her to his girlfriend Debbie.

"Pardon me this is my fiancé. We are getting married during the third week in October."

"Congratulations." Melanie replied.

She escorted them through the living room and into the den. Tango was standing next to Colleen. She still had the baby bundled up in her arms. Leonard walked over to Tango and they quickly embraced. It was a pleasant surprise to see Tango with a new family, new home and new beginning. Debbie joined Colleen as they played with the newborn baby. Tango walked into the kitchen and grabbed a beer for him and Leonard. Leonard followed him onto the back patio so they could talk.

"I appreciate you taking a bullet for me when that one cat was looking for me. I've been trying to keep my nose clean." Tango began.

"Don't even worry about that. You and I go way back and if you noticed the limp has gone away. Did you hear that Drew Dog came up missing? He must have crossed the wrong person because now his body can't even be found. Before that nigga died he killed this Mexican hustler and paralyzed this nigga from his own hood." Leonard shook his head.

"Oh yeah? He was wild just like a lot of people over on the east side of South Central. It sometimes feels like nothing but scandalous shit happens over there." Tango sighed.

"But that's good you have kept yo nose clean. I guess everything comes full circle now. I know you can never replace the family you lost with Loretta, Missy and Samantha but you've been definitely blessed with a second chance. I'm even able to move back into my house again."

"How are you making your money? I got some ways for you to make some money if you want to." Tango offered.

"I'm always willing to make some money. Just let me know what I need to do and I'll be ready to roll." Leonard smiled.

"I know you got that house note so we can make some moves to help you maintain that since you are about to get married and everything." Tango replied.

"When do you want to take care of this?"

"This is something that I wouldn't want to talk about now because we are relaxing and enjoying the good day. But give me a call on Monday and we'll go from there. It'll be better if it is in the evening around eight o'clock; is that cool for you?"

Leonard eagerly nodded while watching Tango turn over the steaks on the grill. Colleen decided to play oldies music while the food was cooking. All three of the ladies went into the kitchen to prepare all the accessories. Tango brought out the cradle holding his son so that he could sit outside with him and Leonard.

"You always wanted a son. I know it won't replace the loss of Samantha but now you can have that legacy you always wanted. Didn't you tell me that Loretta couldn't have any more children?"

"She could have but it would have been dangerous for her. I feel bad because of the shit I was involved in had a lot to do with them being killed." Tango admitted.

"You shouldn't beat yourself up too much. How did you know that kind of shit would happen?"

"Yeah but I knew what came with the game. I understood perfectly well that eventually there would be some consequences. It took me ten years to recognize my own sins." Tango sighed.

"Sometimes it takes a lifetime for most people. It's good not to live with regrets. There was a reason why that happened to them but only the most high knows." Leonard offered words of comfort.

"When did you get all spiritual? I haven't ever seen you acknowledge a higher being like you are doing now." Tango smiled.

"I think when I was in the hospital recovering from that bullet wound. It gave me time to reflect on the different things that have taken place in my life."

"Okay Kevin baby where is the steaks because us girls is ready to eat?" Colleen stepped on the patio.

Tango and Leonard turned around to see Colleen, Melanie and Debbie walking outside with dishes in their hand. Tango smiled before saying anything.

"They'll be ready in a few minutes. Go ahead and fix the plates and I'll have the steaks on your plate in no time."

Within minutes Tango had the steaks piled up for him to assign to each plate. Colleen went into the house and grabbed a bottle of champagne. She grabbed six champagne glasses and sat them at the end of the table.

Tango opened the champagne bottle after he gave out the steaks to everyone. He poured champagne into all the glasses then lifted his glass. Everyone followed suit and lifted their glasses until they were all touching.

"There is nothing more valuable than friends and family. When you think the whole world is against you; real friends and family will be there to catch you when you fall. So I'm giving a toast to new beginnings and to new hopes and dreams."

Tango had never felt so at peace since his wife Loretta and daughter Samantha were still alive. Leonard glanced at him with admiration and Tango bowed his head in the same respect. The streets were behind them so now they were able to live life to the fullest and enjoy the fruits of their labor.

19

A MAN'S WEAKNESS

If you decide to wage a war for the total triumph of your individuality, you must begin by inexorably destroying those who have the greatest affinity with you.
Salvador Dali

Leonard made his way onto Tango's neighborhood street. To his surprise Tango was already outside waiving for him to follow. Tango fired up the engine and took him through the side streets. They finally arrived after twenty minutes of driving at what appeared to Leonard to be a warehouse. When Tango got out of the car he pointed for Leonard to follow. He put his index finger over his mouth indicating that they should be quiet. Leonard was both nervous and excited. They opened the door into a dark room. There were stacks of boxes on both sides of the room leaving a narrow path for them to walk. They reached the end of the room and Tango used a key that opened another back room. This room was empty but just as dark. There was a couch near the wall but Leonard could barely see what was going on. Tango still hadn't said anything pointed to the couch for him to sit down. Leonard wondered how juicy this was going to be since Tango was being so secretive. He considered that Tango had always been secretive about his business. There was a large bucket of water sitting next to the couch that Leonard happened to notice.

"What's going…?"

Before Leonard could finish his question Tango covered his mouth with his index finger again. Leonard sighed for a moment growing very impatient. Maybe this was Tango's new thing, breaking into warehouses and selling the goods for cheap. This could become very lucrative. Tango had disappeared for a moment as though he had walked into another room. It was so dark in the room that Leonard didn't know if he was in the same room or not. After a few minutes the image of Tango's silhouette appeared in the darkness. He walked toward Leonard with so much fluidity that it appeared as though he glided to the couch.

"What's going on?" Leonard whispered.

Tango covered his mouth with his index finger one last time. Then out of nowhere he pulled out a nine-millimeter with a silencer at the end. He put the pistol to Leonard head then reached for his shirt. Tango snatched open the shirt making the buttons fly in different directions. Taped to Leonard's chest was a wire that extended down to his pants. Tango snatched the wire from off his chest. Leonard slightly yelled from feeling the pain of his chest hairs being ripped out. The pain was quickly ignored when he realized he had been uncovered. A tape recorder was barely poking out of his pants but Tango grabbed his pants and snatched the recorder out. He still had the pistol to Leonard's head. He then took the wire and tape recorder and dumped it into the large bucket of water.

"Get undressed." Tango whispered.

Leonard did as he was told as Tango backed away with the pistol pointed at Leonard's abdomen. In a matter of seconds Leonard was out of everything except his boxers.

"Pull yo boxers down then squat and cough."

"You are treating me like we in the county jail and shit." Leonard protested.

Tango cocked the hammer back on the pistol. Leonard quickly did as he was told. After Tango was satisfied he motioned for Leonard to move back over to the couch.

"How did Drew and Shook know where me and my family lived?"

"I don't know."

Tango walked a little closer then put a bullet in Leonard's foot. He shot off three of his small toes and part of his foot.

"Fuck; I told them where you lived with the promise that they cut me in on the score."

"They used that little bitch Tidbit to get in good with you, right?"

"Yeah man but I didn't know those niggas was going to do all that. I didn't know they were going to kill them and rape yo daughter. You got to believe me, Tango, it wasn't like that." Leonard pleaded.

"Why you pleading for yo life when you know I got to kill you? At least stand up and take it like a man. You always been weak for pussy. You've been working for the police since you got cracked when I first got locked up, huh?"

Leonard nodded still holding his foot. Tango paced the floor as calm as a lion savoring the moment he slaughtered his prey.

"Why didn't Drew ever get around to killing you? I don't see him letting you live so long and you knew too much about what he did."

"That was how you got cracked in the first place. He was the one that told the police who you were and that you were about to serve to Fat Rat. The police didn't have anything on him so he was able to back away from them without any problems. He didn't want to kill me because he knew you might get out one day. So he had Debbie watch me when Tidbit got pregnant by one of the Blood niggas." Leonard explained.

"So he kept you alive so that you can help him bring me down if I ever went after him?"

"He knew I was working for the police and he knew that I knew what he did to yo family. If I died there was something that I had on tape that could link him back to the murders. If I was dead I could release it but as long as I was alive he knew that it would incriminate me as well." Leonard explained.

"So that was why you took the bullet for me that day on yo porch. You didn't think that he would kill you, but he decided to shoot you instead." Tango finally understood.

"You can't kill me Tango; they know that I came to meet up with you today. If I come up missing you are going to be the first person they are going to look for. We can work something out."

"What does Debbie have to do with all of this?" Tango ignored his pleading.

"She ain't got shit to do with this except for the fact that Drew sent her to watch me at first. But she grew to dislike that nigga because of his ways. I'm telling you Tango it would be wise to just let me go. I won't even say anything about this gunshot wound. I'll claim I caught a stray...Debbie is innocent of all this shit." Leonard began to panic.

Tango didn't have a response to his ranting. He continued to pace the floor trying to piece together what he might have missed. He watched Leonard through his peripheral with his finger firmly planted on the trigger.

"So you couldn't do a little jail time for the dirt you were doing, huh? You couldn't stand to be away from pussy for a few years. You've always been a weak muthafucka. You were the one that tipped Drew to how my operations ran. You were the one that told him that Fat Rat was going to start working for me."

"I wasn't making enough under you and I had caught a charge. Look man we can go our ways, I'm about to get married...so you killed everybody by yourself? You killed Drew, Shook, Tidbit and everybody else for that matter, huh?"

"Thought you knew?"

"You thought I knew what?"

"Killers don't talk!"

Tango pointed the pistol at Leonard and let off five shots into his abdomen and chest. Leonard's body slumped into the couch. He walked over to the door on the other side and opened the door. A man walked in and nodded when he saw Leonard lying dead on the couch.

"We can wrap him up quick and get rid of this couch all at once."

"What about the boat, Lazy? You have that ready like before?"

"Yeah everything is ready to go. All we have to do is clean up the warehouse and get rid of the body and the couch."

"Well let's move this shit fast. We might have police looking for him and me so it would be good to leave the car abandoned somewhere in L.A. County."

They began the process of cleaning up the body and any evidence of a murder. They wrapped Leonard up in plastic and slid him into the trunk of a car. Then they grabbed the couch and put it on the back a of pick-up truck.

"Okay you get rid of the couch and I'll get rid of the body. Be sure to burn that muthafucka to a crisp. We'll meet back up in a couple of hours so we can get rid of Leonard's car." Tango explained.

It took about three hours for them to take care of everything. They met back up at the warehouse after everything was dispose of.

"Don't say anything while you are driving Leonard's car because if I know that weak nigga he might have some recording device in there as well. Make sure yo gloves is on and you keep that wave cap on yo head. We don't want any evidence to be traced back to you or me." Tango explained the plan.

"Yeah I figured that any particle of hair or fingerprint might tie us both so I brought gloves. But I wasn't expecting him to have a recording device in the car as well as on his body." Lazy replied in disbelief.

"I don't put anything past that nigga. He is responsible for getting my family killed and me and him was boys from way back. It took me awhile to put him in because I couldn't get past him not being loyal. My sister Missy told me before she died that the only person outside of our family that knew where we lived was Leonard."

"What happened to loyalty and the code? I would blame it on this generation, but some niggas just don't have it in them." Lazy shook his head.

"Yeah, he might have a Lo Jack on his car as far as I know. Speaking of loyalty, I want to reward you for yo loyalty to my cousin and my family. I'm getting out the game and raising my family. That key that my niece saved for me provided a little savings for me to live for the rest of my life. I'm going totally legit so I'm giving my connect to you."

"Are you serious? That's good looking out Tango."

"You've more than earned it. Now this nigga I'm about to connect you with believes in loyalty, respect and has an ardent belief in the code. Don't cross him and don't ever underestimate him."

"For sure." Lazy nodded.

"You will probably never know his government name but he goes by the name 'Big Black'. He has more connections than you could ever believe. I'm going to prepare you to meet him before I make the introduction. Now let's get rid of this car." Tango walked toward his car.

They drove down the 10 freeway until they reached the city of Altadena. Lazy parked Leonard's car on the side of the road and left the keys in the car. He made sure the door was unlocked and wiped down everything with a rag just in case. It took another hour before they made it back to the warehouse. They embraced then talked about linking up again soon so that Tango could connect Lazy to Big Black.

It was close to four in the morning when Tango finally pulled into his driveway. He knew to cut off his lights before he even hit the block. It would be best that most people didn't know what time he got in that night. When he walked inside his wife was in a deep sleep. He checked on his son to see him sleeping peacefully.

"I'm going to make sure I keep you from this life." He whispered.

He carefully and meticulously got undressed; putting everything away as carefully as possible. He took a hot shower for twenty minutes then climbed in bed with his wife. An hour went past when he heard a pounding on the door. It woke him and Colleen up out of a deep sleep. Before they could answer the door they could hear the door busted open. There were loud screams announcing that they were the police. Colleen rose up in bed but Tango laid her back down. Within seconds the police had piled into the bedroom with their pistols drawn. One of the cops pulled out a piece of paper.

"Kevin Davenport we have a warrant for your arrest."

Tango didn't expect them to respond as fast as they did. He was in his pajamas so they allowed him to grab a pair of shoes before they handcuffed him.

"What did he do? What are you charging him with?" Colleen asked.

"Murder in the first degree."

They escorted the handcuffed Tango to the closest police vehicle. Tango observed that some of the neighbors were looking outside their window because of all the noise the cops made. Colleen got up from the bed and walked out on the porch. Tango blew her a kiss and she knew what to do.

20
TESTIFYING

Anything that has form can be overcome; anything that takes shape can be countered. This is why sages conceal their forms in nothingness and let their minds soar in the void.
Huainanzi

"Your honor, I would like to bring to the stand Debra Hunter."

Debra approached the stand and was instantly sworn in. She was obviously nervous so she avoids eye contact with Tango.

"Ms. Hunter, is it true that your fiancé when he left your house indicated to you that he would go visit Mr. Davenport?"

"Yes, he did."

"Did he tell you why and what was it that he was supposed to meet with Mr. Davenport concerning?"

"He had a job for Leonard. It was supposed to be extra money for him to be able to make."

"What else did he say to you before he left?"

"If anything happens to me remember that I was with Tango."

"Let the record show that the defendant, Mr. Kevin Davenport goes by the alias Tango. The name Tango is also a name that is infamously mentioned in a dozen murders that includes a young woman named Beverly..."

"Objection your honor! That is speculation and conjecture." Tango's defense attorney responded.

"Sustained counselor; Mr. Davenport is on trial for only one charge of murder."

"No more questions, your honor."

"Your witness." The judge said to the defense.

"Ms. Hunter, did you actually hear the defendant tell your fiancé that he would offer him a job on the day in question?"

"No, but I know that's what he said because Leonard wouldn't lie about that."

"Do you know of Beverly Simms?"

"Yeah, I know her as Tidbit, what about her?"

"Did you know that before she was brutally killed, she and your fiancé had an affair?"

"Objection your honor, this is hearsay." The prosecutor protested.

"Your honor this goes to the credibility of the victim in his relationship with his fiancé."

"I will allow it counselor, but be careful."

"Yes sir. Could you answer the question Ms. Hunter?"

"No I didn't know nor do I believe he messed with her." Debra viciously replied.

"Your honor I want to enter into evidence criminal records that later proved that Leonard Davis was charged with Statutory Rape of one Beverly Simms. I also would like to enter into evidence that blood sample was taken from Mr. Davis that proves that he is the biological father of Ms. Simms' only son even though another man signed the birth certificate."

"Did you know about this Ms. Hunter?"

Debra sat on the witness bench stunned and disoriented. She went off in a daze remembering when Drew Dog suggested that she watched Leonard and she would be compensated. After awhile she developed feelings for the man. Andrew must have known all the time, she considered.

"Ms. Hunter, did you know about this?"

"No I didn't know." She admitted.

"So it would be safe to say that he wasn't totally honest with you?"

Debra grudgingly nodded her head. She was trying her best to hold back her tears. She felt desperate and alone.

"Ms. Hunter, if you recall the defendant's niece Melanie Braxton testified that there was a woman that came to the door the night the defendant's family was killed. The prosecution's whole case suggests that the motive behind Mr. Davenport allegedly killing Mr. Davis was because he felt that Mr. Davis was responsible. Only one man knew where the defendant lived, is it possible that Beverly Simms was the one that went to the house through information told to her by your fiancé?"

"Objection, your honor."

"Sustained. Watch it counselor." The judge firmly replied.

"No more questions, your honor."

After closing arguments it took three hours for the jury to return with a verdict. The judge announced that the foreman could stand and read out the verdict.

"On the count of murder in the first degree?"

"Not guilty!" The foremen replied.

Tango turned around and glanced at Colleen to see her crying with joy. Tango's attorney looked over at him.

"I knew they couldn't convict because they had nothing on tape. If you were on tape then they could have had a strong circumstantial evidence case against you. With only a motive they didn't have any weight." The attorney whispered.

"Well I never talk that much anyhow." Tango replied.

The lawyer looked at him in disbelief and shook his head. Debra glanced at Tango with contempt then walked out of the courtroom. Colleen came over to hug and kiss him. It was finally over.

"We can go home now." Tango smiled.

"I'm glad to hear that." Colleen replied.

THE END

PaPa Sak eventually sat down to write his first novel, after many years of running from his calling. He experimented with many different genres, and then decided to write about the things that he was most passionate about. He found that his passions lied in stories that reflected his experiences in love, street life, and struggle. He began to write the stories of those that have been subjected to violence, poverty, despair, abuse, and unhealthy love. He wanted his stories to be a beacon light for society to recognize the social ills that plague us. His first published novel was published in 2005, 'The Wages of Sin', a gangster story. Ever since his first published book he has hit the ground running. Though his genres may change, he will always stay true to the voice of his community. He will stay true to the passion, pain, dialect, culture, love, richness, vantage point, and glory of the Black experience through his literature.

PaPa Sak is a voice for the streets and the Black community for those that are usually misrepresented and misunderstood. His goal is to bring humanity to these characters and to bring understanding to other unpopular perspectives. His characters come from people he has known or interacted with at one time or another. One of his main focuses is to shed spiritual insight on stories that should be told in the Black experience and abroad. He is also a profound orator and inspirational speaker ranging in spoken word poetry, gang & street lifestyle, male and female relationships, manhood training, spirituality, Hip Hop and history. He is definitely a literary force in the new Millennium. You can also find him on my space at URL: http://www.myspace.com/papasakkingpen, Facebook as Novelist PaPa Sak, Twitter as Sak Dog71 and www.ensbooks.com

Coming soon

@ www.ensbooks.com

Coming soon

@ www.ensbooks.com